# dawn &devilry

Other titles by S. Usher Evans

*The Razia Series*
Double Life
Alliances
Conviction
Fusion


Empath


*The Madion War Trilogy*
The Island
The Chasm
The Union


*The Demon Spring Trilogy*
Resurgence
Revival
Redemption

# dawn &devilry

### The Lexie Carrigan Chronicles

## S. Usher Evans

Sun's Golden Ray
Publishing

Pensacola, FL

Line Editing by Danielle Fine, By Definition Editing

Sun's Golden Ray Publishing
Pensacola, FL
www.sgr-pub.com

For ordering information, please visit
www.sgr-pub.com/orders

# The Lexie Carrigan Chronicles

Spells and Sorcery
Magic and Mayhem
Dawn and Devilry
Illusion and Indemnity

Available in eBook, paperback,
hardcover, and audiobook

# Contents

# Dedication

To anyone who's ever made a mistake

# part 1
# dawn

# One

"Gavon, good man. Look sharp."

Cyrus was taunting me, but that was nothing new. My superior in magical power, technique, and confidence, he was taking great pride in showcasing all three during our morning sparring match in the empty arena. Our daily training sessions were supposed to prepare us for the day the New Salem Warrior's Guild would re-enter the world from which we'd been banished generations before. But more often than not, they were an excuse for Cyrus to show off how much better he was at sparring than me. After all, he was the Chosen One, the Warrior who would bring great victory to our Guild, long suffering in this land of darkness and magic. I, on the other hand, was simply the spare.

Another of his gray fireballs landed hard against my shoulder, taking advantage of my disinterest. I'd bested him only once in the past three years. It was a mistake I wouldn't make again. For a man who'd been handed everything, his ego was rather fragile.

Still, I had to make it look like I was trying, so I flung a few deep purple attack spells in his direction. He blocked them with ease, as I predicted, then released several of his own. I deflected two, but let the last one hit, knocking the air from my lungs and sending me to the ground. Three more came behind it, each landing like a bag of stones against my defenseless body.

"Cyrus, that's enough."

Cyrus turned toward Alexandra, awaiting the praise that was most assuredly coming. Our mistress, a fierce woman in her mid-forties with graying hair and a black wool dress, betrayed no emotion as she approached the center of the arena. Her sharp brown eyes landed on me for a moment before turning to my partner.

"Cyrus, you're too cocky," she said. "Confidence serves you, but too much will be your downfall. Return to the Manor and begin your chores."

From the look on his face, Cyrus had only heard the praise, whatever little there was to be heard. Or perhaps he'd noted that he'd been dismissed, and I had not.

"My lady." He bowed and disappeared in a puff of dark gray smoke, but not before I saw his smirk.

I braced myself for the criticism, but instead, she said softly, "Walk with me, son."

Son, that was a first. Alexandra had given birth to me eighteen years ago, but as customary for Warriors, she'd handed me to her master, another Warrior named George Jones. He was already in his late sixties when I'd arrived on his doorstep, and I'd been more nursemaid than apprentice. He'd died three years ago, and with no other Warriors in the village, I'd returned to my mother's home to continue training with Cyrus.

I snuck a glance at Alexandra, seeing much of myself in her face. But that was where the similarities ended. She was Guildmaster; she held the respect and deference of the entire village. She could dispatch both Cyrus and myself without a second thought.

"Your performance leaves a lot to be desired," Alexandra said, after we'd walked for some time.

"Cyrus is my superior—"

"He's not. He's your equal in power but your inferior in intellect," she said. "His ego will be the end of him."

"I thought you liked his confidence," I said.

"Why aren't you trying against him?"

I thought about my words, running through them in my mind to make sure they wouldn't come back to haunt me. "Because he will be Guildmaster."

"That's not set in stone. You're both Warriors and will be inducted in a few months. When I grow old, the Guildmastership will be available to whomever is the best for it."

My jaw fell. "A few months?"

"Oh, look at you, so concerned now," she said with a short laugh.

"I'm not interested in the Guildmastership, but I would very much like to be inducted," I said, hoping my cheeks wouldn't betray my anger. In generations past, eighteen was the age a Warrior was inducted, but eighteen had come and gone some months ago. "I think it's past time, don't you?"

"It will be time when you show some interest in becoming

more than you are, Gavon."

And that was all she said, walking the rest of the way into the village in silence.

My mother's words sat unhappily in my mind for the afternoon, even as I chased the thoughts away with chores and studies. After we engaged in a rigorous morning of sparring, Alexandra liked Cyrus and me to scrub the Manor, the home of the Guildmaster since James Riley had arrived in this prison created for him and the rest of the Separatists. Although our magic could've completed the task in a matter of moments, it built our tolerance and humility to scrub the wooden floors on our hands and knees.

"You missed a spot," Cyrus said, lounging on a chair as a feather duster swept across the tops of the books in the library.

I sat on my knees, scanning the dark floor for what Cyrus had noticed and finding nothing. I knelt back down and continued scraping the brush across the floor.

"You were pathetic today, Gav," he said, leaning back on the chair and squinting at the window. A wet rag appeared and slid across the glass, not doing much to dispel the grime. "Mistress Alexandra says I'm nearly ready for induction," he said. "Suppose they'll want us to fight each other."

"Mm," I said, reminded again of what she'd said to me. It should've pleased her that I didn't want to usurp her precious Cyrus. So why was she delaying my induction? The sooner I was inducted, the sooner she would be rid of me. What could she be waiting for?

"I know it must not seem like much, this life of a second-class Warrior," Cyrus said, lazily scratching his stomach. "But I promise it won't be so bad. Maybe if you sire a Warrior, I'll keep you off the Council so you can do whatever it is you do."

"How generous of you."

Alexandra appeared in the center of the room in a puff of deep purple magic. "Cyrus, I thought there was to be no magic."

He pulled himself to stand. "My apologies, Mistress."

The rag fell to the floor with a loud *squelch* and Cyrus' impassive face grew angry. I hid a smirk; Alexandra had bound his magic. It was a typical punishment for a young magical, and one Cyrus was well acquainted with.

"Gavon," she said. "You may use the afternoon as you wish. Cyrus, finish the chores by yourself."

I stood as quietly as I could, placed the brush in the wooden bucket of soapy water and left quickly without meeting either of their eyes. It was a short reprieve, one Cyrus would punish me for later. But it was something.

Once I'd left the library, I used magic to transport myself far away, the farthest spot I could travel to in the confines of New Salem. Our world had been created by magic in 1692, when a magical war ended. My ancestors had lost and had been banished. For the Warriors, it was our solemn duty to be ready for the day the magical barrier broke, and we could reclaim the land that was ours.

This other world had been something of an obsession of mine since I was a little boy. I'd stumbled upon a collection of nonmagical books, very rare in New Salem, that had described more than just magical theory. Mathematics, physics, books on civilizations thousands of years before even the Two Years' War.

Plays that talked of great love and wars, faraway lands like England and Greece.

I wanted to see these lands for myself. For the past few months, I'd been playing around with potions, albeit in secret. Brewing potions was expressly forbidden, except in the case of healing potions for Warriors. And that restriction had only been lifted recently; our lone healer was very ill. Even though I could brew a potion to cure him, there was no arguing with Alexandra. Old prejudices didn't disappear easily.

I opened my journal to the last page where I'd written notes on the potion I'd tried. It wasn't much of anything—just some spider's web, three legs of a toad, mixed in a solution of vinegar. Today, I would try four legs of a toad, and perhaps two spiderwebs.

"Hm…" I scratched the growing stubble on my chin. What if four toad legs and one spider web did it?

I had been on these ingredients for a few weeks now. Each time, it had resulted in something simple—a flash of light. Something was better than nothing, though. The first time it had occurred, I'd used one toad leg, one spiderweb, and a splash of vinegar. Using the scientific method, I'd recreated the potion four times, and it had had the same effect. A flash of light, a ripple, then nothing.

Ever since, I'd been adding and removing ingredients, carefully documenting the results. It was painstakingly slow, but patience was something I had a lot of. After all, there was nothing else to do in town except drink and play nasty tricks on the lesser magicals in the village.

*It will be time when you show some interest in becoming more than you are, Gavon.*

Alexandra's words came back to my mind. It had been rather jarring to hear her judge me his equal, no less. Perhaps she had left the door to Guildmaster open for me. After all, Cyrus would be a cruel Guildmaster. His loyalty was to himself first, and his power second.

But did that mean I should take his place? If I did, how would he react? And why now, after all this time, was Alexandra showing an interest in me?

My potion hissed and I closed the book, careful to keep the scrap of paper to mark my place. With care, I ladled some of the white potion out of the cauldron and poured it in a circle on the ground.

Nothing. As expected.

A semi-circle. Nothing, again.

The last bit of potion I poured in an infinity loop. The air sizzled and popped, and a shimmer appeared for three breaths. Then the world was silent once more.

I jotted down the results then flipped back a few pages to compare. The infinity loop was the key, I could feel it, but the exact combination still eluded me. Sadly, I'd been away from the house long enough. Until I was free from Alexandra's attention, I couldn't devote more than an hour to this study per day. But one day, hopefully soon, I would be inducted and could spend the rest of my days toiling and brewing until death took me, too.

# Two

I awoke to yet another day in the drab world. Years of needing to help Master Jones to the privy had trained my body to an early rise, which worked well in Alexandra's house. I dressed quickly and set about doing the morning chores—including rousing my fellow apprentice.

His was the room next to mine, and I took great joy in pulling back the curtains to let in what dismal light there was. That joy was short-lived, as he wasn't alone in his bed.

"Be gone with you," he said to the girl, who vanished before I could get a good look at her face. "And you, as well."

I shrugged and continued the morning ritual, heading down to the kitchen to help the cook with breakfast. Alexandra would be pleased that he was trying his best to create another Warrior. Although I, too, had a duty to the clan to sire another of my specialty, I hadn't gone about the village spreading myself, as it were. Yet another reason Cyrus would be Guildmaster, and I would not.

After opening all the curtains upstairs, I set to work making the breakfast, assembling the bread and picking the mold off our cheese. Our cupboards were running a little bare, so I would have to find an Enchanter to make more. Our original captors had seen fit to give us livestock, but without a sun to grow crops, our village relied on Enchantment magic to turn dirt into bread, tea leaves, and food for the animals.

Cyrus arrived in the kitchen just as I was finishing, as usual. He plucked the full tray off the table and walked into the dining room. I followed with the tea and, after pouring into each of the waiting cups, settled down to eat my fill.

"We will spar this morning," Alexandra said. "Gavon, I hope your performance will improve."

I nodded. Perhaps I'd try a little harder, just to keep her from criticism.

"The Council will be watching."

That got my attention. The Council was the governing body, making decisions for the village and staving off ruin. Traditionally, there were supposed to be five Warriors, but now it was just Alexandra and the four strongest Enchanters and Charmers. Cyrus and I would be added as soon as our formal induction was concluded.

But I couldn't remember a time there'd been an audience for our sparring matches. Even our introduction match at fourteen had been witnessed by her and Jones alone.

"If I may ask…" I began, dipping my head. When she didn't cut me off, I continued, "Why?"

"Because Cyrus is almost eighteen, and I've decided it's time for him to be inducted. And, perhaps, you as well."

Joy and hope surged through me. Perhaps something had changed since we'd last spoken. "When?"

"The exact date will be determined after they watch you fight," she said, sipping her tea carefully. "I suggest you both try your hardest to impress them."

As excited as I was to finally see the end of my apprenticeship, there was still the bare cupboard to contend with. In New Salem, commerce occurred through bartering; the Enchanter made bread for the Charmer, the Charmer gave them milk from their cows. But for the Warriors, we existed merely to… be in charge, I supposed.

I stepped inside an Enchanter's house where a pretty, young girl with curly brown hair seated at a table. I'd seen her around the village, but never got her name. She released a loud squeak when she saw me, jumping to her feet and toppling over the stool.

"Good morning, Master Gavon," she said as her cheeks turned rosy. "What can I do for you today?"

"Good morning," I said. "Just a loaf."

She stood and sauntered to the large barrel in the back, making sure to sway her hips for my attention. She plucked a single morsel of bread from the barrel and grabbed a handful of dirt from the floor before returning to sit at the table. Her fingertips glowed a light blue color and the small crumb levitated, as did the dirt. She closed her hands around the mixture, then released them. It was now a small loaf, dark brown and crusty. With her hands still glowing, she stretched the edges of the bread until it was long and thick.

"That's enough," I said.

"Is it?" she said with a coy look as she handed it to me. "Seems big enough for me, too."

I caught the double-meaning and flushed. "Thank you for the bread. I'll see you next week."

I hurried out of the shop, praying that John the Charmer wouldn't do a dance for me as well. I supposed I should've been flattered, but I saw right through the attention. Despite my reserved nature, I was still desirable. Any woman who had a child with me might eventually be the mother of a Guildmaster.

For Alexandra, the act of sex was a duty—something that should be done without much thought for pleasure. Cyrus, judging by what I overheard from his room, was all about pleasure with the duty a distant second. But my mind was addled by the nonmagical books. Romeo and Juliet, two star-crossed lovers defying everything to be together was what I thought love to be.

I glanced behind me to the Enchanter, who was sadly doodling in the dirt pile left behind. She was pretty, but I wasn't sure we'd have anything to talk about. Still, perhaps a girl like her was all I was meant for. I was just the second.

Which reminded me: I had a sparring match to attend.

The ring still bore the skid and burn marks of our match the day before, and my body still ached from the effort. But if this would get me closer to induction, I didn't mind. The council members had already arrived, each wearing a long black cloak. I counted only four of them—Enchanter Perry seemed to be missing.

"Where've you been?" Cyrus said with a scowl.

"Since you neglected to pick up bread from the Enchanters yesterday, I had to," I said.

In the stands, Alexandra rose then appeared in front of us, her hands resting on her hips. "I trust you're ready, Gavon."

"Where's Perry?" I asked. "Shouldn't we wait for him?"

"No," she said. "Begin."

My questions were lost in a barrage of attack spells. Cyrus, it seemed, wasn't taking any chances. Unlike the day before, I didn't have to feign distraction; I was very curious about why the Council was one man short. Could it be they'd already kicked Perry off to make way for Cyrus?

A gray bomb tore through my magical defenses and flung me across the ground. I coughed for a moment, cursing Cyrus and his pressing need to show off.

Alexandra had retreated to join the rest of the council, and they weren't even watching. What could they be talking about, other than Perry's disappearance?

"If you're not even going to try, what's the point of you being a Warrior?" Cyrus said, standing over me.

"Aren't you the least bit concerned that Perry's missing?" I asked, coming to stand. "If we were to be seen by the entire council, why continue if a member isn't here?"

Cyrus shrugged, as if it hadn't crossed his mind. "It doesn't do to question, Gavon. You'll need to learn that before I become Guildmaster. I won't be as forgiving as your mother."

He surely wouldn't, and the horrifying thought of him lording over me the rest of my life got me back to my feet and fighting. I'd done a good job up until that point of ignoring what was to come—and how life would be when Cyrus was in charge. I just hoped he might leave me alone as long as I didn't challenge him.

"Enough," Alexandra called, coming to the center of the arena. "The Council has seen plenty."

I climbed to my feet gingerly, grateful today's torture was complete.

"Cyrus, they are most impressed with you," Alexandra said with a nod. "You've truly done well. You are ready to be inducted."

I waited for her to turn and tell me the same, but she said nothing to me. The silence stretched out until finally she nodded and began to walk away.

"W-wait," I said, stepping forward. "What about me?"

"You're not ready to be inducted."

A cold wind blew by, and I was sure I'd misheard. "Not ready?"

"No," she said, ignoring Cyrus's sniggers. "You've not demonstrated to me that you will be a useful member of the Guild. Therefore, you will remain my apprentice until you can prove otherwise."

Anger surged in my veins, my face growing hot and I spat out my response. "And how, pray tell, shall I prove my mettle, *mistress?*"

The quick rise of her brow boded nothing good. Even Cyrus had never spoken to her thus—not that I'd seen. But I was weary of these games. Of being treated as a second class magical to Cyrus. For no other reason that I was born Alexandra's son and couldn't be trained by her.

"To begin with, you will show deference to your Guildmaster," she said evenly. "And if you raise your voice again, I will make sure you regret it for a very long time."

I swallowed, readying myself.

But to my surprise, she disappeared in a plume of purple smoke without another word. Her torture would be to make me wait for punishment, to let my mind come up with a litany of possibilities. Would it be a week in the magic-less cellar? A month with magical binding, forced to do chores? Or would it be something more—physical pain? I'd rarely seen a lash, but the few times I had left a mark.

Or perhaps my punishment would simply be to remain her apprentice, bound to do her bidding.

"Hmph," Cyrus said, tossing me a smug look. "Tough luck, Gav."

It was all I could do to keep my mouth closed. Wisely, I left the sparring ring, as fighting outside a monitored match was expressly forbidden, and I wasn't all that sure I could beat him anyway.

Instead, I left for my sanctuary, knowing that if Alexandra wanted me, she could use her power as my mistress to call me to her. The apprenticeship began to chafe like never before, knowing I was no closer to freedom than the day it had begun.

When I'd first turned eighteen, and Alexandra told me I wasn't ready, I hadn't even thought to argue. But now? Cyrus, who never lifted a finger, Cyrus, who could fight in a ring but did little else valuable, Cyrus was getting inducted? I wanted to scream.

I paced in front of my cauldron, unable to breathe under the weight of Alexandra's yoke. There was nothing I could do, and that was the worst thing. I was stuck. Stuck as her apprentice, stuck as Cyrus' second and lesser magical. Stuck in this stupid world with the gray sky and cold wind.

As I marched over to the cauldron, I began summoning ingredients. Lavender, spider webs, frog legs, beer, wood, whatever my magic could bring me. All of it went into the cauldron. Gone was my scientific approach—now I just wanted results. After the cauldron was nearly overflowing with black, viscous potion, I levitated it and carefully began pouring the infinity loop.

Then I gathered the rest of my energy and threw it at the line on the ground, just as the bright flash of light split the world.

Only this time, the flash came with an incredible force of power. I flew backward, slamming into the hard, rocky ground and lay there for a minute, pain singing through every inch of my body. I blinked at the dark sky above, my ears ringing. Now that my magic had dissipated, so had my rage, and I felt rather stupid for what I'd done.

Presumably, I'd be sparring in the morning, so expelling all my magic in a tantrum was very irresponsible. Besides that, I'd used up much of my potion-making materials, which meant I'd have to answer some uncomfortable questions with an Enchanter tomorrow. Not to mention, someone in the village had probably seen that bright light, and they might come here to find me working in potions—

*Pop.*

I shook my head. That was an odd sound—almost like the hissing of a teapot, or the crackle of magic. My magic had severed when I'd released the attack spell, so it shouldn't still be hanging around.

Gingerly, I lifted my head. There was…for lack of a better term, a *tear* in the air. A white, writhing dangerous-looking thing suspended above the cliff face. Magical bolts crackled from the center as it rolled into itself, undulating as if it were alive.

Slowly, I came to my feet. What had I done?

I observed the rippling creation for a few minutes, trying to time the crackling, but there was no rhyme or reason to it. Cautiously, I crept closer, jumping back when a bolt hit my shoulder. It was magical, but painless.

With trembling fingertips, I reached toward it. There was nothing but energy between my fingers.

Then something hooked around my navel, and I fell forward.

# Three

I landed hard on a surface that gave easily under my fingers. Coughing, I spat the gritty dirt from my mouth and wiped my face. But there was something off—the smell. The air was salty, but also with a pungent, sulfur odor. The dirt I was lying in was a lighter shade than I'd ever seen before. I grabbed a handful and watched as it slid through my fingers. It moved like water.

Tilting my head up, I took in the sky—no longer gray and overcast, but black. Black and expanding as far as I could see. And twinkling with…

Stars.

I was looking at stars for the first time.

Tears sprang to my eyes as I took in their beauty. It was more incredible than any book had described it. I was accustomed to seeing stars in constellations from astronomy books, but I could no sooner discern a pattern as count them all.

But if there were stars, did that mean…was I…

Had I returned to the old world?

The sound of laughter drew my attention. I gathered my wits and stood, brushing the dirt from my clothes. As gracefully as I could on shifting ground, I drew closer to the sound, which included laughter and movement.

It was just as I came across them that the first moan of pleasure echoed through my ears, and I realized I had stumbled on something private. But it was too late.

"*Oh shit,*" the girl screamed, grabbing her shirt and covering herself. "What the…? Get out of here, you perv!"

I froze, unaccustomed to seeing a woman in that state of undress. She wore nothing but a pair of pants that had been cropped close to her rear, and a white shift that covered naught but her bosom. Her scrambled attempts to cover herself only revealed more of her naked body, and I could do nothing but stare.

Until her paramour stood, fists bared.

"Ya deaf? Get outta here!" he said, marching toward me.

My defensive instincts kicked in, and I fired off an attack spell. The purple fireball hit him square in the stomach, and he fell backward, unconscious immediately.

"What the fuck is wrong with you?" the girl screamed at me, rushing to cradle her lover's head. "You can't just use magic in front of a nonmagical. And you can't attack them! How did you even do that anyway?"

I stuttered like an idiot, my gaze drawn to the skin on her lower back, where her backbone was visible.

"Well? What do you have to say for yourself?" she demanded, standing and marching toward me with her shirt still clutched in her hand.

I might've had something to say, had I not looked into her eyes. They were the bluest color I'd ever seen, and the spatter of freckles along her tanned face took my breath away. She was unlike any girl I'd ever seen, her golden hair falling to her shoulders and framing her heart-shaped face perfectly. But it wasn't just her features, it was the way her nose crinkled in anger, how she stood in front of me undressed and unashamed. She was as fierce as Alexandra—and I was terrified.

"Hello?" She was now waving her hand in front of my face. "Are you there, pervy?"

"What is that?" I choked out.

"What is what?"

"Pervy? I've never heard the term."

She blinked once, twice, three times. "Are you high?"

I glanced at the ground, where my feet were planted firmly on the sand. "I don't appear to be?"

"Dude, what is your deal? Are you foreign? What's with your clothes?"

I could've asked her the same thing, but decided not to, as it might draw my gaze down to her breasts once more. "I'm from New Salem."

"What the actual hell is New Salem?"

I blinked. "It's…um." A question I'd never had to answer before. "It's a town where magicals live."

"Yeah, I've lived in Salem my whole life and never heard of it," she said, quirking a brow and crossing her arms. I wished she hadn't, for it propped the tops of her breasts upward, and I was already struggling not to stare. "What are you doing here? And how'd you use magic on Renny? I've never seen magic like that before."

"I don't know what I'm doing here," I said honestly. "I don't even know where here is…"

She chewed her lip and finally covered those beautiful breasts with another shirt. It didn't help much. "I don't really know what to do with you, but I know you can't use magic in front of a nonmagical. That's like…impossible."

I looked down at the man I'd attacked, finally realizing what I was looking at. "You mean…he's a nonmagical?"

"Yeah, duh."

I couldn't believe it. "I've never met a nonmagical before. They look…just like I do."

"Of course they do, dumbass," she said, running a hand through her golden locks. "Man, this is some shit. You're talking about some town called New Salem, and you don't know what a nonmagical is. Hell, I've tried to use magic in front of Renny before and I can't. And you with your weird magic…"

A worried tone had come through in her voice, so I held up my hands. "I'm not…I mean, I won't hurt you."

"Yeah, well, you hurt him," she said, nodding to the unconscious form below.

"I promise, it was unintentional," I said then cleared my throat. "I didn't mean to…interrupt your lovemaking."

She coughed roughly. "Uh, that's not what we were doing. We were making out at most."

"Making…out?"

She huffed, but then lost her anger when her paramour grunted and moved. "Look, you're obviously lost. Let me take you to my mom and see what she thinks."

"What will happen to your friend?" I asked curiously.

"Renny is…well, let's just say he's baked all the time, and this won't be the first time he's woken up half-naked on the beach," she said with a half-hearted shrug. Then, she paused and chewed her pink lip. "Please don't mention any of this…"

"Any of what?"

"Us making out. She'll totally wig out on me."

I didn't understand any of what this girl was saying to me, but I assumed she meant that I'd found her and the boy in a compromising position and that her mother would be upset. How could language change so much in…

"What year is it?"

She stopped and I nearly ran into her. "You don't know what year it is?"

"I…"

She sighed. "It's 1989."

"Nineteen…" I couldn't believe my ears. The Council hadn't kept good records of the time that had passed, believing it to be immaterial. The general consensus was that it hadn't been that long since we'd been banished.

But it had been three hundred years almost exactly.

"Are you okay, dude?"

"Yes, of course. My apologies."

"So Goddamned formal…"

The shifting terrain turned into a hard, black substance, on which houses sat in front of vibrant green pastures. Even though it was dark, the world was illuminated by magical balls of light in boxes all along the streets—and, surprisingly, inside the homes.

"Is magic known here?" I asked, breathlessly. "This thing, is it magic?"

"Dude, it's a lamp," she scoffed. "Electricity? Do you know what that is?"

I shook my head, and she rolled her eyes.

"You're buggin'," she muttered. "I'm buggin'. Maybe I'm still high."

I was beginning to wonder if she wasn't referring to her elevation. "You said that it's impossible to use magic in front a nonmagical."

"Yep," she said, eyeing me.

"I don't understand," I replied. "What do you mean impossible?"

"Meaning I couldn't even summon a Tootsie Roll if a nonmagical was standing in front of me," she said. "I can't even speak about magic to a nonmagical. Makes me feel like my throat is closing up. There isn't magic in front of nonmagicals. Period. End of story. That's all she wrote."

"That's…incredible," I replied. "But does that mean… The nonmagicals don't know about magic?"

She shook her head. "Not even a little bit. We have to hide it. Sometimes it's just easier not to use it, you know? I forget I have it sometimes, especially when I'm out with my nonmagical friends."

I slowed, stunned. For me, magic was always there to grab onto. It was another tool, like a pen to paper. I could never just "forget" about it.

"Things are much different in New Salem," I said after a long pause.

"Like Amish different?" she said.

"I'm sorry, but—"

"You don't know what that is. I'm starting to understand."

She stopped in front of a large house with bright light shining from all the windows. I followed her onto a small porch, observing the gray wood as she fumbled with a set of keys and jammed them in the door lock. Then, with a grunt, she pushed the heavy door open and beckoned me inside.

"Moooooooom."

I started at the sound. Children in New Salem never addressed their parents in such a way. Alexandra would've strung me up by my ankles.

"Mora, what..." The woman who appeared was incredibly powerful, but she was no Warrior. Her magic was the oddest I'd ever felt. It was Warrior and Healing and Charming and Enchanting all rolled into one. But, as I looked at her daughter, I sensed no magic from her. Or rather, I did, but it was bound tight. No wonder she'd thrown me off.

"Mora, what the hell did you bring home?" the woman asked, increasing her power with every step down the staircase.

"I dunno, Mom. Some weird kid who appeared when I was out for...a walk. I thought you'd want to know."

"Go finish your homework," the woman barked. As the girl darted up the stairs, the woman grabbed her by the arm. "And I smell weed on you. Have you been hanging out with that boy again?"

"No, Mom."

"Lie to me again, and you'll be without magic for another

month."

Ah, so that explained the lack of magic from the girl. Well, at least that brand of punishment hadn't changed in three hundred years.

The woman continued down the stairs, and even though I was fairly sure I was more powerful than she, I still backed up a step. I wasn't as brave as my new blonde friend.

"And who the hell are you?" she asked, as she reached the bottom step. "And what kind of magic do you carry?"

I licked my lips nervously. "My name is Gavon McKinnon. I'm from New Salem, but—" I winced as her magic surrounded me, ready to expel me from her house, "but I promise I mean you no harm."

"New Salem has been kept separately," the woman replied. "How did you get here?"

I picked my words carefully, While the younger woman had no idea what New Salem was, and our history, her mother certainly did.

"I don't…know exactly. I'd been experimenting with potions and magic, and then it just happened."

"What?"

"A t-tear between our worlds, I suppose you could call it." I swallowed hard, stepping back once more. "Next thing I knew, I stumbled upon your daughter and…"

"And her pothead boyfriend," the woman finished with a glance up the stairs. "Are there more of you?"

"More of… In New Salem?" I nodded. "We number a few hundred, maybe."

"And do they know what you've done?"

"N-no," I said, then, as her magic flooded the room, I quickly added, "And I won't tell them."

She snorted. "As if I could trust the word of a Separatist."

"I'm not a Separatist," I said with a hearty laugh. "My ancestors were, but they're long since dead. I doubt many in New Salem even know this world exists."

"If you know what's good for you, you'll keep it that way. Now get the hell out of my compound."

Warm magic surrounded my body, and before I knew what was happening, the world shifted around me, and I was back to the sandy place where I'd first entered the world. It took me a moment to realize what had happened, and I marched toward the bright lights of the city, but found I couldn't go very far. This older magical had some power in her—although it still paled in comparison to the power of my guild.

I sat on the shifting sands, the sound of the water pushing against the sand a soothing backdrop to my thoughts. I wasn't sure what I was waiting for. More magicals? But there was nothing more than the waves and a cool breeze.

I gazed at the beautiful stars in the sky, my heart racing in my chest. Fear, excitement, curiosity—every emotion I could name—coursed through me. I had done what others couldn't. I'd broken through the magic that had bound us to this world and returned to the realm of our ancestors.

I wanted more of it.

One magical woman wasn't going to keep me from exploring every inch of this world. I closed my eyes and let my magic travel as far as it could—visions of places completely unfamiliar coming to my senses. Transporting had never felt so freeing before; there were so many options. Where would I begin?

A gentle tug brought me back to reality. Alexandra was sending feelers for me to return to the Manor. It appeared her control over my magic extended beyond the tear, unfortunately. If I didn't return immediately, she would come looking for me. And since I wasn't quite ready to share this beautiful new world with anyone else, I returned to New Salem.

# Four

"You're distracted this morning, Gavon." Alexandra peered at me from the head of the table. "Something on your mind?"

Oh, how little she knew. She probably thought my silence the result of petulance—anger at her for not allowing me an induction match. I'd arrived back at the Manor to a silent house and woken to the same. I'd rushed through my morning chores with vigor, impervious to Cyrus' digs about his impending induction match. Now, more than ever, it was more important for me to get out of this apprenticeship.

"My apologies, Mistress. Did I miss a question?" I said, plastering on the most pleasant smile I could muster.

"I simply noticed your distraction, nothing more." She turned to Cyrus seated across from me. "We shall spar at midday."

"We?" he said, glancing in my direction.

She nodded and tapped her napkin against her lip. "Since it's clear Gavon will not be inducted soon, we will need to continue your preparations."

If she expected a rise from me, she was mistaken. It was easy to escape into the recesses of my mind and imagine the new world I would get to explore as soon as I was free of her grip. Not to conquer it, as Cyrus would, but to appreciate it. To visit the places I'd only read about. To sit on the banks of the ocean once more and see every shade of blue. To gaze upon the stars and try to find one of those constellations. To see Venice, Rome, London.

"Gavon." Alexandra's voice cut through my daydream once more. "Are you listening?"

"I apologize," I said, averting my gaze to look chastened.

"Fetch the Healer," she said with a look of disgust. "See if he's healthy enough to heal me after our morning session so that we may spar again this afternoon."

I nodded. "And if he isn't?"

"Then I suppose you may brew one of those infernal potions," she said, waving her hand.

"Yes, ma'am," I said, dreading the number of chores. I wanted to get back to my new world.

"Cyrus, finish your meal and meet me in the sparring ring." She disappeared in a puff of purple, leaving us to our usual after-meal conversation.

"Such a shame," Cyrus said with a shrug. "It appears you'll be destined for potion-making your whole life. What a fate for a Warrior."

I bit my tongue so as not to spill the secret of the newfound world. When it was safely kept in the back of my mind, I responded with, "Unfortunately, any potion I make for you would be less potent. There's a correlation between magic and family." I paused before landing the blow. "Alexandra and I share the same blood, you see, and that makes all the difference."

Before Cyrus could retort with something equally biting (or a spell), I transported out of the house to the center of the town. It was rare I got the last word, so I considered that a good omen for the rest of the day.

First, I had the dubious task of visiting the sick house. Magical rot was a vicious disease that slowly drained the magic, and then the life, from a magical. It was an affliction of the middle aged, mostly. It was rare for a magical to live past fifty.

I covered my mouth with a kerchief as I entered the dark space. The stench of death was everywhere, but so was the earthy smell of the rot. Dying magicals lined the room on makeshift beds made of hay with a single sheet atop them. They gasped for air through purple-tinged lips, black, inky lines drawing lower down their necks. Some were well enough to take food, others were just waiting for death.

Councilman Perry lay on one of the cots, gasping for breath as he stared at the ceiling. I supposed that explained why he'd been missing from our match. At least Cyrus wouldn't have to fight for a spot.

A woman was crying from the other room and I ventured closer. It didn't sound like the normal dying sounds—rather, a painful whimpering. I peeled back the curtain to see a young girl not much older than I with her legs spread. She was biting down on a stick, her face shiny with sweat. An older woman knelt before her, and although I couldn't see exactly, I had an idea what was going on.

"Wh-what is it?" the new mother whispered.

"Enchanter," the woman said. "But stillborn."

The girl's eyes filled with tears and then she fainted—either from exhaustion or grief. But the baby was squirming—it was very much alive. There was no magical signature, which meant...

"Smother it," came the weary directive from the midwife. She handed the baby to another older woman, who left the room with it. I swallowed the sickness in my stomach. It was a mercy, then, that the girl would believe her child had died.

"Can I help you?"

I jumped at the voice, turning to see the mistress of the sick house staring down at me with beady eyes. I'd heard once that she and Alexandra shared a mother, which would make her my aunt, I supposed. They certainly shared the same disgust for me.

"I'm looking for the Healer," I said, finding my tongue.

"He is dead," she said, lifting her chin higher. "Died three weeks ago."

"Oh," I said, with a soft exhalation. "I will inform the Guildmaster."

The woman raised a brow. "She was already informed. She was here when it happened."

That was curious, but I didn't feel like pressing further. With a soft thank you, I hastened from the sick house, needing to breathe fresh air and rinse the soft cries of the now-dead baby out of my ears.


When I returned to the house, Alexandra was in the library, lounging on her chair and nursing a rather large bruise on her forehead, and a cut on her lip. Without saying a word, I summoned the healing potion and handed her the vial.

"What did you see at the sick house, Gavon?" she asked, her voice weak.

"I saw…" Should I tell the truth? Would she think me weak to worry about the new mother and her child? "The Healer is dead. Councilman Perry is close as well."

"Is that all?"

I finally turned, tempering my tongue before it got the better of me again. "I'm not sure what I should say, Mistress."

"Did the girl Ann give birth to her child?"

My mouth fell open. "Sh-she did. But it was a Potion-maker."

Alexandra nodded. "I knew as much. Elise told her it was stillborn, did she not?"

Again, I could scarcely believe my ears. "Yes, she did."

"We are cursed with one Potion-maker for every six births— and of the remaining five, many more are born dead." She looked at the vial in her hand then tossed it into the fire. "I believe it is part of the curse John Chase laid upon us."

I didn't dare ask if she considered not killing Potion-makers; there were some lines that even I didn't cross.

"Our village is dying, Gavon. How the village celebrated when you and Cyrus were born. But not a single Warrior has been born since. Before we were banished, our numbers were in the hundreds of thousands. Now? Only three." She sighed as the purple bruise faded.

"Is that why you sent me to the sick house?" I asked. "To witness the birth?"

"I wanted you to think very clearly about your decision not to be Guildmaster," she said. "What might you do differently if you were responsible for these five hundred souls?"

I honestly didn't have an answer, because it was never something I'd thought about. "But Cyrus—"

"Ah, Cyrus," she said with a soft chuckle. "My dear apprentice, who right now is on the prowl for another girl to lie with." Her sharp eyes pierced me. "That girl? Ann? That was Cyrus' child she gave birth to."

I frowned. "Did he know?"

"He would've known if it was a Warrior, I'm sure." She pushed herself upright and rubbed her temple. "I believe he's had three to survive birth so far."

Three children. It hardly seemed possible.

"I have watched Cyrus grow from a precocious child into a man that I hardly recognize. He's callous, he's cruel. He only cares for people who can give him something in return. Is that the kind of man you wish to lead this Guild?"

I didn't know what to say. I'd never thought I had a choice in the matter. "Are you saying you'd rather I be Guildmaster?"

"I would like to see you fight for it," she said, coming to stand. "Even though I didn't raise you, you're still my son. The product of my bloodline."

"Then why did you decide against my induction match?" I asked.

"Perhaps I wanted to see your reaction to it," she said with a coy smile. "It's not my desire to keep you in my house for longer than necessary. After all..." She placed her long, white fingers against the black fabric of her hips. "Cyrus isn't the only young

Warrior in need of coupling. You, my son, have a legacy to continue."

"I'll do my best."

"See that you do," she said. "You will complete all the chores today while Cyrus and I spar."

"Yes, ma'am," I said, dipping my head. "And if I may ask—"

"I haven't changed my mind," she said. "When I can look upon you without embarrassment, I'll reconsider your induction."

As a Warrior, a mother's love was never something I'd experienced. So Alexandra's comment to me slid off my back like water. Besides that, as much as I cared what happened to the villagers in New Salem, I had other things on my mind. Greater things.

I sped through my afternoon chores. Alexandra was gone, so I used magic to scrub the floors and windows, making them sparkle in the drab light. As I worked, I thought about all the things I wanted to see, writing a list to myself. Rome was the top of my list, as was Athens, Alexandria—all the great places of knowledge that existed in my books. I'd seen the sea briefly the day before. But today I would jump in the water. I would find myself a piece of actual bread, comparing the flavor to that which was magically created.

Speaking of bread, I would have to bring a small piece to that young Enchanter. The remnants of real bread had long since been used, and the morsels they used to craft bread were nothing more than using magic to build more magic. Perhaps one day, when I understood this new world, I would have fresh loaves for every belly in my village.

But I was a long way from that. In just the few minutes I'd spent there, I'd been completely overwhelmed with new changes. I wanted to understand everything first, then…perhaps I'd tell them.

Perhaps.

When the house sparkled, I transported to the other end of New Salem, grateful that the tear remained as vicious and unrelenting as it'd been the day before. Without any trace of fear, I walked into it and fell into the new world.

# Five

Bright light assaulted my eyes, and for a moment, I thought I was dying. But slowly, my eyes adjusted to the light. Heat seeped through the fibers of my shirt, much like a warming spell. Sweat broke out on the back of my neck and my wool socks became uncomfortable in my black boots.

But all of that was nothing compared to the view.

What had been dark and beautiful was now blue—the most vibrant color I'd ever seen. The water glittered in the light like sparks off an attack spell. And the water, oh, how it moved. Rushing toward the brown sand with unlimited energy, then slowly rolling back to the depths. It was so vast, so infinite. Tears welled in my eyes. There were no barriers, no ends. Nothing to stop me from walking to every corner of this land and exploring everything it had to offer.

I struggled over the sand, marveling how it gave way under my feet, until the terrain changed to the blacktopped hard surface I'd seen the night before.

A loud blaring caught me by surprise, and a giant box-like carriage barreled toward me. I transported myself out of the way just in time, but my heart pounded all the same. The monstrosity was followed by three smaller ones, each whizzing by me as fast as an attack spell. I waited for more to come, but heard nothing, so I continued on my way.

I wanted to avoid that girl and her mother at all costs, and even felt something of a barrier spell on my consciousness when I tried to recall where I'd been taken. It was a pitiful spell, easily breakable if I put my mind to it, but I opted to let it stand. I didn't feel like looking for trouble.

After a while of walking along the black road, I came into the village—or what I could only suppose was a village. Houses made of red bricks rose two stories in the air with carriages of different sizes and shapes parked out front.

I craned my neck to examine them closer, when fevered whispering reached my ears. I turned as a couple openly stared at me, scampering away when they caught me looking. But it was I who stared at them—they were nonmagical. As was everyone else on the street.

It was the oddest sensation, as if the living, breathing humans walking by didn't have souls. Even the Potion-makers had the faintest magical signature, and when Cyrus was magically bound, I could still sense his presence. But there was nothing in these people. No wonder my ancestors thought them inferior.

I, however, was fascinated. Having grown up with magic in every aspect of my life, I'd never once considered what it might be not to have it. To have to walk great distances instead of transporting. To get up and look for something if I couldn't find it. From what I could see, the nonmagicals had been able to accomplish plenty without it.

Another group walked by, giggling and pointing at me as they passed. Following their gaze, I realized my clothes—black cloak, black leather boots, black pants—seemed a little out of place here. The other men on the street wore white shoes and bare legs. I was still observing the world, but I would be much more comfortable if I changed. So, I ducked into a dark space between two buildings and observed the passersby—specifically the men. Most wore shirts with short sleeves and pants cut off at the knee.

With a quick charm, I mimicked a set of clothes. The material breathed much easier than the wool, but the feel of a starchy collar against my neck and a breeze up my pants was strange. Even the shoes—brown leather without socks—made for a different gait. The last piece was a hat—similar to the one a young man was wearing across the street. At least now I could walk without the bright sun in my eyes.

Confident that I had built myself a timelier outfit, I strode out into the sunlight once more. Now, ignored by the townsfolk, I took my place beside them.

The carriages that had frightened me earlier now rolled along slowly, stopping at intersections and allowing other carriages to pass. I watched the dance for a while, amazed at how everything worked without magical interference. I took out my notebook and jotted down observations—a green light meant the queued cars could move forward—a red meant they stopped. After a few moments, I still couldn't figure out the yellow light, but I left a note to investigate further.

I explored the village shops. One assaulting my senses with a barrage of smells that gave me a headache. Another seemed to be a place where the nonmagicals got their hair trimmed. Still another had blinking windows that displayed the same person in every one. I was mesmerized as they mimicked each other in perfect synchronization, but hurried out of the shop when a man stopped to ask me what I was interested in.

Finally, I spotted a place I understood—the library.

A cool breeze blew against my face—the entire library seemed to be in some kind of a permanent winter, but after the heat outside, I wasn't too upset by it. Not with the sight of thousands of books—perhaps hundreds of thousands—all lined up in rows and columns.

How could so many books exist? I'd thought Alexandra's library daunting. But this? There would be no way I could read every book in this library in my lifetime. Just thinking about all the knowledge found in this one building took my breath away.

I wandered to the stacks, running my finger along the spines and reading every one. Economics, science, something about a man named Ronald Reagan. Seeing books just fueled my thirst for more knowledge. I had no idea where to begin with it all; I could spend my entire life on this one bookshelf.

I pulled a book off the shelf, Introduction to Economics, and quickly scanned the front cover. Which was when I heard a sharp intake of breath on the other side of the stack.

I looked between the books and saw a pair of familiar blue eyes staring back at me.

"You're back," she said.

"H-hello again," I said, unsure why I was nervous to see her. Her magic was still bound tightly, and she carried no other weapon I could see. She chewed on a pink lip, surveying me with a mix of apprehension and curiosity.

"I'm supposed to tell my mom that I saw you," she said. "The whole clan is looking for you."

"Are they?" I looked around, expecting more magicals to appear. "Why?"

"You're evil or something," she said with a shrug.

"E-evil?" I blinked; I was the least deserving of that moniker. "I told you I'm not here to harm you. I told your mother that, as well."

She huffed and disappeared between the books, reappearing around the corner. Yet again, she wore the shortest pants I'd ever seen, and a shirt with nothing but two thin straps keeping it on her frame.

"What are you even doing here?" she asked, placing a hand on her hip. Her nails were…green? "Like, actually. What are you doing here?"

"Right now…" I motioned to the book. "I thought I might find out what economics are."

She tilted her head, as if she couldn't understand me. "Are you really from some alternate dimension where all the evil magicals were banished three hundred years ago?"

"The story I was told was that we were trying to live freely, lost a war, and were banished," I said. "But yes, I am from New Salem."

"What do you mean, live freely?"

"Live in a world where magic can be practiced in the open,"

I said, pressing the book to my chest.

"That sounds like a great world to me," she said with a huff. "But Mom said that James Riley wanted to enslave humanity or something like that."

"He might have," I said, recalling it being mentioned once or twice in my history lessons with Master Jones. "But it's been three hundred years. He's long since dead."

"Do you want to enslave humanity?"

My brows shot upward. I was at a loss for words.

"So last night, we had a big clan meeting about…well, about you. Mom stood up in front of everyone and told them to be on the lookout for you 'cause you're here to cause trouble. But…" She tilted her head. "I mean, I guess you're powerful. But you don't look evil."

Still at a loss for words, I looked down at my clothes then back at her.

"I mean, look at you. More like a lost puppy. A really preppy lost puppy. Where'd you get that get-up?"

"Get-up?"

"Your clothes," she said. "You look like you just stepped off Martha's Vineyard."

"Are these not typical?" I asked, looking down. "I tried to mimic what I saw on the street, but—"

"Oh, well, yeah. There are a lot of rich boys in town right now on summer vacation," she said. "You know, beach and all that. But I guess you sort of fit that vibe."

"I honestly have no idea what you just said," I replied, as my cheeks warmed.

To my surprise, she smiled. "You really aren't from around

here, are you?"

"No, I'm afraid not."

She took a hesitant step toward me, then another—then held out her hand. "I'm Mora. Mora Carrigan."

"Gavon McKinnon," I said, shaking her hand. Her skin was soft, unlike mine, which had borne the brunt of cold winds my entire life. "If I may ask, what's your specialty? I can't seem to figure it out."

"What's a specialty?"

"It's the type of magic you have," I said. Perhaps they called it something different now. "Some people are Warriors, some are Charmers or Enchanters…"

"Oh, right. Mom said something about that," she said with a nod. "We don't have any of those anymore."

"I'm sorry…what?" No specialties? That was ludicrous. "How is that even possible?"

"Apparently, there was some agreement right after…well, all you guys had your big war or whatever. Everyone on this side agreed to get rid of specialties."

I furrowed my brow. "That's the most ridiculous thing I've ever heard."

"So is Warrior magic." She snorted, but there was no malice in her gaze. "That's the dumbest thing I've ever heard of."

Again, we shared a smile and my cheeks were now growing warm, although it might have had less to do with my embarrassment and more with this bold girl in front of me. From this angle, I could see down her shirt, my gaze drawing to the separation of her breasts, nestled in a corset—

"Well, you're still a guy, I guess," she said, placing a hand on her hip.

"I'm sorry, you just...don't look like anyone I've ever met before. Your clothes are..." I cleared my throat. "Aren't you a bit indecent?"

She burst out laughing, her guffaws booming and loud, but somehow still endearing. This girl wasn't meek or mild, and I rather liked that about her.

"You and my mother could start a club. But it's hot outside."

"Right," I said, rubbing the back of my neck. It still felt warm to the touch. "There's no sun in New Salem, so this warmth takes some getting used to."

She made a sound and there was pity on her face. "There's no sun?"

I shook my head. "The land is dark, barren. No water other than a magical wellspring. The food is only what we can breed and create with magic."

"So you've never even had a burger?"

I shook my head. "I don't know what that is."

The curiosity grew on her face. "So, you really have no idea what anything is, do you?"

"I do have an education. I know physics and mathematics and—"

"Ugh, like that'll help you in the real world. I mean like TV and burgers and cars and..." Her grin widened. "Are you hungry?"

"I...suppose?"

"I'm starving," she said. "If you promise not to enslave humanity, I'll show you a few things. Starting with lunch."

# Six

It was rather fortuitous, I thought, that I'd happened upon Mora. I had thousands of questions about everything, and she seemed willing to answer all of them. As well as she could, anyway.

"A car," I said.

"Yeah, you put gas in it, turn on the ignition, step on the pedal, and vroom-vroom!" she said, guiding me down the street. "They also have airplanes—which are like cars, but they fly in the sky. Like a bird."

"Fascinating," I said, watching these so-called cars rumble by. "The nonmagicals really are quite adept, aren't they?"

"I guess," she said, taking my hand. "C'mon. I'm starving."

She dragged me into a dimly lit building that smelled absolutely delicious. She leaned against the counter and smiled as the pockmarked teenager blushed and wrote down what she said.

"Thanks, Timmy," she said with a sultry wink. How she

could get away with such acts was beyond me, but it was fun to watch her work. She took two white paper cups and sauntered over to a dispenser of sorts, where fizzy dark liquid came out.

"What's this?" I couldn't help but ask.

"Soda," she said, handing me one. It had a tube sticking out the top, so I pulled off the lid. She sighed and placed her hand on top of mine, sucking the tube. I followed suit and grimaced as a vile, acidic taste filled my mouth.

I coughed. "What is this?"

"It's Coke," she said. "You don't like it?"

I licked my lips. After the initial shock wore off, what was left was a sweet tang. I tentatively drank more. "No, it's not bad. It's different."

"This is so ridiculous," she said, leaning against the table and chewing on the tube. "You have no idea what anything is. Not even a straw."

"Which part of this is a straw?"

She flicked the tube on my drink then turned as the pockmarked teen called a number. She retrieved two bags from him and beckoned me to follow her out into the sun once more. We sat underneath a multicolored shade, and she handed me a warm bag that wafted a delicious aroma my way.

"Do I gotta show you how to eat or…?"

"I think I understand this part," I said, fishing a long, yellow piece out of the bag. "What am I about to put in my mouth?"

"Potato," she said. "Heard of that?"

"In a book," I said, taking a bite. It burned the roof of my mouth, but it was so delicious, I didn't care. It melted in my mouth, and I savored every last drop. Truly, I had been underprivileged to have never had food not touched by magic.

"You seem to be enjoying that," Mora said with a giggle.

I swallowed and took another bite, closing my eyes. "Most of what we eat, besides the meat, is created by magic."

"How does that even work?" she asked, slowly dragging her brown nugget-like food through a red sauce.

"Well, Enchanters have the ability to stretch and grow things," I began, picking up another stick. "So they could take a small piece of this potato and turn it into a thousand more."

"Oh wow," she said. "But I thought you can't create new things from magic?"

I smiled. A girl who knew her magical theory. "Exactly. So they fake it with…other things. Our bread is made from a tiny speck of bread and…dirt."

"Gross," she said, scrunching her nose. "You mean, you guys eat dirt?"

"It tastes…well, I suppose I've never really had bread not created by magic, so I don't know the difference."

"Here." She picked up the other part of my meal and handed it to me. "That's got bread in it."

I took a bite, my eyes widening as the flavor exploded in my mouth. Every piece of meat I'd had before then had been a cheap imitation of the real thing, the bread no more than the dirt from which it had been made. I chewed slowly, savoring every moment, before washing it down with the soda once more.

"Well?"

"Incredible," I replied. Her gaze rested on me, warming my cheeks as she toyed with her food, an unreadable smile on her face. "What is it?"

"I've just never met anyone who's had an orgasm after a bite of a burger before," she said.

I blinked. "A what?"

"Like, when you're having sex, and you, you know…" She closed her eyes and made a few noises. I quickly reached across the table to quiet her, my face growing even warmer.

"Oh yes, I'm quite aware," I said. "Was that how I looked eating this food?"

"I mean," she giggled again, and I liked the sound, "kind of."

"I'll have to be more careful," I replied, picking up the meat again. I kept my gaze on her and took a bite, a smile teasing the corners of my mouth as she watched expectantly. "How'm I doing?"

"PG," she said.

"PG?"

"Like, at the movies, when you go, there's a rating system," she said.

I shook my head, confused.

She sighed and put her chin on the heel of her hand. "Never mind."

As I ate (making sure to school my face), it was my turn to watch her. Even without free magic, she had an energy that was addictive. Her gaze danced around the restaurant, landing on the shop across the street. There was a little bit of red sauce on the corner of her mouth that I wanted to wipe away. Her golden hair swung from the gathering at the top of her head when she moved. Nothing against the girls in New Salem, but I think I preferred Mora.

"What?" she asked, catching me staring. "Do I have

something on my face?"

"No," I said, swallowing. "I just find you interesting."

Her lips parted and her blue eyes widened, giving her something of a younger expression. A nervous chuckle rumbled through her words. "Why? You don't know anything about me."

"I'd love to learn more," I said. "About you, about this place. The name of whatever I'm eating."

The shock wore off. "You're eating a burger—hamburger. This place is Salem and it's boring as hell. And me..." She shrugged her brown shoulders. "I'm not that interesting."

I certainly begged to differ, but didn't push the point.

"I'm in high school," she said after a moment. "I'm gonna be a senior in the fall. Still not sure where I want to go to college. Um...I hate physics."

I perked up; finally, something I understood. "You're studying physics?"

"Studying?" She snorted. "Barely passing is more like it. Math has never been my strong suit."

"I wonder how much of it has changed," I asked. "After all, if there's burgers and...cars, and all this change, I'm sure the world of physics has matured."

She held out her hand, as if summoning something, then grimaced. "Oh yeah. I'm fucking grounded."

"Grounded?" I put two and two together. "You mean a magical restriction?"

"Yeah, grounded." She huffed and dipped another potato stick into the red sauce. "I had to go to summer school 'cause I failed physics. And..." She shifted and cast a wary glance in my direction. "Technically, I'm supposed to be at the library studying. And technically, I guess, I'm supposed to go back to the compound if I run into any evil men."

I actually found myself grinning. "I'll certainly keep my eye out for any."

Her eyes lit up, and she stole another potato. "If she knew I was out with you right now, she'd kill me." Somehow the punishment didn't sound so bad. I wondered if Mora was one of those children who delighted in giving their parents trouble. But it had been several hours since I'd left. Presumably, Alexandra would notice my absence once she and Cyrus finished sparring.

"I should probably return home," I said with a sad sigh. "My mistress will be wondering where I've run off to. Until I'm officially inducted…"

"Inducted?"

"Yes, it's the last step before I become an official member of my Guild."

She reached across the table and took a potato stick from my dwindling pile. "And then what?"

"I…" I furrowed my brow. "I don't know. Up until a few days ago, I was going to continue experimentations on the magic binding us to New Salem." A smile grew on my face. "Perhaps now I'll learn what I can in this new land. I'd love to see Rome. I wonder if it's anything like Julius Caesar." I tilted my head. "Do you still read Shakespeare in your time?"

She snorted. "You have to be the biggest nerd I've ever met. Next time I have a book report, I'm coming to you."

"There's precious little to do in New Salem," I said. "Reading nonmagical books is strictly forbidden."

"Ooh, rebel," she said, leaning across the table and taking

more food. "Well, if you're going to be exploring the world, you should definitely expand beyond Shakespeare. Go to music festivals. Concerts. See a movie! Go to Disney World!" She began counting off other things on her fingertips, and I had no idea what any of them were.

"Would you go with me?" I found myself asking.

Her counting ended, and her eyes grew wide. "What?"

"I know nothing about anything," I said. "I could use a guide to help me make sure I'm getting the most out of it."

She grinned. "That sounds like a better way to spend a summer. You do the magic, I'll tell you what's a burger and a French fry."

It was faint, the tug from Alexandra, and I sighed. "This may have to wait. I have to return to New Salem."

"Are you gonna come back?" she asked.

I smiled. "As soon as my chores are done tomorrow. I'll meet you here. It should be around the same time."

"It's a date."

New Salem was bleak and hopeless compared to the shimmering daylight of the new world. Perhaps it was also the lack of Mora that added to its dullness. The girls in New Salem were certainly pretty in their own way, but they lacked that rebellious fire. I couldn't wait to return to the world to see more of her.

Before all of that, though, there was the matter of my induction to be concerned with. Now, more than ever, I wanted to be free of this cursed tether to Alexandra. It wasn't just a nuisance—it could lead her to the tear. And I wasn't quite ready to share it with anyone yet.

The house was quiet when I returned, and I crept down the hall to Alexandra's study, not wanting to rouse Cyrus, if he were home. I listened for the rustling of papers then softly rapped on the door.

"Enter."

I cracked open the door and slipped inside. The study was filled to the brim with books. On days when I cleaned her room, I'd had a chance to peer at her titles, but today, I kept my gaze on the woman herself. She was lounging on a chaise, her black boots crossed at the ankles and a large tome in her lap. Her brow was quirked up in curiosity as she waited for me to speak.

"You called for me," I said.

"Yes, because it's late, and I can't have you gallivanting around the village," she said, eyeing me. "Where have you been?"

"Around."

She closed the book and considered me. "Am I boring you with my questions, Gavon? Is there somewhere more important you'd rather be?"

There was, but I couldn't very well tell her about it. But there was something I could do.

"I want to be inducted," I said simply. "What do I have to do?"

She chuckled and leaned back on the chaise, surveying me with sharp brown eyes. "What do you think you have to do?"

"I…don't know, that's why I'm asking."

"Gavon, you're a smart boy."

I didn't like it when she played games with me, but I kept

my temper down. "You said to prove to you I should be inducted. I don't know how I can do that."

"A good first step is coming to ask," she said, tilting her head. "What else do you think I want from you?"

*Damn it, just tell me.* "I honestly have no idea."

"I suggest you do some thinking," she said simply, returning to the book.

That wasn't an answer—it was more of the same. Anger burned a hole in my tongue, but I kept my lips closed except to utter, "Yes, Mistress."

# Seven

A night's rest calmed my rage somewhat, but it still simmered beneath the surface. Alexandra enjoyed torturing me —why, I had no idea. Perhaps it was merely because she was, as she said, embarrassed by me. Embarrassed or not, Alexandra wouldn't keep me as her apprentice forever.

Dutifully, I did my morning chores and put the kettle on for morning tea. The key to my induction couldn't be demonstrating servitude, for I'd done that in spades for years. Perhaps one morning I would stay in bed and let Cyrus bear the brunt of Alexandra's rage.

Instead, I assembled bread and cheese on the serving plate and walked out into the dining room.

Alexandra was already there, as was, surprisingly, Councilman Rogers, an old Enchanter way past his prime. Wiry gray hair grew out from all angles of his head and came out of his bulbous nose. His face was always a shade pinker than everyone else's, a testament to his love of beer, most of which he made himself. He'd yet to pass on his spellcasting knowledge to any younger Enchanters, and therefore was the only beer-maker in the village, probably why he remained on the Council.

I summoned a fourth tea cup then set the bread and cheese in the center of the table, quietly greeting him with a nod.

"These boys have been taught well, Guildmaster," Rogers said, looking at Alexandra. "A humble Warrior is a strong Warrior."

"Indeed," Alexandra said, glancing in my direction.

I helped myself to the food. I took one bite of the bread and almost spat it out. It had no flavor, or perhaps, having tasted something more palatable, going back to my magically-created diet was a shock. Everything at the table looked gray, ashen. Unappetizing.

"Something wrong, Gav?" Cyrus asked, seeing through my attempt. "You look as if you've swallowed a fly."

"Not at all," I said as evenly as I could. I imagined the beautiful blue ocean I'd seen the day before to steady my pulse. The waves rolling to the shore then back again, as if magic imbued their very form. But water wasn't magical. I'd have to ask Mora how it worked. Thinking of the new world was a salve to the reality of sitting in a room with an old Enchanter, a smug apprentice, and my infuriating mistress.

"Sad news today," Alexandra announced when we had all settled. "We've lost Councilman Perry."

I frowned, but Cyrus puffed out his chest. "Such a shame. Magical rot? Happens to the best of them."

"In this case, I don't believe it does," she said, gently breaking off a piece of bread. "Perry had long since become more of a ceremonial councilman. Wouldn't you agree, Rogers?"

The old Enchanter coughed and nodded. "Yes, ma'am."

"I dream of the day when we might have a full council of Warriors," Alexandra said with something of a wistful tone. "Alas, we have what we have." Again, her gaze darted in my direction.

"Does that mean my induction match will be now?" Cyrus asked.

"I don't believe you're quite ready yet," she said. "But we may consider it soon."

I waited for her to say the same about mine—after all, if there was a vacancy on the Council, surely whatever vendetta Alexandra was waging against me would be put to the side.

"Gavon." My hopes rose, "Today, I'll need you to take the census of the village. I want an updated accounting of every villager."

This time, it was much harder to keep my face void of emotions. But perhaps if I accomplished the task quickly, I could still make my meeting with Mora. I thought of every question I was going to ask her instead of how much I wanted to throw something magical at Alexandra.

Cyrus snickered. "Such important work, Gav."

"Indeed it is," Alexandra said. "A Guildmaster should know his guild. And every person in it. Therefore, Cyrus, you will be assisting him before our sparring match."

His smug face dropped like a sack of dirt. "But I have to prepare for our sparring match."

"If you have to prepare for a sparring match, perhaps you aren't ready to be inducted," Alexandra said.

I wished I could argue with her—to say Cyrus should rest before stepping into the ring. To do anything that would keep him from accompanying me. But when Alexandra made a decision, that was that.

I cleaned up after breakfast with a scowl, then I summoned a quill and leather-bound notebook from Alexandra's office, waiting for Cyrus at the front door. Predictably, he took his time joining me.

I thumbed through the previous entries, going back at least twenty years. When Alexandra had first taken the census—presumably as an apprentice herself—the villagers numbered seven hundreds. Last year, there were barely five hundred, and Cyrus and I were the only magicals born in that period not an Enchanter or Charmer.

It was a bit disconcerting.

The front doors opened, and Cyrus finally made his appearance.

"Let's hurry up and get this done," I snapped, turning on my heel toward the village below.

"Oh? Do you have some place to be?" Cyrus drawled. "I, personally, love walking amongst the filth. Surprised we don't all get magical rot, breathing their air as we do."

I gritted my teeth. There would be little unnecessary conversation with Cyrus today, because the more he talked, the longer this task would take. I did have better places to be. Things would've gone faster had I divvied up the village and allowed Cyrus to account for his half. But I didn't think it fair to unleash my fellow Warrior on them. And if the final census was incorrect, Alexandra would blame me. So together we went.

At the first cluster of houses, I rapped on the door and announced myself. The door cracked open a hair, but revealed nothing, until a pair of dark brown eyes caught my attention. The little girl was barely knee-high, and her dirty face still held an angelic look.

"Sarah, get away from the door." The girl's harried mother, her belly swollen, came rushing to the door and pulled the child away. She hastily swept her brown hair back into a bun and straightened. "Masters Cyrus, Gavon. It's an honor."

"I'm sure," Cyrus said.

"We're here on behalf of the Guildmaster," I said, ignoring my partner. "The annual census."

"Ah." The worry melted from her face. "Yes, it's just myself, Sarah, and my husband."

"Husband?" Cyrus snorted as he wandered into the work room. "Is there really such a thing still?"

The woman blushed and straightened. "Among the Charmers."

Cyrus might've found their marriage ridiculous, but I was jealous. This little girl would grow up knowing her mother as a mother, and not a calculating mistress who enjoyed toying with her son's desires.

"So, yes. There's just three of us," the woman repeated, with a wary eye on Cyrus, who was looking in their cupboards as if he owned them. "And the baby."

I nodded, casting a look down at the child. "Any sign of magic?"

The woman nodded, rubbing her belly. "Another Charmer.

I'm sure of it."

"Excellent," I said, marking it on the list. I turned to last year's count; Alexandra had also noted their livestock. "And your farm?"

"Oh, we've had three calves this year," she said with a grin. "If they survive to adulthood, we'll have more milk than the village can drink."

"Thank you," I said, marking it down. Then, as we were leaving, I added, "And good luck with your new child."

She beamed and rubbed her belly.

We walked out of the house and Cyrus made no effort to hide his disdain. "Another Charmer. As if we need more rabble in the village."

"And what do you propose we do with them?" I asked as I rapped on the next door.

"Smother them like we do the Potion-makers," Cyrus said. "We already have too many mouths to feed."

The door opened to an old woman, who, by the size of her eyes, had heard the conversation. I made sure to smile genuinely when I informed her of the reason for our visit.

"Come in, come in," she said. The Enchanter, Mary, sat at a table drinking tea. She rose quickly, knocking the cup over then cleaning it with a quick spell.

"M-Master Gavon, it's so nice to see you." Cyrus cleared his throat behind me, and she quickly added, "And Master Cyrus."

"Just here for the annual accounting," I replied.

"Just us two," the older woman said—her mother or sister, I wasn't sure. "Enchanters both."

I flipped to the previous page, finding that Alexandra had

asked about their bread stores. "And your stores?"

Mary fidgeted, but the older woman silenced her with a look. "They're good."

I paused, sensing they weren't being honest. "Are they?"

"No, Master Gavon," Mary blurted. "The bread we make…it just falls apart."

"So make more with magic," Cyrus drawled. "Isn't that what you do?"

"Yes, but…even the bread we have now, it's not the… It's magic made from magic. I don't even know if there's real bread left in the crumbs."

"Hush, girl," the older said. "This is Enchanter business. We don't need to bother the Guildmaster with it."

I paused and marked a note that they needed more. "I'm sure there's something we can do. I will check with Alexandra."

The older woman nodded, looking down. "Please don't take this as a sign of our inability to cast."

"Of course not," I said. Perhaps I would add a crumb or two from my journey to the new world today. That I had the ability to actually help these people left a smile on my face as we walked to the next house.

"What are you grinning about?" Cyrus asked. "Did you roll with that girl yet?"

"No," I said, casting him a look.

"I did," he said with a grimace. "It was forgettable."

"I'm sure it was."


Our canvassing had taken much longer than I'd wanted, as Cyrus had dawdled and languished at almost every house. I would probably miss my meeting time with Mora. Nevertheless, when we arrived back at the Manor, I hurried through the list for Alexandra.

"So that's three hundred Charmers, two hundred forty-one Enchanters, and three Warriors," I said. "Fifteen pregnancies—twelve of which are known Charmers or Enchanters, and three are too early to tell."

"Too early?" Alexandra asked with a quirked brow.

"Potion-makers," I admitted. "Or stillborn."

She sat back in her chair, her fingers intertwined above her lap. "And no Warriors or Healers?"

"Not one, Mistress."

She nodded and tilted her head toward Cyrus. "And what do you think of this, Cyrus?"

He straightened, as if he hadn't been paying attention. "What?"

"I asked what you thought of our numbers." Her face gave away nothing, and for once, I was glad I wasn't on the receiving end of her questioning.

Cyrus swallowed his surprise in favor of a smug look. "Too much rabble. We came across a woman who had seven children —seven. All Enchanters. What a waste."

She nodded slowly. "Why do you think they're a waste? Charmers and Enchanters create the food you eat. They're an integral part of our village."

"Yes, but do we need three hundred of them?" he asked. "It seems a lot."

"Very well. Meet me in the sparring ring. I will join you momentarily."

And he was gone in a puff of gray.

"And what do you think of our numbers, Gavon?" Alexandra asked. "Do you think it's a waste?"

I honestly had no answer for her. To my eyes, the villagers seemed happy. They might not know how to read, or understand magical theory, but they were still good magicals with every right to their small plots of land.

"No," I said finally. "I don't."

Something like amusement lit her eyes. "You may dust my library today."

# Eight

As soon as she was gone, I used magic to dust every inch of that library and wash the windows. When it was finished, I transported myself to the tear then dove in head-first.

This time, the bright sun didn't bother me as much. I once more charmed my clothes to the shorter clothing favored by the men of this era then closed my eyes. I'd probably missed Mora, so I sought her out using magic, praying she wasn't beyond the confines of her mother's magical barrier.

No, she was in the library. Sitting at a table, reading a book with a furrow in her brow. My magic sang as it transported me to the seat across from her.

She looked up and yelped in surprise.

"It's me!" I said, momentarily terrified she'd forgotten me—or worse. "Gavon, remember? I'm still not here to harm you!"

"Holy crap," she cried, placing her hand over her head. "Dude, you can't just..." She lowered her voice. "Transport in the middle of the library. You can't use magic in front of the nonmagicals. What if somebody'd seen you?"

I opened and closed my mouth. "I...don't know? What would happen?"

"If you ask my mother, the apocalypse," she said, her shock slowly fading into a smile that eased my tension. "For whatever reason, you don't have to stick to the same rules we do, but... you have to be more careful. Just...don't use magic outside your house."

"That...seems impossible," I said, shaking my head.

She laughed, her previous annoyance disappearing. "It's not so bad doing things nonmagically. I mean, especially when you've got all nonmagical friends, it's not hard to hide your magic." Her smile faded to a scowl. "Or when you're grounded and you can't use magic anyway."

"But how do you get anywhere?" I asked. "If you aren't allowed to transport to nonmagical places?"

"Cars," she said. "Remember? Those things you were so interested in yesterday? Airplanes, too."

I frowned. "But if I wanted to go to Rome?"

"I mean," she leaned across the table, "you can use magic. Just gotta be careful no nonmagical folks see you, that's all. Like appearing here in the library?" She shook her head. "Can't do that."

"I obviously can..."

"Yeah, Mom was talking about that last night," Mora said. "Apparently, you're not bound by this whole agreement they made in the seventeenth century. Like me? I couldn't transport here even if I really wanted to. And attacking Renny like you did?" She shook her head. "But since you're able to do all that and a bag of chips, you aren't under that same agreement."

I'd nearly forgotten about her paramour. "I apologize for hurting him."

"Eh," she said with a shrug. "It was kind of over anyway. I mean, he's fine. But he's an ass. Nonmagical guys are always a pain to date. Can't ever talk to them about family functions or anything like that." She tilted her head, something like mischievousness on her face. "And besides that, you're a lot more fun than he is."

"Am I?" I looked down at my shirt, for lack of anything else.

"Oh yeah," she said, leaning over. "Not at all what my mother said you were."

I swallowed. "I'd be happy to speak with her. I don't want to cause any undue trouble for you or her."

"Don't bother," she said, shaking her head. "My great uncle is retiring soon, and my mom wants the Clanmaster spot. I'm sure she thinks this is a good opportunity to showcase how badass she is." Her shoulders drooped. "Politics. It sucks."

"I am quite aware," I said with a laugh. Finally, something we had in common. "My mother isn't much better. And Cyrus —"

"Who's he?"

"He's the other Warrior in the village. My mother's primary apprentice. I'm just the... My former master died three years ago, so I was sent to finish my training with her."

She lifted her head. "You make it sound like you didn't even live with her."

"I didn't." Her eyes widened, as if the admission were shocking. "Warriors are traditionally trained by someone other than their biological parent. It makes the transition of power much easier, and removes any emotional attachment. My own mother cares more for her apprentice than she does for me."

"Sounds like Irene. All she talks about is getting Clanmaster. My existence is enough to piss her off these days."

"What about your father?"

She grew a bit somber. "He wasn't magical. Divorced my mom a few years ago after Jeanie was born. Guess the pressure of having such a ballbuster was too much for him. We don't see him a lot—but he calls sometimes."

I heard the loneliness in her voice but decided not to press. "My father died a few years ago. Magical rot. A curable disease, if one opted to brew a potion every once in a while."

"So why didn't you?"

"Potion-making is illegal," I replied. "Has been since we arrived in New Salem."

"Hm." She slid her hands along the book pages. "So…are you hungry?"

"Another burger?" I asked.

"Nah, I have something else in mind," she said. "We should probably get out of Salem, with all the magicals roaming around here looking for you. But you're gonna have to drive."

"Drive?"

"Use your magic," she said, slinging her bag over her shoulder. "C'mon, I know a good hiding place."


With Mora's directions, I transported us to a distant city, in a dark alley away from nonmagical eyes. She called it Glow-ster, and dragged me into something called a 'pizza place.' The room was very dark with an enticing aroma that made my stomach rumble. We sat down at a table covered in checkered red and white fabric that slid under my fingers. A man came to speak with us, and I let Mora do the talking. She promised she was ordering us something good as the man left. I nodded and continued to inspect the cloth, contemplating what it could be made of.

"What?" she asked, chewing on her straw as she sipped her soda. "Is the tablecloth interesting?"

"It's…different," I said, looking up at her then smiling at the look on her face. "I can stop, if it's bothering you."

"Nah, I kind of like watching you experience the world," she said. "It's like…everything's brand new to you. Nothing's boring."

I grinned and turned to the left, where a framed drawing of the Colosseum hung. "That's familiar. I've read many books about Rome."

"Oh yeah?" She plucked the frame from the wall and handed it to me. "You like ancient history then?"

"To me, it's regular history," I said with a laugh. "But I want to see it with my own eyes. To know if it's as magnificent as they say."

"What else have you read about?" she asked.

"Venice," I said. "Verona—"

"Like Romeo and Juliet?" She giggled. "You've read Romeo and Juliet?"

For some reason, my cheeks warmed. "Yes, it's quite good."

"Dude, it's two teenagers who meet at a party once, get married, then die for no reason," she said with a scoff. "Like…

the world's worst love story."

I'd never considered it that way before. "I suppose. Then tell me, what do you enjoy reading?"

She shrugged. "My mom thinks it's stupid, but I really love Anne Rice. *Interview with the Vampire*? Lestat? Yum."

Any further questions I had were quelled by the appearance of a circular loaf of bread covered in white cheese and red circles. It looked incredible, but smelled indescribably delicious. I mimicked Mora as she plucked a pre-cut triangle from the center, then brought it to my mouth.

"Careful!" she said just as I bit down. Pain sliced the roof of my mouth and I nearly spat out the bread. "It's hot," she said with a frown. "Are you okay?"

I nodded and struggled to swallow the bite.

"You may want to wait a minute," she said, handing me the black soda. I sucked it down and let the cool liquid fill my mouth to salve the burn.

"I guess I should have noticed that," I said sheepishly. It was steaming fairly obviously.

"Here." She handed me a miniature bread loaf that had come with it. "Try this."

I took a hesitant bite, and the most glorious taste filled my mouth. I had no words for it, having never tasted anything similar in my life. It was pungent and salty, the bread soft and doughy in my mouth.

"Yeah?" she said with a smile. "You like that?"

I nodded. "What is this amazing thing?"

"Garlic bread," she said, taking a bite of one herself.

"Garlic bread." I lifted the half-eaten loaf in the air. "Imagine the Enchanters making one of these. There'd be chaos."

"You guys don't have garlic either, I take it?"

"No. No spices whatsoever," I said. "I'd read about them in a book, but this…"

"Well, you ain't seen nothin' yet," she said, picking up the cheesy triangle that had burned me before. "Try this now."

I closed my eyes and bit off a tentative piece. Like the garlic bread, it was an unfamiliar taste, but delicious.

"Good, huh?" she said, wiping the corners of her mouth.

"Amazing," I said, furrowing my brow. I'd had cheese for breakfast nearly my entire life, but it had never tasted so rich and full. Perhaps even our livestock had suffered from a lack of non-magically grown food, as we had. I'd never thought about the food the Charmers gave to their animals. I doubted there was anything real left in the village.

"What's wrong?"

"Just thinking about our food," I said. "I wonder if it's the reason so many of us die from magical rot."

She grimaced. "What's that?"

"It's an illness that slowly drains your magic from your body. It usually sets on around the fiftieth birthday, if not sooner. It's rare for someone in New Salem to age past sixty-five." I looked at the bread in my hand. "And I'd wager eating magically-enhanced food might be the cause of it."

"Geez," she said. "My great-uncle is ninety. I think. We don't die early."

I nodded, but my mind was back in New Salem. "I wonder if I could bring food back to them."

"I mean…why can't you?" she asked.

I envisioned Alexandra's face when I handed her a piece of garlic bread—or pizza. "I'll have to be covert about it. They don't do well with change. And they might ask questions I'm not ready to answer…"

"So, like…you haven't told anyone about the tear yet?" she asked.

"No, and I'm not sure how to tell them about it," I said. "Or even if I should. My mother and my fellow apprentice, Cyrus, are one thing—they are fairly well-read and at least understand that this world exists. But there are five hundred others, and many can't even read. To bring them here? They might die of shock." I looked at the bread again. "But that doesn't mean I shouldn't try to help them, if I can."

She picked at the tablecloth. "You aren't going to tell anyone at all?"

I imagined Cyrus swaggering down the street. He wouldn't be bothered by the differences—and wouldn't care about Mora's desire to keep magic secret from the nonmagicals. He'd start flinging attack spells as soon as he could. Besides that, there was some selfish glee at knowing I'd done what he couldn't.

"I suppose I could never tell them," I said slowly. "Once my induction match occurs, I'd be free from Alexandra."

"Then what would you do?"

I turned to the Colosseum picture again. "See things like that until the day I died."

"Well, what's stopping you from seeing it now?" She sat up. "We could go. Right now."

"Right now?" I blinked. I'd never considered the prospect. I had no idea how far away Rome was, but I was sure it was farther than I'd ever transported before.

But something about her smile made me ready for anything.

"Sure, let's go."

81

# Nine

"Have I ever transported across the ocean?" I scratched my chin as I followed Mora down another dark alley where we could transport. "No, never. I've only just seen an ocean."

"I've only done it once before, with my mom," she said. "But you seem like a smart guy. I bet you could do it without trying."

Her confidence in me was nice, but my stomach turned uncomfortably. Transporting from one end of New Salem to the other wasn't difficult. But the idea of traveling across oceans and continents?

She took my hands in hers, squeezing them. Once again, her eyes took me captive with a mix of mischievous and kindness. "Hey, if you need a refresher, I can help."

"Perhaps," I admitted, grateful she didn't seem to think less of me for it.

"So it's all about letting your magic go," she said, sliding her fingers through mine and sending chills up my arms. "Mom always says it's smarter than I am, so you gotta just let it do what it does."

"Alexandra says the same thing," I murmured then inhaled deeply. "Very well. Let me see what I can do."

With her hands tethering me to the ground, I retreated into the recesses of my mind and let my magic loose. It was tentative at first, sharing my trepidation, like a baby taking its first steps. Together, we reached the edge of the village, finding water.

And then I let it go.

My eyes grew wet as my magic took in the whole world—all of it. I'd thought the stars in the night sky had been vast. The ocean, too. But it was nothing compared to mountains and valleys, green pastures so verdant they couldn't possibly be real, sights so beautiful I had no words to describe them. I wanted to see the world, but now—just as with the library—I became aware of my own mortality.

Mora swiped my cheek with her fingertips. "Why are you crying?" she asked.

I opened my eyes to gaze into hers. "It's just...I never thought things could be so beautiful. And I want to see it all, but I don't think I'll ever live long enough to."

She smiled and wiped my other cheek. "Then why don't we start now, and see as much as we can? Starting with Rome."

I nodded and closed my eyes once more, asking the magic to find the place in my mind's eye—and then to find us a desolate spot. Then, once I was confident, I enveloped us both in my magic, taking extra care to surround Mora with more magic than previously, and physically pulling her into an embrace. She rested her head on my shoulder and for a brief moment, I forgot what I was doing.

Then, I let the magic transport us to the darkness. As soon as my feet hit the ground, I regretted using so much magic, for it left me dizzy and swaying. Luckily, Mora's embrace kept me on my feet, and she giggled.

"You all right?" she asked, stepping back just enough to look me in the eye.

I nodded, even as I blinked away spots. My sluggish brain achingly resumed normal speed. More senses caught up, too—smells, sounds, how she felt in my arms. I shook my head once to clear the rest of the fog then noticed things were much darker here.

"What's wrong? Why is it dark here?" I asked with a frown. Could something horrible have happened to Rome in the past three hundred years?

"Probably because it's like nine at night," she said, gently stepping out of my embrace. "Time difference."

I furrowed my brow. "Time…difference?"

"Oh boy, I'm gonna have to get you a book or something," she said, although the smile on her face said she wasn't annoyed. Once again, she threaded her fingers through mine as she led me out of the darkened alley. She explained how the world rotated, and how each section of the globe had a different time, but I lost her about halfway through the conversation. As much as I enjoyed hearing her talk, the bustle of the city was too much. The cars that had been in Salem were present in Rome, although they looked much different here. Everything was different, in fact. The central road was less a road and more a hallway, with towering buildings on either side.

"C'mon," Mora said, tugging at my hand.

We walked along a tall wall resembling a castle with turrets and long walkways along the edge. I lazily dragged my hand along the stone, scarcely able to believe this was real. I was really in Rome. Not for the first time, I wondered if this was a dream. Perhaps Cyrus had hit me too hard during a sparring session. For how could someone like me have traveled through the tear to a place as beautiful as this, with a blonde beauty guiding me down the street?

If it was a dream, I'd enjoy it until I woke up.

The passersby spoke in a language I'd never heard before, which Mora explained was a language called Italian. She stopped two of them and asked for directions, a comical episode that featured a lot of hand waving and pointing, but she returned to hold my hand.

Newer buildings had been constructed around the older buildings, giving the scene a mismatched appearance. I drank in the sights and smells—even the unpleasant ones.

"So what do you think?" she asked. "Is it better than you read about in your books?"

"I think…" I swallowed hard. "I think it's better than I ever could have imagined."

"Oh yeah? Well, look over there." She pointed.

I turned, and my heart stopped. The massive stone structure was crumbling, but the parts that still stood towered over the street. We walked closer, the Colosseum growing with each step. Finally, we stood beneath it and it was all I could do to just stare. I would never get enough of this feeling.

Mora stood beside me, her fingers intertwined with mine. I snuck a glance at her; her eyes were wide and there was a smile toying on her lips.

"I would've thought this boring to you," I said.

Her cheeks reddened. "I've never seen it before either. It's pretty cool up close, you know?"

"Thank you for bringing me here," I said softly.

"You brought us here," she said. "I just gave you directions."

"Yes, but…" I turned to her. "Thank you. This means a lot to me."

She grinned. "Want to see what else we can find?"

With Mora leading the way, we walked down streets and alleys, gaping at structures and statues that rose from the streets. Mora pointed out a few she knew, and we guessed at those that she didn't.

"And that over there is the statue of Peter the Perturbed," she said, pointing to a large man standing. "He was memorialized for telling kids to get off his property."

I laughed, more at the way she'd lowered her voice and furrowed her brow. I was fairly sure that one she was making up.

"I can't tell if you find me funny because you don't know any better, or if you actually think I'm…well, funny," she said after a moment.

"I'm a little behind, but…I'm not laughing at you, if that's what you're thinking."

She shrugged. "I don't know, it's just…nobody's ever found me this funny before." She half-smiled. "Then again, I've never had this much fun with anyone before, either."

I couldn't disagree. Despite most of our conversation centering on explaining things to me, talking with Mora was easy. I was enjoying the world, but I was also enjoying the company.

"This has been the best day of my life," I said honestly.

She beamed, and we kept walking. "So, like…do you have a girlfriend back in New Salem?"

"Girl friends? There are girls, but none I'm very close with."

"No, I meant like…a girlfriend," she said. "Someone you go out with?"

I shook my head, still not understanding.

"Like someone you kiss?" Mora said, her face growing redder as she stumbled over her words.

"Oh." Realization dawned. "No, I'm afraid it's not really something Warriors concern ourselves with."

"Really? Why not?"

"Love is weakness, or so they say," I said. "It's the reason my mother sent me to another Warrior to raise. Attachment gets in the way of…well, whatever Warriors do."

She frowned. "That's horrible. So how do you get married and all that?"

"Warriors don't get married," I said with a hint of sadness. But her questions piqued my curiosity. "Why do you ask?"

"No reason." She turned her red cheeks away from me.

I was about to press further, but we'd reached a crowded square. There, in the center, was a sculpture that seemed too lifelike to be stone. The center figure's cloak floated effortlessly in a permanent wind, his gaze angry and strong toward the other figures. Each of the statues erupting from the earth as if coming from the depths of hell itself.

"This is…incredible," I said after a moment. "What is it?"

"The…Trevi fountain," Mora said, squinting at a book on a nearby stand. "Made of marble."

I shook my head. "They had to have used magic to create this."

"Nope," she said, smiling up at me. "Nonmagicals made it. Carved it from stone."

It seemed impossible that stone could be manipulated in such a way. I couldn't even fathom how a nonmagical would even begin to do something so complex. The statues were practically moving, yet remained frozen.

"You're crying again," she said, wiping my cheek.

"I'm just so…stunned," I said, bowing my head. "I'm sorry if—"

I turned, and yet again, was taken with the sight of her. The freckles on her face, the upward turn of her lips. She was full of energy and beauty. And I knew if I never returned to this place, I would treasure the memory of her face, just as it was in that moment, for the rest of my life.

"You keep looking at me like that," she said, her voice quieter than it had been. "Like you can't believe you're looking at me."

"I can't." I wrenched my gaze from her to the stone structure before me. "I can't believe any of this exists. I know soon I'll wake up and be back in New Salem. I'll have to scrub the floors and make the fire to boil the water. Then, I'll be forced to spar with Cyrus morning and afternoon. And then, I'll be back at the edge of New Salem, trying different potion concoctions to create a tear to a girl I dreamed about."

She smiled. "And if this is only a dream, what else would you do?"

I was about to answer, but I was bumped by a couple giggling with each other. They spoke in a language I didn't understand and held something between them. Then with their backs turned, they tossed the metal into the water once, twice, then, with a look at each other, three times. They shared a kiss, and walked away, holding each other as they did so.

"What are they doing?" I asked, noticing others were also throwing metal with their backs turned. It wasn't just couples, either—families young and old were throwing things into the fountain.

"Superstition," said an old man nearby. He was the same one selling the thick books with Rome plastered on the front of them. "Throw one coin," he said, mimicking the movement. "Return to Rome. Two coin, new romance. Three coin, marriage!"

"We should do it," Mora said, taking my hand and pulling me closer to the fountain. She procured a small metal coin from her pocket and handed me one.

"So what are we doing?"

"It's like…a myth," she said. "If you throw one coin in the fountain, you'll definitely return to Rome. Two…" She glanced up at me from beneath her thick lashes. "You'll find new love. And three, you'll get married."

All of those sounded like great things to me. Together, we turned and stood shoulder-to-shoulder then chucked the metal coin with our right hand over our left shoulder, as others were doing.

"That's one," Mora said, a little breathlessly. "That means

we'll return to Rome."

"I think I'd return here anyway," I said.

"Do you…want to throw another in?"

The nervousness in her voice drew my attention to her face, which had turned pink. Her breath was coming in shorter bursts, but her eyes—her beautiful blue eyes the color of the ocean—were full of excitement.

"What was the second?" I asked, noticing how close we stood, and how very soft her lips looked. The freckles that playfully dotted her cheeks. The golden locks that brushed against my fingers as I slid my hands around her cheeks.

"That we'd find new love," she whispered, her gaze dropping to my mouth.

"I don't think I need a coin to do that," I said.

And with a move that was mostly instinct, I pressed my lips softly to hers. The quiet exhalation exhilarated me, as did the sweet taste of her.

Just as I let myself fall deeper into this feeling, there was a small tug at my magic and my heart dropped into my stomach. Even across the ocean, I remained tethered to Alexandra.

"What is it?" Mora asked.

"I have to go," I said, wishing with everything I had that it wasn't so. "Alexandra is calling."

"Bummer," she said, chewing on her lip.

I couldn't help myself and I kissed her again. She responded, sliding her lips over mine and tangling her hands in my hair. I never wanted this moment to end—but Alexandra tugged with more fervor. The last thing I wanted was for her to come searching for me and find the tear on her own.

"I'm sorry," I whispered. "I wish…I wish I could stay."
"Will you come back tomorrow?" she asked.
I grinned. "Absolutely."

91

# Ten

"Where have you been?" Alexandra asked as I walked into her office. "It's not like you to miss dinner."

"I apologize. I was detained."

Alexandra stared me down, and it was all I could do to keep a grin off my face. I hoped she couldn't smell Mora's scent on me, for it was filling my nose. I could even taste her on my lips.

"Go to bed," she said, returning to the book she'd been reading.

I practically floated to my room, my mind filled with dreams of what was to come. Would we go back to Rome? Would we instead go to Verona? Venice? Somewhere else entirely?

Nothing in my life had ever been so exciting and distracting. Just thinking of Mora's face—especially when the corners of her pink lips turned upward—sent my heart pounding. I understood why love could be a weakness to someone like Alexandra or Cyrus. Mora took up every one of my thoughts, even crowding out the desire to be inducted. Even though I'd only known her a short time, I was oddly willing to do anything for her. How quickly this all-encompassing feeling had settled in. And how sad that it was frowned upon in New Salem. Had Alexandra ever felt this, or was she so cold she'd never allowed the telltale flutter? Did she feel anything for my father, or was my birth mere duty?

I slept little, but it didn't bother me much. Even Cyrus had noted my happy demeanor, trying in vain to disrupt it with his snide remarks about sparring with Alexandra. But nothing would deter me. Not when I had grand plans to return to Mora today and explore the world further.

"Gavon," Alexandra said. "You will continue cleaning the library today. It has become dirty again."

That broke my reverie. "I cleaned it top to bottom yesterday."

She sipped her tea. "Do you believe me to be simple, Gavon? Or believe I couldn't discern a magical cleaning job from a manual one?"

"Well, you let Cyrus get away with cleaning magically all the time. I thought it might be the key to my induction match," I said before I thought better of it.

Alexandra put down the book and clicked her tongue—and my magic was gone. Or rather, it was tightly bound away from my grasp. The food I'd so carefully prepared had also vanished before I could take my first bite.

"Get to work," she said.

Cyrus snickered as I rose from the table and walked out as calmly as possible, but inside, I was a raging storm. Not only did I have to clean the library, a task which took hours, but I wasn't to have any magic. And most infuriating of all, I wouldn't be able to see Mora today.

Doing chores without magic was always difficult. I had to walk all the way down to the water well, pump a bucket by hand, then carry it back to the Manor. Even more embarrassing, the well was in the center of the town, so the whole village would know I was being punished.

I found the bucket and brush where I'd left them the day before and trudged down to the center of town. I felt every gaze as I clomped by, grateful the cold on my cheeks could have been the cause of my flushing. Even Cyrus had never had to walk to the well. Conversations followed me as the onlookers stood around their small houses, whispering to each other. A cold wind blew through my shirt, reminding me I'd left without my cloak. But alas, without magic to summon it, I pressed on.

I put the bucket on the ground under the pump and grasped the metal lever. The frigid metal bit into my fingers but I held on, working it up and down. Magically, this would've been a simple task. Even if I'd walked all this way, I could've summoned the water to the surface.

As I worked, my arms aching from effort, I thought back to what Mora had said about the nonmagicals. This would've been normal for her—especially if all the villagers hadn't had magic.

I'd never seen New Salem as anything antiquated, but having seen the progress in the other world—the world without magic —our own technology seemed quaint. There, liquid came at the press of a button. And not just water, but that delicious soda with bubbles and sweetness. The nonmagicals had created cars to get them from place to place without magic. In a way, theirs was a world that made magic obsolete.

Footsteps broke me from my musing, and I straightened to see Mary, the young Enchanter, behind me. She wore her cloak tightly around her body, shielding her from the cold wind. And I was sure she also had a warming charm on her shirt.

"Hullo, Master Gavon," she said, bowing her head. "Would you like me to pump your water?"

"No, of course not," I said, grasping the handle. When a flash of hurt crossed her face, I softened my expression. "I mean, it's obvious the Guildmaster has a punishment in mind. It would be wrong to ask you to circumvent it."

She nodded and kicked the dirt with her scuffed boots. "Did you…have a chance to talk to Guildmaster McKinnon about our grain stores?"

I hadn't—I couldn't even remember what I'd promised. "Forgive me…"

"It's all right," she said with a forced smile as water finally came from the pump. "We'll figure something out. We always do." She turned to walk away, but stopped and turned back. Her ruddy face scrunched up as she came back toward me. "Master Gavon, I'll just say it: I would like to couple with you so I might pass on your Warrior magic."

The bucket fell out of my hand, spilling all my hard-earned water on the ground. "I'm sorry?"

Her face turned even redder. "My mother was a powerful Charmer before the rot took hold. I think I could make a Warrior if you would have me."

Was this the sort of thing Cyrus dealt with? I worked my jaw as I had no idea how to answer her.

"I…will consider it," I finally said.

She grinned, and I regretted even leaving that door cracked.

"But why not go to Cyrus?" I said as she walked away. "He'll be Guildmaster."

"Oh, don't say that," she said with an unmistakable grimace. Then she gasped and covered her face. "Forgive me, Master Gavon. I didn't mean to speak ill of your fellow Warrior."

"It's all right, I speak worse of him," I said. "I take it you aren't looking forward to the day Alexandra steps down?"

She glanced around, as if checking for Cyrus around the corner. "Most in the village hate Cyrus. He takes what he wants from us. We'd much rather you be Guildmaster."

I frowned. "I'm no match for Cyrus in the sparring ring, though. Wouldn't you rather have a leader who could protect you in battle?"

"Battle," she scoffed. "What battle? We'd much rather have someone with kindness in their hearts who cares about us. You care about us."

"Cyrus…cares about the village," I said, although we both knew it was a lie.

"Not like you do." She took a hesitant step toward me. "I've been with Cyrus before. He treats it like a competition only he can win." She batted her eyelashes. "You, I believe, would at least make it fun."

I swallowed hard, again at a loss for words.

"You know where to find me," she said, sauntering away with swinging hips.

To say I was rattled by Mary's forwardness was an

understatement. I purposefully avoided walking by her house on the way back to the Manor, hoping to avoid any unintended messages that I was interested in coupling with her.

Less surprising was her opinion of Cyrus and wishing I would ascend to leadership in his place. But as far as I was concerned, his Guildmastership was set in stone—no matter what Alexandra thought. I only hoped I was far away from New Salem when that day came. That thought happily lifted me out of my sour mood as I finished pumping the water.

When I returned to the house, Alexandra and Cyrus had concluded their morning session. Cyrus was snoring in his room, and Alexandra was in the library. I didn't bother to ask if I should return later. She would delight in watching me toil, so I would let her in order to hasten the end of my punishment.

I knelt on the floor and scrubbed at the new layer of dust—presumably, she'd magicked it in to give me more work to do. For a long time—at least an hour—the only sound in the room was the brush against the wooden floor. I didn't know if the floor was getting cleaner or if I was merely pushing dirt around, but I did know Alexandra was watching.

Then, out of the blue, "I am reviewing your notes from the census."

As I scrubbed under a bookcase, I readied myself.

"These numbers are concerning," she murmured.

I paused my scrubbing and sat up. Was she going to critique my math now? "How so?"

She didn't lift her gaze from the page, the crease deepening in her forehead. "Crumbs aplenty for the Enchanters, but from what are those crumbs made? Magic." She sighed. "The

Separation might not have killed us immediately, but it will kill us eventually. Every year, we grow weaker and weaker."

"I had no idea things were so bad," I said quietly after a moment.

"Didn't you?" Alexandra asked, tilting her head. "Was there no sign in your privileged position?"

"I…" I swallowed. "I knew things were difficult. But what I heard was…more than I thought. The village is dying—truly dying."

She nodded. "And I can't do anything to stop it."

I rested on my knees. I didn't disagree with her—especially after tasting the food on the other side. There was a vibrancy to it, a feeling like it was more than just dirt and magic. If I brought some of it over, and if I told Alexandra about what I'd done, it would solve all our problems.

And yet, I hesitated. I didn't want to tell her outright what I'd done, not until I'd had my fill of it. But perhaps there was a way to gauge her reaction.

"Have we ever tried…breaking the barrier between this world and the old one?"

She lifted her gaze to mine, a smirk on her face. "Breaking the barrier? You believe it to be as simple as that?"

"I don't." I averted my gaze, lest she read something in it. "But if we're dying, we might try expending some energy toward freeing ourselves from this prison."

"It has been tried by magicals much smarter and more powerful than you or me," she replied. "Our captors made a prison to last eternity."

I continued scrubbing, still wanting to broach the subject,

but not quite sure how to. Without any other ideas, I decided to just get straight to the point. "What…might you do if we did break it?"

She inhaled and straightened her shoulders. "I'm not in the business of discussing imaginary situations."

"No, but…" I schooled my features, even though I had my back to her. "I'm curious. Would you indulge me?"

"I suppose I would gather food for the villagers," Alexandra said, after a moment's thought. "Then continue Riley's goal. To live under the sun in a world run by magicals. And to take revenge on those who put us here."

I couldn't hide my grimace and was grateful for my position on the floor. Perhaps Mora's mother was right to be cautious of us. "You would go to war just when we get salvation?"

"I told you, I'm not in the business of discussing imaginary situations." She finally stopped and turned to me. "What is more pressing is how we will save our village within the confines of our magical bounds now. The more we focus our energy on anything else, the more will die of magical rot."

I closed my mouth and nodded. "Understood."

"I know you've read all of Jones's nonmagical books," she said quietly, almost pensively. "And I don't want you to pine for a place you may never see. A man could waste away with that kind of yearning."

I straightened, finally turning to her. "You've read them, too?"

She nodded. "When I was a girl. Cover to cover, repeatedly. Jones was a good master, but there were no other Warriors in the village. You're lucky you have Cyrus to train with."

Lucky wasn't the word I'd use.

"But that's neither here nor there. We have a dying village and we must do whatever we can to keep ourselves alive."

I paused mid-scrub. "Whatever we can" gave me a small opening. I wasn't yet ready to tell her the whole truth, but perhaps I could still help.

"What if I were to find a potion?" I asked slowly. "One that could bring back the original properties of a piece of bread or meat?"

She lowered her journal. "Do you know of such a thing?"

"Not...exactly," I said. "But I have been experimenting. Perhaps I might try something when I've finished with my chores."

She didn't reply immediately, and I feared I'd said the wrong thing. But as I scrubbed, magic returned to my body. Alexandra had undone her containment spell.

"See what you can come up with," she said, before disappearing in a puff of purple smoke.

# Eleven

Not wanting to test Alexandra's patience, I finished cleaning the library without magic. Mora would be waiting, and I would yet again have to apologize for not making our meeting on time. I had come up with quite a list of ways to apologize, and most of them involved staring into her eyes and perhaps kissing her lips.

I arrived in the new world, thankful for the heat and the sun. The cold, biting air of New Salem melted from my skin as I changed my clothes into shorts and a shirt.

My new task from Alexandra should've been simple, but I had no idea how to find the nonmagicals who baked breads, or anything like that. I would have to talk to Mora—something I couldn't wait to do anyway. This time, I decided to honor her wishes not to use magic around the nonmagicals. Instead, I found a private room inside the library and transported myself there.

I strolled out of the room, acting as if I didn't know what I was looking for, though I knew exactly where she sat. It was rather fun, this pretending to be nonmagical.

I leaned against the bookcase and watched her for a moment as she cursed under her breath, flipping angrily through a book. With a huff, she threw down her writing instrument and sat back. Her cheeks reddened when she saw me.

"How long have you been standing there?" she asked.

"Not long at all," I lied, coming to sit across from her. "What's troubling you?"

"Well, I'm doubly grounded now," Mora said, slumping into her chair. "On account of skipping class yesterday."

I grimaced. "That's my fault."

"No, it's not. I didn't want to go, so I skipped." She slid her hand across the table to take mine. "Besides, I had more fun with you anyway."

Electricity slid from where her skin touched mine as I closed my hand around her. Was it too early to kiss her? Probably so.

"I, too, was punished for staying out too long," I said, my gaze falling to her pink lips. "I had to scrub the library without magic."

"Is that why your hands are so pruny?" she asked, gently turning my hands over and dancing her fingertips along my palms. "You sound like Cinderella over there. All you need are some mice and a fairy godmother."

I was too preoccupied by the gentle brush of her fingers against mine to be bothered to ask her to explain further. "How are you doubly grounded?"

"Well, Mom's gone to the Clanmaster," she explained, drawing circles on my palms and glancing up every few moments to catch my mesmerized gaze. "You know how that goes."

"Mm…in theory," I said, shivering as she drew a long line down my hand. "But all I know about clans are in books, and I believe things have changed."

"Well, so my great uncle is the Clanmaster," she began, her voice low. "And he can take the power of Clan Carrigan to enforce stuff."

"Mm…"

"So she's asked him to keep a tighter leash on me," Mora said. "He knows where I am at all times—Mom can't do that by herself." She released my hand and blew air out between her lips, breaking her spell on me. "And so I gotta stay in the library or my ass is grass."

I smiled at the imagery and nodded to the open book. "What are you reading?"

"Physics," she said then stuck her tongue out. "Kill me. I didn't get it during the school year, and I'm certainly not going to get it now."

"That's not true," I said, drawing the book closer to me. Although the colors and images on the page distracted me momentarily, soon, the structure became familiar. "This is Newton's law of motion, isn't it?"

She nodded. "I have to solve all these problems. Every time I try, I get them wrong. I don't know what I'm doing wrong."

I pulled the paper over to me and read the first one.

*An airplane accelerates down a runway at 4.3 m/s2 for 45.2 seconds. What is the distance traveled?*

"What's an airplane and a runway?"

She chuckled, explaining the concept. While I didn't get the specifics, it did clear up what we were looking for. I walked through the problem then found her error—she'd forgotten to square the time. "See, here it is."

"Ah, son of a bitch," she said, pulling her paper back and working through it. Finally, she sat back with a grin. "God, I hate math."

"Why?" I asked. "It's just a puzzle."

"I'd rather do a jigsaw puzzle or a crossword puzzle," she said, tapping her pen. "Finding the square root of fifty? Who the hell ever needs to know how to do that?"

"Maybe not in practice, but mathematics is good for the mind," I said, reviewing the rest of her answers. "And a sharp mind makes a sharp magical."

"You are the world's biggest dork." Based on her tone, dork meant nothing good.

"As I told you, there's not much to entertain in New Salem," I said as my cheeks warmed. "So solving these puzzles was sometimes my only entertainment."

"You poor, poor baby," she said then grinned. "Say…you might be able to complete all these problems for me. My mom charmed my paper so I can't use magic to complete it. But I'll bet that it doesn't apply to you, does it?"

I laughed. "I'm sure it doesn't, but I believe that's cheating. Otherwise, how will you learn?"

"I don't need to know physics," she said. "It's not like it's going to be useful in adulthood. And unlike where you're from, there are plenty of other things to entertain us here."

"I'm sure, but I don't think it's right."

She blew air out between her lips. "Well, then, will you help me? At least check my math?"

"That, I can do."

I'd never had the pleasure of teaching anybody anything before. Perhaps it was my student, but I found it satisfying every time Mora nodded in understanding and was able to solve an equation by herself. Before either of us knew it, we'd completed every one listed in her book.

"You're a great teacher," she said. "That made more sense than anything anyone else ever said."

"This," I pointed to her book, with the graphics and colors, "is too much information. When I learned physics, all I had was a book." I grinned and looked around for nonmagicals. Then I summoned my only copy of Newton's *Principia* from my library. It took a moment, but it appeared in my hand.

"Wow," Mora said, gingerly taking the book from me. "This thing is ancient. An antique!"

I smiled. "I don't know if it would help you learn anything more. But you can read it, if you want."

"I don't want to take your books, Gavon," she said, carefully turning the pages.

"Books are meant to be read," I said. Giving her this book was like giving her a piece of myself, and watching her carefully turn each page warmed my heart.

"Then how about this. Stay here for a sec." She rose and disappeared through the stack of books, returning a few minutes later with a book in her hands. She slid it across the table.

"*Interview with the Vampire?*" I said with a laugh. "This was the book you told me you loved."

"Well," she tucked a strand of hair behind her ear, "I know this old physics book probably isn't your favorite thing to read, but…maybe you'd like to read mine." Her face warmed as she picked at the pages.

"There's nothing I'd love more," I said, sliding my hand across her cheek. "And if you wanted to know my favorite book…" I sat back, never pondering the question before. "I'd say it's probably *Julius Caesar*, or my potions book."

"I think we have a few potion books floating around," Mora said. "But you're in luck. I had to read Julius Caesar in tenth grade, if you want to read my book report on it. It's not as riveting as *Interview with the Vampire*, but it's close."

"Anything you write is fascinating, I'm sure," I said, as her hand slid across mine once more. I couldn't help myself. I leaned across the table and captured that lower lip. She smiled and pressed her hand to my neck, drawing me in closer. Oh, this glorious sensation. It was even better now than the day before, especially when she swept her tongue across my lips. I followed in kind, pulling her closer. I could've lived in this moment forever.

"Ahem."

I sprang apart from her, turning to the sound of the voice. An older nonmagical woman was glaring at us from the other side of the stacks. Mora swallowed, her face bright red and she scooted away from me, picking up her physics book and hiding behind it. I mimicked her, gathering her vampire book and pretending to read.

"Oh my God, that was embarrassing," she whispered. "I've

never gotten caught making out in the library before."

I couldn't share in her embarrassment, not when I had her taste on my lips. "I feel it was worth it."

She grinned. "Yeah, it was. A good reward for all the hard work I've done today."

"I'd be happy to help you study some more," I said. "Perhaps somewhere more private where I can kiss you more often, rewarding you after every solved problem."

She made a face. "Then I wouldn't get any work done. We'd just be making out the whole time."

"I'd make sure we used our time wisely." I slid my hand across hers, savoring the feel of her soft skin.

"I'll consider it," she said. "But I think maybe you should go. I don't want Madame Snootface throwing me out of the library. Or my mother finding out I was making out with a boy." She batted her lashes at me. "Even if he is a really good kisser."

"Am I?" I asked, closing my eyes and leaning into her hand. "I haven't had much practice."

Her lips brushed against mine once more. "An excellent kisser. Who's going to get me in so much trouble."

"You don't sound too upset over that..."

She grinned. "Maybe I'm not that upset about it."

And like that, we were kissing again. She knotted her fingers in my hair and opened her mouth against mine. I sank back down into my chair, pulling her closer with a hand sliding down her back. The thrill of getting caught meant I savored every second of her kiss, the sound of her breath, and the new feeling of completeness.

"Miss Carrigan."

We broke apart at the sound of the older nonmagical, who had her hands on her hips.

"I will thank you to keep your hands to yourself in my library," she said, raising herself straighter. "And your mother called. She needs you to pick up milk on the way home. Which should be now."

"Yes, ma'am," Mora said, her face growing bright red as she gathered her things.

"I told her you were here making out with a boy," the woman said. "She's very upset with you."

"Hopefully not this boy," Mora muttered under her breath.

The librarian turned and left in a huff, and I began to laugh at Mora's embarrassment. I couldn't help it; she was even cuter with pink cheeks and an averted gaze.

"Stop it," she said, slinging her backpack over her shoulder. "You're going to get me in so much trouble."

"I thought you didn't mind trouble," I said.

"Maybe not," she said then grinned. "Wanna see if we can get into more trouble at the grocery store?"

"I have no idea what that is, but I'd love to."

# Twelve

"Oh…my…"

More food than I'd ever seen in my entire life was laid out before me. Brightly colored orbs of various sizes—reds, blues, purples. Greens. Yellows. I could scarcely believe such things existed. Glancing around at the nonmagicals around me, I touched one of the red fruits and inhaled. It smelled fresh, like a cool blast of wind.

"Okay, okay, don't eat the food," Mora said, plucking it out of my hand and putting it down. "You really don't have this in your world?"

I shook my head. "Meat and cheese is about my entire diet. Some milk for dinner on occasion."

"Wow," Mora said, threading her hand through mine. She let me drink in this new wonderland she'd dubbed a grocery store, answering my questions as they came up and gently redirecting me when she thought I'd become a little too enamored. If I brought home just one fruit or vegetable to

Alexandra, I'd be Guildmaster in a week.

We came to a wall of white, the placard above reading "Dairy" and Mora opened the glass door to pluck one of the containers from a wall of them.

"So this is how you get milk," I said. "It's incredible how far things have come."

"What, do you have to milk a cow or something?"

I nodded. "Yes. Although the Charmers do fairly well with convincing them to stand still during."

"So you know how to milk a cow?"

"Not me, specifically. The Charmers do that," I said. "I suppose it's about the same for me. I go to their house with an empty container and they give me a fresh one."

"Hm," she said.

"You know…" I said, recalling my promise to Alexandra to find a solution to our food problem. "Where is the bread?"

"The sliced bread or the bakery?" she asked.

I shrugged, at a loss for words. "Whichever would look similar to what we eat in New Salem."

She handed me the cold container and led me to the other end of the building, where a fresh, delectable smell assaulted my nose. There, we found loaves of bread in all shapes and sizes. I picked up one that looked close to what the Enchanters made.

"I don't suppose you have any money for that," she said with a chuckle.

"I don't need much," I said. "Just a little crumb."

"What do you need it for?"

"I'd like to give it to our Enchanters," I said. "But without telling my mother where I've been and what I've done, I can't simply bring food into the village."

"So what will a crumb do?" she asked.

"I may have…lied to Alexandra about using a potion to recreate original magical properties," I said, blushing at the thought of lying to my Guildmaster. "But if I brought back a crumb—"

"And told her it was made from a potion, she wouldn't bat an eye." Mora nodded slowly. She glanced around then plucked a small piece off the loaf and thrust it in my pocket. "There. That should be enough to get you going."

I smiled. "Thank you."

We walked to the front of the store, and Mora handed a man some green paper, which he replaced with several metal coins. As we walked out of the store, she explained the concept of money and dollars, when I asked her.

"So instead of bartering, you have this paper?" I said with a nod. "Fascinating."

"Well, I'd better get home," Mora said. "Mom'll know if I dawdle too long, and I don't want her to get pissed at me. Or see you here and…"

"I understand," I replied. In one movement, I captured her lips for a brief kiss. "Thank you for showing me a grocery store."

As I turned to walk away, she called my name. "Am I gonna see you tomorrow? At the library?"

I dropped my gaze to her, taking in the sight of her holding that jug of milk, the way her shirt molded against her body, the tan color of her legs. She was something I wanted to keep to myself for as long as I could.

"Wouldn't miss it."

The cold New Salem air sliced my skin and I quickly uncharmed my clothes back to the wool cloak and leather boots. I walked the long distance into the village so I could come up with an adequate way to use this small piece of bread in my pocket.

I'd decided to give it to Mary the Enchanter, not because I wanted her to proposition me again, but if she was already infatuated, she might not ask many questions.

"Oh, Master Gavon," Mary said, standing as I walked inside. "Are you here for—"

"Bread," I said quickly. "Just bread."

Her shoulders sagged, and she turned to the barrel at the back of the room. "We still haven't heard from the Guildmaster," she said with a frown. "Our stores are running low."

I chewed the inside of my cheek. "I've been experimenting with something." In my pocket, I magically pulverized the small, fresh piece of bread into crumbles. The flecks landed in the palm of my hand, and I pulled it out to show her. "I'm not sure this will work. But I've been trying certain…" I cleared my throat. Should I should call it a potion? Alexandra may be forward-thinking, but others in the village weren't. "Trying certain charms to bring back the original properties of our magical food. I think I might've cracked it. Try this and see what you can make of it."

She plucked one crumb from the pile and her hands glowed as she made the bread from dirt. Even from looking at the newly formed loaf, I could tell a difference. The color was more vibrant than the other freshly-made loaves right next to it.

She magically sliced a piece off and took a hesitant bite. "This is...oh my." She closed her eyes and moaned. Perhaps that was how I'd looked when I'd first eaten that burger. "Master Gavon, I can't thank you enough. I think you've saved us all."

"I will continue experimenting," I said, piling the rest of the crumbs on the table for her. "Please use these, and let me know how it turns out. If you don't mind, I'd like to take this bread to the Guildmaster."

She nodded emphatically then hesitantly asked, "Will you tell her which Enchanter did it?"

"Of course," I said with a nod. "And thank you."

I stood in front of Alexandra's door, gathering my thoughts and schooling my features before I knocked. It was simple to lie to Mary, but with Alexandra, it was more difficult. I closed my eyes and reminded myself that, if she had a mind to, she could compel me to tell her everything about the tear, the world, Mora. I couldn't give her any inkling that I was lying to her about anything.

I raised my fist and rapped on the door.

"Enter."

I pushed it and walked inside, nodding respectfully. She sat at her desk, an open book before her and a pair of spectacles perched on her nose. I'd never seen her wear them before, but she was growing older.

"Is there something you need?" she asked.

"I think I've made progress on the...task we discussed this morning," I said, walking forward with the bread in my hands.

Alexandra's eyebrow lifted when I placed it on her desk.

"This is…"

"I had Mary the Enchanter work on it," I added quickly. "But I think it might help with some…of the issues we've been seeing."

She summoned a knife and sliced into the bread. She took a hesitant bite and chewed thoughtfully as I waited for my instructions. The back of my neck warmed with my rising nerves. Would she ask me to procure the potion I'd used? Perhaps I'd made a bad decision in bringing this to her. I could have secretly introduced it—

"Well done," she said, breaking into my internal firestorm. "I think it would be wise to keep this discovery amongst ourselves for now. How much did you tell the Enchanter?"

"Not the truth," I said. "I don't think she cared enough to ask for specifics."

"As well she shouldn't. This is far superior to anything she's created in the past." Alexandra chuckled as she gave herself another slice. "And how much of this…special starter did you give to her?"

"A handful," I said. "Enough to be getting on with. It may take me some time to make more—"

"I don't want it to spread in the village that you're brewing potions, so that's the last we'll talk of it," she said, cutting me off with a wave of her hand. "I assume the Enchanter will want to take credit for the improvement in her wares."

I smiled. Mary seemed eager to impress. "Yes, I believe you're right."

"But please continue making…whatever you're making. Our

cheese and grain could also use some infusion." She tutted. "It's possible this is just delaying the inevitable and you've only made our final poison more palatable."

"If so, then a better way to go."

That earned me a rare smile. "Please see to cleaning my room tomorrow. I don't like Cyrus in my things. I will have him in the kitchen."

"Cyrus will be doing chores?" I asked, surprised. "Shouldn't he be getting ready for his match?"

"I might've been too hasty in allowing his match to go forward," she said. "It appears he isn't as ready as I thought."

I tried to hide my smirk as I nodded and turned to leave, but she called my name.

"That Mary would make an excellent partner in childbearing," she said. "She comes from a long line—perhaps descended from Riley himself."

I nodded; half the village claimed that heritage. "I'll consider it."

"See that you do. It would be a shame to see our line end with you."

# Thirteen

Alexandra made no mention of my discovery at breakfast the next morning, nor did she invite me to her sparring session with Cyrus. But his mood was decidedly sour, and I probably wouldn't have wanted to be in the ring with him anyway.

I ran through the rest of my chores as quickly as possible then transported to my tear, diving through to the other side. Pellets of wetness hit me in the face, and for a brief, terrifying moment, I worried the tear had moved, and I was in the middle of the vast ocean. But that fear soon passed as I took in the world around me. The sky was now a drab gray—more akin to what I was used to in New Salem. And the water falling from the sky was presumably the rain I'd read so much about.

I stood, my face tilted upward to fully experience this newest sensation. I wanted to know how it worked—obviously not magic, but it certainly felt like water was appearing out of thin air. A warm breeze blew the water harder against my cheeks, and a loud rumbling echoed from somewhere far away.

My clothes now thoroughly soaked, I used magic to find Mora—she was back in the library. With a smile, I repeated my actions from the day before, waltzing into the room where she was hunched over her physics book.

She raised her head as a look of surprise dawned on her face, followed by that adorable bite of her lip. "Did you get caught in the thunderstorm?"

"I…suppose," I said, wiping the wetness from my cheeks.

"Look at you," Mora said, putting down her pen then coming over to stand next to me. "You're soaked. Why didn't you summon yourself an umbrella or something?"

"I guess I just wanted to feel it," I said, closing my eyes as she brushed her hand over my forehead. "I've never seen rain before."

"Just wait until it snows three feet in April," she said, wiping my cheeks. "At least dry yourself off before the librarian throws you out for getting everything wet."

I concentrated, and the water evaporated from my clothes. "I don't want to get on her bad side again."

"She's been giving me the evil eye all morning," she said with a smirk. "Luckily, Mom just thought I was here with Renny, and she gave me another lecture on why I shouldn't date deadbeat guys."

Perhaps one day, I'd understand every word out of her mouth. But for now, I just wanted to kiss that mouth. So I did.

"We have to be careful," she said, pushing me away. "If I get kicked out of the library, the only place I'll be able to go is home…and you won't be able to go there."

"No, I suppose not," I said. "Are you working on physics

again?"

She nodded. "My teacher was really impressed with the work I did yesterday. Asked me if I'd cheated, too."

"You did most of them yourself," I said, annoyed someone would treat her thusly. "I merely provided guidance."

She kissed my cheek. "Want to provide some more?"

It became something of a routine over the next few weeks. I would do my chores early, transport to the library, and Mora and I would spend the afternoon on her homework. These hours were some of the most peaceful in my memory, punctuated by brief moments of passion as we stole kisses when the librarian wasn't looking. Mora was only allowed out of her house on what she termed the "weekdays," so in between, there were days when I couldn't see her. I would stay in New Salem, devouring whatever book she'd suggested I read to catch up on everything I'd missed in the past three hundred years.

No one in New Salem had said anything to me about Mary's bread, although there had certainly been more conversation about this wonderful Enchanter and her delicious new food. Even Cyrus had begun to pay more attention to her, and bragged to me and everyone who'd listen about how he was trying to bed the poor girl now that she was more desirable. I declined to inform him that she'd propositioned me, or that she'd become rather insistent about it every time I went to see her. Especially as Alexandra still hadn't set a date for his induction match, and any mention of it or anything negative sent him into a ferocious tirade. So I let him talk about how Mary found him so handsome, and his thinly veiled comments about how I'd never be so desired.

While Mary seemed like a nice girl, my mind and my heart were seated across from me at a library table, leaning over a book and chewing on her lip as she wrestled with another equation.

"What are you looking at?" Mora asked.

"Nothing," I said, smiling. "Just thinking. How are you doing?"

"Almost finished," she said, showing me what she'd done so far. "You know, my mom's really happy with the progress I've made so far. And with school starting back next month, she might let me off restriction."

"What does that mean?"

"Means we can do more than sit here," she said, putting her pen down. "Like go to Rome again. Or maybe even just on a real date."

"A real…date?"

"Yeah, you know… go see a movie. Or just sit out under the stars." She took my hand. "Make out a little bit without an audience."

"Do you think you'd be allowed out at night?" I asked, my heart thumping with anticipation of being alone—truly alone—with Mora.

"I could just sneak out—"

"Mora," I said with a shake of my head. "Why would you intentionally put yourself back where you started?"

"Well, I can't very well tell her who I'm going out with," she said. "And she always asks. So I'm lying either way."

"But…" I'd more than proven my intentions. She had to believe I didn't mean them any harm after I'd helped her daughter learn physics.

"Gav." She cradled my face, and some of my angst disappeared with the soft way she said my name. "You don't understand. My mom, she's doesn't listen. All she wants is to be Clanmaster. Anything that'll put that in jeopardy...including me...gets squashed. If I told her about you, she'd go to my great-uncle. Then I'd never be able to see you again."

I wished I could find a lie in her words, but I knew all too well the pressures of having a mother who couldn't be trusted.

"If it were different," she began, but quieted when I kissed her.

"I understand," I said. "If it's what you have to do..."

The tone of my voice must've triggered something, because she made a noise of defeat. "Maybe I could go over her head. Petition directly with Ashley and the rest of the clan. If they give you their blessing, Mom can't go around them."

"That...could work," I said with a nod. "How often do you meet?"

"We've got a quarterly clan gathering at the end of August," she said. "Right before school starts. Maybe I'll talk to my uncle now, though. He's pretty reasonable. *And* he's really happy my grades have improved."

I nodded. "I'd love to meet him."

"You two would get along great," she said, glancing around before climbing into my lap. "He's always telling me to read more books."

I held her by her hips, savoring her closeness. "Smart man. I did finish that book, by the way, the vampire one."

"Oh? Did you like it?"

I winced. "Not terribly. I'm sorry—it was hard to follow."

"You prefer Shakespeare to Anne Rice?" she said with a sigh, sliding her hands through my hair.

"I prefer you to anything else," I replied, capturing her lips with mine. She smiled, opening her mouth to me. Oh, how I couldn't wait for the day when I could get her alone, away from this library with the observant librarians. Even now, this was stolen time that might—

"What the hell do you think you're doing, Mora?"

The voice was young—and the girl it belonged to was as well. I pegged her age at maybe nine, but her magic was bound tightly —tighter than any grounding spell I'd encountered so far. Her short cropped hair gave her the air of a boy, but shared some of Mora's features. There was no mistaking it—this girl was somehow related to her. A sister?

"Hello," I said quietly. "My name is—"

"I know who you are," she snapped. "And I also know you aren't supposed to be here."

"Scram, Jeanie," Mora said. "Gavon, this is my obnoxious little sister."

Although her magic was tightly bound, even I could tell there was very little of it. "Why is her magic so secured?"

"We don't get magic until we're fifteen," Mora said.

Still, the girl had very little to be concerned with. I'd almost consider her a Potion-maker. "Does your magic increase in strength as you age?"

The little girl's face turned white and Mora smacked my shoulder. "No, it doesn't."

"My sincere apologies," I said, knowing I'd made an

egregious error. "Please, forgive me—"

But Jeanie wasn't to be persuaded. "Mom said you're supposed to tell her when you see him, and here you are making out with him." She narrowed her eyes. "He's dangerous."

I swallowed, looking around. "I don't mean either of you any harm."

"I'm sure you don't," the girl replied. "So why are you making out with my sister?"

My cheeks warmed—I had no good answer for that, other than that I was hopelessly besotted with her.

"That's what I thought," the girl said, marching forward as if she had any kind of magic to wield. "I'm gonna go home and tell my mom about you. And then you're both gonna be in serious trouble."

"Jeanie," Mora said, grabbing her sister by the shoulders. "What can I give you so you won't tell Mom?"

The little girl thought then held out her hand. "All you have."

Mora grumbled and dug in her purse for her wallet, handing her sister a wad of cash. "Not a word, understood?"

The girl looked at me then turned on her heel and walked away.

"That was close," Mora said. "I wonder how much I'll have to pay her to keep quiet."

"Hopefully, you won't have to pay for her for very long. You said you'll go petition your uncle, right? Maybe it'll all be taken care of."

"Maybe," Mora said, chewing her lip. "I just hope he's as reasonable as I think he is."

# Fourteen

The next morning, I did my chores but my mind kept wandering back to Mora and her little sister. I suppose I could understand Mora's hesitation; her mother was a formidable woman, magically and otherwise. But I also really didn't believe that Mora's mother would be so prejudiced toward me, especially now, as I'd spent hours with her daughter in the library. That had to count for something.

"Look sharp, Gav!"

I looked up just as I nearly ran into Cyrus in the hallway. He scoffed at me as if I were dirt and continued walking down the stairs. He didn't bother to pretend he was helping me assemble breakfast, so I brought the food into the room by myself. I kept my gaze averted to avoid any unwanted conversation.

"I had a fascinating conversation with the Enchanters yesterday," Alexandra said, her gaze on neither of us, but my ears pricked up regardless.

"Oh? What do the vermin want now?" Cyrus asked.

She chuckled, though the gaze she gave him was anything but humorous. "Those vermin create the food on this table, Cyrus. As you might have heard on your rounds, they've grown concerned about the quality of their bread-making materials." She lifted her gaze to mine. "Gavon, it appears your experiment was a resounding success, and the Council wants to speak with you."

Cyrus's head practically popped off his shoulders. "What experiment? What's he been doing? What—"

"Calm yourself, Cyrus," Alexandra said. "Gavon simply offered to use his free time to conduct experimentations on the bread." She brought her cup to her lips. "You've never shown any interest in magical sciences, therefore I didn't ask you. A Guildmaster must delegate effectively."

The look on Cyrus face was pure jealousy—something I hadn't seen since he and I were boys. "Oh."

"I wasn't aware that my involvement was common knowledge," I said, glancing across the table to Cyrus.

"Councilman Rogers was very persistent, and Mary decided to share the secrets behind her success," she said. "I believe they want to hear more about what your solution might do for others, like the grain stores. You'll accompany me to the Council meeting prior to your sparring match this morning."

I was halfway to nodding when I heard what she'd said. "Sparring match?"

"Yes, Mistress," Cyrus said. "Sparring match?"

"I believe I was quite clear," she said. Was she actually smirking? I must've been seeing things. "Gavon, you will resume sparring with Cyrus this afternoon. If I decide your performance is unsatisfactory, we'll return to our other arrangement of daily matches." She met my gaze and the rest of her statement was clear:

*If you impress me, you'll be inducted.*

If Cyrus had been jealous at breakfast, he'd been beside himself with contained fury as Alexandra and I left for the Council meeting house together. I would deal with his petulance (and whatever he'd do to punish me for this perceived slight) later, because now I had a much bigger problem: What was I going to tell the Council?

Alexandra gave me no indication of what she was thinking, which never boded well for me. If I told them it was a potion, would they want to see it? Would they want to watch how I turned crumbs of dirt into delicious bread? Or would they simply order my execution because I was dabbling in forbidden magic?

Only time—and Alexandra—would tell.

My heart thudded in my chest as the doors magically opened and Alexandra and I walked into the Council room. For the location of all the major decisions in the village, it was incredibly small, containing a single table with five chairs spread around it. Alexandra took the chair in the center, and I stood against the door while we waited for the rest of the magicals to make their appearance.

Timothy Rogers, the Enchanter, was first, appearing in a haze of green. He was the oldest on the Council, and had lost most of his hair. What was left was white and stringy. It wouldn't have surprised me if he'd already been infected with rot.

Elizabeth Humbert was next. A Charmer with the most cows in the village, she hoarded them emphatically and gave only as much as Alexandra made her. She took a seat next to Rogers, eyeing me curiously.

The final living Councilman to join was Roger Mowry, another Enchanter who was fairly young—younger than Alexandra. He'd fallen into his position when Master Jones died, and to my eyes, he never quite looked like he knew what he was doing.

"Very well, let's begin," Alexandra said, glancing for a moment at the empty fourth chair. "Gavon, we've heard from the Enchanter Mary's own mouth that you gave her a pile of crumbs to use in her bread. Is that true?"

I scanned her face, looking for what I was supposed to say. "Yes. The Enchanters mentioned their bread fell apart when they fashioned it. So I sought a solution to help stabilize the bread." *On your orders*, I might've added. I didn't though, as I wasn't sure what game Alexandra was playing at.

"And what was this solution?" Alexandra asked. "A potion?"

My blood ran cold. Was she trying to get me in trouble, or perhaps giving me some legitimacy? Slowly, I nodded. "Yes, Mistress. Just something I've been dabbling with."

"Potions, beh," Rogers said. "How can we even entertain such a thought?"

"One would say that your beer brewing is similar in nature to it," Alexandra said casually. "As it is, our village is dying. Magical rot is taking us younger and younger. I believe it has to do with our lack of real food. We've been here for generations.

We can't grow anything in this dead soil, and what we have is mostly magic."

I could scarcely believe my ears. Was Alexandra defending potions?

"Magic sustains us," Humbert said.

"Perhaps," Alexandra said, her voice lowering to its previous level. "But it cannot be denied that Gavon's discovery has brought hope to our Enchanters."

"It's good bread," Rogers scratched his chin. "Think you could make something for my beer, boy?"

"I could try." I hadn't even asked Mora if the nonmagicals still drank beer. I hoped I wasn't promising something I couldn't deliver.

"And grain for my cows?" Mowry asked. "Half our milk has to be thrown out these days, it's just no good."

I'd seen milk in that wondrous building, but grain? I was sure I could find it. "I'll try."

"How about a demonstration?" Rogers asked. "I'd like to see what this boy is doing to our food before I put it in my mouth."

"I saw you eating a loaf not one hour ago," Humbert said.

"Potions are distasteful things," Rogers said, although he settled into his chair. "I merely want to ensure we aren't poisoning ourselves."

Alexandra held up her hand to silence the argument. "For the time being, Gavon will continue to experiment in private. I don't wish for this to get out to the rest of the Guild. Is that understood."

Something warm slid down my throat—Alexandra was barring us from speaking about it.

"Now, we have other business to attend to," she said, nodding to me. "Gavon, wait for me at the arena."

I exhaled, thankful I'd survived another close call. Luckily, the Council wasn't inquisitive. I would have to figure something out to keep one step ahead of them—or more specifically, Alexandra. But for now, I was safe. No one except the Council would know about the potions, and I could continue to bring new food into the village. Now, the larger problem remained: sparring with Cyrus again.

My mind had been focused on other things these past few weeks, and I was even less confident than usual. As best I could, I shook it off, searching for the Warrior instincts I'd been born with. Deep in my brain, there was a burning urge to wipe the smirk off Cyrus's face. Most days, I let it remain dormant. But for today, in order to move forward with my life and with Mora, I called it to the forefront.

My sparring partner appeared across from me, looking mostly bored and unaware of my internal monologue. "Well, back again, aren't we?"

"I suppose so," I replied.

"Hope you've got some of those healing potions ready," he said. "I plan on showing off today."

"And that's different from any other day?" I muttered, glancing at the empty box where the Council would be sitting.

"Careful, Gav, you're addressing the future Guildmaster," he said with narrowing eyes. "Or do you now have designs on my role?"

I cast him a tired look. "No, Cyrus."

Of course, he didn't hear me, or chose not to. "I hope you got a good look at the Council room, because it's the last time you'll ever see it."

I actually chuckled. "You aren't Guildmaster yet, Cyrus. I suggest you don't let Alexandra hear how easily you take her position."

The woman in question appeared between us in a puff of purple.

"Begin!"

Cyrus must've been nursing an attack spell, because he let it fly before she'd finished the word. This time, I wasn't eager to be his victim, so I batted it away.

"Oh-ho, looking alive today, are we?" he said.

Alive, indeed. Perhaps this is what she wanted—a show from me. Well, a show was what I would give her. Perhaps if I tired Cyrus out, we could end this quicker.

It had been a long time since I'd really pushed the limits of what I could do magically. As Cyrus did his best to outsmart me, I found him lacking. He would feint left, I'd go right to meet him before he could land a blow. He'd transport to another part of the ring, I'd follow his magical signature, having a spell ready when he got there. Perhaps it was true what Alexandra had said—Cyrus was my inferior in intellect.

"Oof!" But power, that he had. He'd finally managed to land a spell in my gut. I slid back a few feet, falling to one knee with the pain of it. Before I could even react, another came in its place, sending me backward. I at least had the presence of mind to transport myself to another side of the ring—but just as I appeared, I was hit again.

"Must be quicker than that." Cyrus barely looked winded.

I gritted my teeth and straightened, struggling to appear as unfazed as he did. But I was already bruising, and I could taste blood in my mouth.

"I'll let you take a swing at me," he said, bowing. "Just to make it interesting."

"I don't need your pity," I snapped.

"Very well."

His magic, dark gray and dangerous, rushed toward me, and I thrust a barrier forward to protect myself. The pressure built around my ears, and my muscles ached from holding the barrier, but I didn't dare let go. This was my chance to prove myself— and if I didn't…

I felt the crack in my barrier a moment before the full force of Cyrus's magic came upon me. I tumbled head over feet, landing in a tangle on the other end of the ring. And there I lay, panting from exertion and fear.

I'd been sure, in the back of my mind, that if I really tried, I could defeat Cyrus.

But I *had* tried. I'd given it my all, and he'd still beaten me. Did that mean he really was more powerful? And if so, did he deserve to be Guildmaster over me?

Cyrus showed no outward signs of fatigue as he waited for Alexandra's praise. In that moment, I truly hated him for the first time in my life.

"Cyrus, excellent work," Alexandra said. "I'm still concerned about overconfidence. You act as if you'll never be beaten."

He cast a glance in my direction and his smirk widened. "Yes, Mistress."

"Return to the Manor," she said. "Mop the downstairs floor and dust the library."

"Yes, Mistress."

"And no magic," she said with a warning glare.

"Of course, Mistress." He bowed low and disappeared in a puff of gray smoke.

I remained on the ground, hating myself and my situation. My only way out had failed—I was still trapped. I wouldn't be inducted. I would be an apprentice forever.

"Today was a good start," Alexandra said softly.

"Start?" I scoffed and pushed myself to my feet. "It was pathetic."

"You tried," she said. "That's the first time I've ever seen effort from you in the ring."

I let my shoulders sag. "I still failed. I tried, and I lost."

"Gavon," she said with a bit of a chuckle, "you've been pretending in the sparring ring your entire life. It should come as no surprise that your first attempt at being more than a recipient of attack spells was mediocre. But you have raw power and the mental discipline. What you lack is the training and the will."

I certainly had the will now. "I'll do better."

"I hope so," she said. "You will fight Cyrus for his induction match in one month. If you win, you'll be inducted, too."

I swallowed, hope filling me. "And if I don't win?"

"I've given him permission to kill you," Alexandra said.

Something thudded in the back of my mind. "W-what?"

Death in an induction match was rare—rarer still now that there were only three Warriors. That Alexandra would be so cavalier with it was horrific.

"You'd have Cyrus kill me? Your own son?"

"I would have him persuade you to fight for your life," she said with a steely-eyed glint. "And there's a reason Warriors don't raise their own. As Guildmaster, I must put the needs of the Guild above all else."

"And killing the only other Warrior will do that?"

"He will only kill you if you let him," she replied. "I suggest you don't let him."

# Fifteen

She may as well have told me to conquer the world. I was more disciplined than Cyrus—more well-read on strategy and fighting techniques—but it still hadn't mattered. And it wouldn't. I would die and Cyrus would be Guildmaster.

I sucked down a healing potion, wondering why I was even bothering, then transported myself to the tear. With little care, I fell through to the other world, landing under a sky streaked with purples and pinks.

Instead of finding Mora, I walked to the edge of the ocean, the salty breeze warming my face. The water lapped against the shore, and I listened to it, trying to keep despair away. How cruel was it that I'd been given this precious gift only to have it taken away so quickly?

"Gavon!"

I closed my eyes. Mora's voice was a welcome respite from all that had gone wrong. I spun just in time for her to fly into my arms. I inhaled her scent, imprinting it on my brain.

"So guess what…" Although it was dark, there was a smile in her voice. "Mom was so impressed with my grades, she took me off restriction." She grinned brightly as she summoned a carrying case with six bottles in it. "Let's celebrate!"

I nodded. Perhaps, it would be for the best that she be forbidden from seeing me again. I wouldn't have the stomach to tell her I was probably about to die.

She punched my shoulder. "Okay, what the hell is wrong with you? I tell you I'm off restriction and all you do is nod?" She swallowed. "Do you not like me anymore?"

I spun, shocked—and even more to see tears in her eyes. "Of course I do, Mora."

"Then what's wrong?"

"I…" I warred with myself, whether I should tell her. But if I died, and she thought I didn't care for her, that would be a worse fate. "Alexandra has allowed my induction match to go forward."

"That's great, though," she said with a hand on my shoulder. "Right? That's what you wanted?"

"The match, yes," I said. "But she's also given Cyrus permission to kill me if I lose."

Her hand twitched. "W-what? How? Are you serious? Why the hell would your mother do that?"

I honestly had no idea. "She's always considered me inferior. Perhaps this is just her way of proving that."

"You should tell her about the tear." She crawled under my arm, and I held her to my body, feeling better to have her close. "Then she'd shut the hell up."

"I wish I could," I said, resting my chin on her head. "But I fear if I did, it would cause more trouble. Your mother might not be wrong about the rest of my clan. Alexandra wants to continue what Riley started. It would be reckless to tell her about this world. And besides that, my induction would still go on as planned."

"This is bullcrap," Mora said, plucking a bottle out of the pack she'd brought and sitting down on the sand. "I just got off restriction and now you're going to die?"

I had to laugh at her serious face. "You certainly have a way of phrasing things." I joined her on the ground, taking another bottle and allowing her to open it for me. Beer, I could smell it right away. But with one swig, I knew this was yet another thing I'd never really tasted before.

"I really like you, Gavon," she said after a minute. "You can't die."

"And I've fallen in love with you."

Her fear was immediate, or perhaps it was just shock. Her eyes sprang open and her jaw dropped as she slowly turned to me.

"You…love me?"

I nodded. "Is that all right?"

"I mean, it's kind of sudden," she said, her blue eyes wide and uncertain. "We've only known each other a few weeks."

"Romeo and Juliet only knew each other for a few days."

She glared. "I'm not doing a suicide pact with you."

Again, I laughed, but only to keep from thinking about my induction match. "Perhaps you're right. I've never been in love before, so I don't know the rules. But I know that when I see you, my heart feels like it's going to burst. I think about you all the time—about talking with you, seeing new things. Kissing you." I swallowed. "I suppose I thought that's what love was."

She cupped my cheek and tilted my head to meet her gaze. "Do you really mean all that?"

"Of course I do," I said. "Why wouldn't I have—"

She captured my lips, and this time, there was no hesitation. With gentle strength, I crushed her to me. Perhaps I would die —perhaps her mother would be successful in keeping us apart. But for the moment, I had her in my arms, and I intended to take advantage of it.


There were many benefits to a girl from the modern era. One of them happened to be her knowledge of all things sexual. I was a willing and attentive student, and learned more in those few hours than in my entire life before then. When we'd had our fill of each other, we lay under the stars, content to hear the ocean waves and count the bright lights above.

"You'll tell me when it's appropriate to love you, right?" I asked, twirling a lock of her hair around my finger

She chuckled and pressed her hand against my chest. "You said you've never been in love before. Never even had a crush on someone? Like, felt something for them?"

I thought of Mary in the village. "I told you. Warriors don't get the luxury of love."

"Why not?"

"Because this…effort is only supposed to be for procreation," I said.

She slowly lifted her head. "Dude, you did not just try to—"

"No, no, of course not," I said with a laugh. "This was…to

put it mildly, because I cannot seem to keep my hands off you. Though I suppose if you were with child, Alexandra would be pleased."

"Not gonna happen. I'm on birth control." She lay back against my chest. "They really want you to start having kids now?"

I gathered another lock of hair, letting it slip through my fingers. "I believe my fellow apprentice has three children already, but that could be a lie."

"Ew." She made a noise. "Three kids. I'm not ready for that."

"To be honest…I'm not either," I said. "It's one of the many reasons I'm grateful I found this world. I feel like here I have a choice. I don't have to be a Warrior and adhere to traditions I don't agree with." I kissed her forehead. "I can lie with the woman I love and ask her to marry me."

"Gross. I'm seventeen. We just met."

"Well, I'm eighteen, and I still want to marry you."

"Gavon, marriage is for old people. Thirty-year-olds. I'm…I mean, maybe one day, but slow your roll."

"I don't think I can wait twelve years to be with you," I said with a small whine.

"But you are with me," she said. "Right now, you're here with me."

I let the sigh loosen from my chest as reality came back to me. "I am. Tonight. But I could die soon."

"So…is it a foregone conclusion that you're gonna die?" she asked quietly.

"No, in that I can fight for my life. Yes, in that Cyrus outranks me in magical strength." I told her about the sparring match, and how even though I'd tried, I'd still failed. "Ergo, my death is…all but certain."

"Bullshit," Mora said, sitting up. "You can defeat him. You gotta just want it bad enough."

I trailed a line down her bare back. "I do want it badly. I wanted it badly the other day—"

"No, you kind of wanted it," Mora said. She began dressing herself. "And maybe that's what your mom is trying to get you to see. She wants you to earn the Guildmaster, and she thinks the only way to make you want it is to save your own skin. I mean, Cyrus seems like a total ass—"

"He is."

"And didn't you say he's like…a shoo-in for the Guildmaster?" she asked, and I nodded. "Then there you go. I doubt he'd be okay with you just taking over his spot. You gotta earn it. No nepotism and all that."

Although I only understood about half of what she'd said, she did make a lot of sense. "There are other ways to motivate people."

"They're barbarians," she said with a shrug. "And I think saving your own ass is a pretty good incentive."

"I can think of another one," I said with a smile. "Getting to see you again."

She sighed. "Do you really want to win? Really, truly?"

I nodded.

"And you don't think you can beat him magical to magical, right?"

"No. Even if I were to give it my all, he's had many more months of training," I said. "I would tire quickly matching him blow for blow."

She pursed her lips. "But what if you tire him out first? Like, make him think you're on the ropes, then knock him out!"

"On the…ropes?"

"It's a boxing thing, don't worry about it," she said. "The point is he already thinks he's more powerful than you are. So, what you do is make him expend a lot of energy. Let him think he's beating you up. But you just conserve your energy. Then, when he's tired, you let him have it."

I scratched my chin. "I suppose that might work, but only if he's stupid enough to fall for it."

"He sounds like a dick, though," she said. "Somebody who thinks really highly of himself."

"Oh, yes, he's very selfish. Incredibly full of himself and confident." I considered that for a moment. "In fact, Alexandra thinks too confident at times."

"See?" She poked me in the chest. "What else could you use?"

I thought some more. "He's very jealous of my relationship with Alexandra. Not…that we have one, but that she's my mother. It bothers him when she pays attention to me."

She grinned slyly. "Oh, does he? You can work with that."

"Can I?"

"Just be an asshole to him," she said. "Like, remind him how he's just there because he wasn't born to Alexandra. Get in his head, make him make a mistake."

I allowed myself to think about how I might defeat Cyrus on my own terms. In a battle of wits, he was unarmed, as it were. Quick to reaction and quicker to jealousy, Cyrus outside the sparring ring was an easy opponent. I'd spent my days avoiding confrontation to keep myself away from his petulance. But what if I turned that petulance into an asset?

I furrowed my brow. "I suppose that might work."

"I know it'll work," she said. "My sister does it all the time. You should find a book on reverse psychology and read all about it."

"I doubt the answers I'm looking for are in a book."

"I'm serious," she said. "Psychology. It's the science of the mind. You can use it against him. Reverse psychology is when you get someone to do something by telling them not to do it."

A new voice echoed across the beach. "Kind of like when I tell you to stay in the house, and yet here you are, out with a magical man."

# Sixteen

We jumped at the sound of Mora's mother behind us.

"Mom, don't freak out—" Mora said, jumping to her feet.

"Somebody should be freaking out." Irene stood behind us with her arms crossed, the nearby light from the tear giving her an ethereal glow. "Because it seems I didn't impress upon you the dangers of associating with this man."

"Mom—"

"Home. Now."

Mora didn't even have the chance to scream before she disappeared in a cloud of yellow magic. And as soon as she was gone, I lost track of her magic, too. Wherever Irene had sent her, it was far away from here, or behind a potent barrier.

"You won't find her, so stop looking."

I scowled, fixing the harshest glare I could on the woman. "Please explain to me why I'm so dangerous. I keep hearing it, but I'm just not understanding."

"Your very existence is dangerous. Don't think I don't know

what your kind have been planning—"

"Do enlighten me," I snapped. "As no one but myself has any knowledge of the tear or where it is. I've done nothing to warrant this ridiculous vendetta against me. Unless loving your daughter and helping her improve her grades is somehow worthy of all this hate."

Irene tutted and crossed her arms across her chest. "Then perhaps it's you who's been fooled. My daughter doesn't date men because she likes them. She does it to see how angry I get. If you felt something for her, it was one-sided, I'm sure."

I licked my lips. I wasn't very experienced in love, but I knew Mora felt something for me. Perhaps her mother was trying to distract me.

"Such a shame that you speak so poorly of your own child."

"Lucky for me, she's my child and I can speak of her however I want." She straightened and leveled a stern look in my direction. "Since I cannot seem to control my child using parental magic, I've gone to our clan master. He has used his powers to keep Mora within the protections of our clan. I've also asked for his blessing to permanently bar you from setting foot in our clan ever again."

I blinked, parsing her words. "Just your clan?"

"Yes," she scoffed. "Why?"

"If you're that concerned about my intentions, why not take concrete action against me? Why not engage us in a match…" I nodded, understanding. "You can't, can you?"

Her nostrils flared. As powerful as she was, I sensed she lacked the ability even to form an attack spell, even though she probably sorely wanted to. That explained her penchant for barrier spells. Those offered some protection, although I could still get through if I wanted to.

"If you know what's good for you," she said, her face betraying nothing, "you'll stay away from this place. You'll forget about my daughter and leave us out of whatever schemes you're planning."

"My only scheme seemed to be improving Mora's grades," I said, dully. "As I've said repeatedly."

Instead of arguing further, she disappeared in a puff of yellow smoke. For a moment, I forgot where I was, and why I was standing on this beach. With a shake of my head, my mind brushed up against Irene's magic, and the barrier spell she'd enacted. It took very little effort to knock it down, freeing my recollection. But Mora's magic was still hidden from me, and as hard as I tried, I couldn't find it.

She was gone.

"You look upset, Gavon," Alexandra said the next morning over breakfast. "I'd think you would be happy to know your apprenticeship will soon be over."

I lifted my gaze to her, unable to wipe the look off my face. I'd spent the night walking the length of Mora's town, searching for her magical signature, but had come up empty. I'd just come back in time to make breakfast once again and have Cyrus take all the credit for it. And now Alexandra was taunting me by asking me to be happy about a match I had no chance of winning?

"I'm thrilled," I said, tearing off another piece of the bread Mary had made. Even with the fresh crumbs, it tasted like ash in my mouth.

"Oh, be nice to him, Mistress. It can't be easy to know you're facing the gallows," Cyrus said with a smirk. "I promise I'll make it quick, Gav. Just lie there and let it happen."

I rose from the table abruptly, in no mood to listen to him or Alexandra. And to her credit, she didn't stop me as I walked out of the house. Perhaps she, like Cyrus, assumed I was merely going to surrender. But my sour mood had nothing to do with my own impending death and everything to do with Mora. I wasn't going to die without seeing her one last time.

Although I'd canvassed the entire town the night before, the library had been closed (as had everything else), so, with hopeful thoughts, I ascended the stairs into the building. The librarian who'd always interrupted us was at her desk in the front. I hadn't said a word to her before, but perhaps today was as good as any.

"Hello," I said quietly.

She raised her gaze from her book, giving me the once over. "Hello. Can I help you?"

"Um…yes, have you seen…Mora?" I swallowed. "The girl —"

"That you're always making out with?" She shook her head. "Haven't seen her in a few days. Saw her mom this morning, who told me you were bad news and that I should kick you out if I saw you."

I frowned. "I'm not bad, just…worried about her. If you see her, can you tell her…"

Tell her what? That I was sorry? That I would think fondly of her over the next few days before my untimely death at eighteen?

"Look," the librarian pulled her glasses off her nose, "you seem like a nice kid. I heard you helping her in there when you could keep your hands off her."

"Thank you?"

"She did come by this morning, before her mother," the librarian said, coming out from behind her desk. "Irene had asked me not to tell you, but I can tell you care a lot about her. So here, Mora wanted me to give you this book for some reason."

*Managing Difficult People*

I blinked, turning the book over in my hands.

"Maybe she thinks it might help you with her mother?" The librarian said with a shrug.

"Thank you," I said with a smile.

"Good luck." She cast me a look. "I'm a sucker for a good romance."

I tucked the book under my arm and wandered back to our room, knowing she wouldn't show up, but hoping she might. After at least an hour of staring sadly at the door and envisioning her blonde tresses bouncing as she walked through, finally I slid the book over to me and opened it.

There, I found a folded up, handwritten note.

*Gav,*

*My mom's forbidden me from leaving the house, so I hope this note gets to you at the library before she catches me. Mom compelled Jeanie to tell her what I'd been up to, so I can't blame the little twerp for ratting me out. But now Mom's gone to Ashley to petition for your permanent banishment. Ashley's agreed to meet with me sometime this week, so maybe he'll reconsider. I think I might have a case since he's not insane like my mom is.*

*I don't know if you're reading this before or after your induction match, but if it's before, I hope you kick that guy's ass. I asked the librarian to give me some books for dealing with difficult people. I don't know if it'll help you, but I still think this guy is an insecure little prick and you could trip him up. You're probably twenty times smarter than he is. Use that, too.*

*I want to see you again. Please don't die.*

*Love, Mora*

*PS: You can't die, because the fountain in Rome said we'd be coming back.*

I barked a laugh as her voice filled my mind. And while I was heartened at the thought of her searching for books to help me in my induction match, the one she'd chosen didn't seem very helpful. I was hopelessly lost within the first few pages. She'd left scraps of paper marking several chapters, all on the narcissist.

> *The narcissist, named after the Greek myth of the man who fell in love with his own reflection, is a person with an overinflated sense of self. They may use demeaning comments, attention-seeking behavior, and obsess about fantasies of them being successful. A narcissist most often uses their bravado to overcompensate for a lack of something in their lives, usually parental affection.*

That certainly sounded like Cyrus.

> *The narcissist relies on others to provide them with attention and self-worth. They may consider themselves invincible, either ignoring real issues or convincing themselves they can't be hurt by anything. Criticism may be taken out of context, and should be avoided. Some narcissists earn pleasure from watching others suffer, so try to keep your comments positive and your appearance unruffled.*

Although it wasn't necessarily new information, it did get me thinking. For all his strengths and abilities, Cyrus was incredibly insecure. It was easy to draw his ire with a comment about how he wasn't Alexandra's son, or anything having to do with his magical abilities. He'd certainly become immune to Alexandra's critiques, but for me, it was especially easy to get a rise out of him. I normally didn't because I didn't want to deal with the consequences.

In a match, would it make him more focused, or might he make a mistake?

I reread the passages, trying to glean what Mora was trying to get me to understand. I could try to remain unconcerned by him in the ring; that tended to drive him mad. But would it result in his making a grave mistake?

Rubbing my face, I sighed wearily and picked up her note once more, imagining her hasty scribbles and the way she furrowed her brow when she concentrated.

*Please don't die.*

Such a simple phrase, but it was enough to light a fire. She'd said perhaps I hadn't wanted to win enough, and that was why I'd lost. But now, knowing my girl would be waiting, I owed it to her to try with everything I had.

I summoned a pen and blank piece of paper.

*Mora,*

*Induction match is in two weeks' time, and I'm hoping for a miracle. If something happens to me, or you're unsuccessful in convincing Ashley, I want you to know I've treasured these past few weeks with you. If I somehow make it out alive, I'm taking you to Rome so we can throw the second and third coin in.*

*Love, G*

The librarian was still at her desk, and she looked up with a smile as I approached with the book in hand.

"Did you find it interesting?" she asked as I handed it to her.

"I did," I said with a nod. "But perhaps you could give it back to Mora. I think—"

"Or maybe I'll just give her this note." She plucked the note out from between the pages and shook her head. "As if you two are the first to try this trick."

My cheeks warmed. "You'll give it to her, then?"

She nodded. "Now get out of here before I change my mind."

"May I…may I borrow that book, actually?" I said, thinking.

"Sure, just fill out this application for a library card," she said, handing me a paper form. "You're local, right?"

"In a manner of speaking," I replied, unsure of what she wanted me to do. "Actually, I'll just come back tomorrow to read it."

"Suit yourself," she said with a shrug.

Before I returned to New Salem, I summoned the book

before falling through the tear.

# Seventeen

Our induction match was quickly approaching, and since Alexandra was allowing us to rest and prepare, there was little to do but contemplate. Despite what Mora had said about finding Cyrus's weakness, I doubted he would be stupid enough to goad into making a mistake. If anything, my sniping might increase his focus. Then I'd be dead and he'd simply be smug.

Still, I'd been brewing healing potions and taking them morning and evening, hoping to boost whatever latent magic I had. He'd been bragging on that strength for days now; whenever I'd see him in the hallway, he'd make a comment about how he'd be sure to make it quick when he killed me. The more I read about narcissists in the book Mora had given me, the more I began to notice Cyrus's predictable behavior. He did consider himself superior, and although he had some evidence to support it, he was also a little too confident. About everything.

Of course, there was nothing in the book that would help me defeat the man in a ring. Most of the chapter dedicated to narcissists seemed to recommend capitulation—make eye contact but don't insult, don't disagree, don't criticize, don't show weaknesses. Short of turning over and letting him kill me, none of the tips seemed very helpful.

Cyrus was in his element in the town, surrounding himself with magicals who fawned over him with compliments. Alexandra had forbidden us from visiting the local taverns—saying it was in our best interests to keep free from drink while we were in our apprenticeship. Cyrus was openly flaunting that order now, swaggering in drunk every evening as I put together our dinner.

"Such a shame your last days are being spent in here," he said, slurring his words. "You should get out, lie with a woman. See what you're missing before the world goes dark on you."

Thus far, I'd ignored his comments, but in light of all I'd been reading, I thought I might try a different tactic.

"I do believe you're right."

He stumbled then turned to look at me. "What did you say?"

"I said you were right," I said, with a shrug. "I should get out and enjoy the world, shouldn't I? Perhaps I'll pay that Mary a visit. She said she was interested in me. Perhaps I'll sire a Warrior before you kill me."

He blinked as his inebriated mind worked through what I'd said.

"I mean, after all, I do have a bloodline." I snuck a look and held in a smile at the open anger growing on his face. "Alexandra said it was my duty to continue what she'd started."

Cyrus snatched the tray off the table and stormed into the dining room. I followed with the tea kettle, pleased I'd won that round, at least.

Alexandra was already seated at the table, her gaze narrowed on Cyrus as he clunked the tray down and slid into his seat.

"Such grace, Cyrus," she said, before turning to him fully. "Have you been visiting Humbert's tavern, by chance? I can smell the ale on your breath."

He blanched and my eyebrows went up. "No, Mistress. Of course not. You forbade it. I would never disobey you."

Which might've worked had a beer-soaked belch not come from his lips.

"And the day before your sparring match," she said with a shake of her head. "One might get the impression you're not taking this seriously."

"Gavon—"

"What? Did he force your mouth open and pour the alcohol down your throat?" Alexandra asked. "He has been here, studying and preparing for the match."

Cyrus's face now resembled one of those strawberries I'd seen in the grocery store, and it took every ounce of self-control to keep my face passive.

"Go upstairs," she said, removing his food and drink from the table. "I don't want you to get sick over my table."

With a snarl, Cyrus shot up and stormed out of the room, the slamming door echoing in the room as I waited for Alexandra's next move.

She picked up her tea cup and took a hesitant sip. "Interesting."

"What?"

"Cyrus frequents that tavern at least once a week, but he

normally has the sense to fake illness instead of joining us here. I wonder why he came to dinner today, then?" Her eyes sparkled with something like amusement as she surveyed me over the rim of her cup.

"Perhaps he made a mistake," I offered.

"Be careful, son," Alexandra said. "You push him too far, it might result in something undesirable."

"I'm not doing a thing," I replied with a look.

"Make yourself useful, then," she said. "Mary has asked you to bring her more bread tonight, so she'll have plenty to sell tomorrow for the match. If you're to die, as Cyrus is suggesting, perhaps you'll bring her enough to be getting on with."

Although I knew I shouldn't invite it, I couldn't help myself. "And why aren't you asking me to give you the potion I've been using, if I'm to die?"

She lifted a shoulder. "Maybe I'm optimistic you'll survive."

As long as I lived, I would never understand Alexandra, but I ventured into the village anyway, looking for Mary. The villagers, normally in their homes at this hour, were milling around, carrying mugs of ale and openly cheering when I walked by. I waved at them weakly, not wanting to engage any of them in conversation or, worse, be forced to drink with them. If Cyrus wished to be sick for our match, so be it.

"Master Gavon," Mary said, jumping to her feet when I walked through the door. "Oh, this is a surprise. I'm so sorry things aren't clean here for you."

"Alexandra said you wanted more bread," I replied.

"Of course, but..." Her cheeks had grown rosy. "I didn't

expect you to come tonight. I mean, of course, I'll take it, but..."

I handed her another pile of crumbs, the last of bread I'd been slowly breaking pieces off. I didn't miss the disappointment on her face.

"It isn't enough?" I asked.

"It's plenty," she said, gathering it in her hand. "But... perhaps..." She averted her gaze and walked to the two barrels in the corner, opening her palms. "I'd hope one day we could fill this entire barrel with them."

"We could, still," I said lightly. It would take another trip through the tear, as I hadn't yet mastered the art of summoning through the magic there. "Would you like me to see what I can do tonight?"

"Oh, no, please." When she turned to me, her smile was bright. "You need your rest for the match tomorrow. We're all looking forward to it. Are you feeling very good about it?"

I didn't have it within me to tell her the truth. "I believe so. I think it'll be a nice competition."

"The Guildmaster has invited the whole town," she said, twirling her hair. "I've never seen a sparring match before. Is it quite exciting?"

"It is very bright," I said with a nod. "Lots of attack spells flying around."

"Is it dangerous?" She leaned forward, revealing more of her breasts to me. "Sarah says that your attack spells may fly into the village. Is that possible? Should I be prepared?"

"In a duel, there will be a dome," I said, mimicking the shape above our heads. "It keeps most of the magic contained until the match is concluded."

"And…is it true that Cyrus may kill you tomorrow?" All her breathless excitement was gone, and in its place was a wide-eyed terror I couldn't lie to.

"He may. The Guildmaster has given him permission."

"Please, Master Gavon, you can't let him win," she whispered. "He will ruin this village. You must beat him and become Guildmaster."

"We're merely dueling for induction," I said. "Alexandra will be Guildmaster for a long time. She's still young."

"Magical rot comes on quick. And if you're dead, there will be no one else to protect us from him." She took my hands. "Please, Master Gavon. You must win."

I patted her hands, noting they were rough and calloused compared to Mora's soft ones. Mary's pale skin was sallower, too, and even though she carried weight on her cheeks, the purple bags under her eyes told of her overall health. And yet, she actually looked haler to me now than a few weeks ago.

"I will do my best," I replied. "If you'll give me a moment, I'll go fetch more of that bread for you. I might have a couple extra loaves for you."

Perhaps Alexandra was a lot more cunning than I'd given her credit for. If she was trying to prove a point about why I should want to survive with Mary and her bread, she'd made it. Cyrus would make a terrible Guildmaster, and the only thing keeping him from villagers like Mary was me.

Still, even if I'd make a better Guildmaster, I still had to defeat him.

I crossed the tear and transported myself to the grocery store Mora had taken me to. The rich bounty of food took my breath away for a second time, and my stomach grumbled at the woefully inadequate dinner of bread and cheese, especially as I walked by a case filled with delicious smelling roast birds. But my focus for today was bread; if I survived, I'd help myself to something truly decadent.

As before, there were many different types of bread to choose from. I kept an eye on the nonmagicals shopping nearby then sent several loafs to sit at the front of the tear. Then, deciding I might as well, I took the rest of them, leaving the baskets empty.

"I'm gonna call a manager."

I jumped, turning to find Mora standing right behind me, a sly grin on her face.

"Mora!" I cried, pulling her into my arms. "What are you doing here? I thought I was banished?"

"I don't have a lot of time," she said breathlessly. "Long story short: Ashley told Mom she couldn't magically imprison me in the house, and Mom thinks I'm in my room, so I don't have a lot of time, but—"

I didn't care what the reasoning, I was just glad to see her. I kissed her soundly, but she pushed me away gently, glancing around at the nonmagicals who'd become curious at my outburst.

"How did your match go?" she asked, her voice low.

"It's tomorrow," I said, running my hand through her hair. Was she always this pretty, or had I just forgotten how blue her eyes were?

"And did you read the book? Figure out how you're going to

beat him yet?"

"I read the book, but as far as beating him…" I sighed. "I'll do my best, but I feel even if I make him angry, he'll still beat me."

"That's why you work him. Get him riled up then make him make a mistake." She gripped my face. "Just…promise me you won't give up. Promise me you'll try to come back to me."

I cupped her cheek, grateful for her confidence in me. "I will try with all my heart."

"I mean, you're a Warrior, right?"

I nodded.

"And I bet Warriors don't whine. They just do. So go do. Just win, Gav." She jumped. "Crap, gotta go. And hey…I do love you, too. I'll hopefully see you tomorrow, okay?"

She pressed a wet kiss against my lips before dashing around a corner to presumably transport back to her house.

I stared at the space she'd left, wondering if I'd dreamt the whole thing. But I had the taste of her on my lips still, and her scent lingered on my shirt. It wasn't much, but it was yet another reminder that I had something very important to live for.

*Warriors don't whine, they just do.* I'd have to use that from now on.

# Eighteen

My goal was clear: win. Win for Mora, so I might be able to kiss her more often without Alexandra's tug. Win for the world I would get to explore in greater detail. Win to bring more fresh food to the village and to save them from a Guildmaster who cared more for himself than for them.

Win to wipe that smirk off Cyrus's face.

The next morning I spent sitting on the beach, watching the waves crash against the shore. I'd hoped that Mora might appear, but it seemed I wasn't very lucky. As the hour drew closer, I rose and dusted my pants off, taking one final, long gaze at the world I'd only just begun to explore.

I transported myself to the tear, dove through, then continued on to the sparring ring. Where I'd expected silence, perhaps a howling wind, there were raucous voices. I craned my neck, taking in the sight—there was an audience for our match today. Our entire village had come to watch the show, it seemed, which unnerved me, but also gave me a little boost. I knew they, like Mora, were rooting for me to best Cyrus. They wanted me to be Guildmaster, not him.

Perhaps I had allowed Cyrus to convince me I wasn't worthy of my specialty. Perhaps I'd still die in the ring, but I wasn't going to go out without a fight.

Alexandra appeared in the center, her face betraying nothing. When she opened her mouth, it echoed across the open space, magically amplified.

"Welcome to today's induction match. A very special day, indeed. Cyrus Fairfield and Gavon McKinnon. Our two Warriors, the first born in twenty years, and the only born since. They will prove their mettle through the traditional Warrior duel. One will be a victor. Both, should they survive, will be inducted."

I tried not to look annoyed at that comment.

"The match will end when one is unable to continue or is dead."

I strode up to Cyrus and jutted out my hand.

"See you on the other side, brother," Cyrus said, his voice dripping with sarcasm.

"We'll see," I replied evenly. Our hands joined, and a burst of magic rose upward, doming around us. A mix of dark gray and purple, it would contain our spells while still giving our audience a view of our activities. The last time I'd been in a match, during my introduction match, my side had been a yellowish green, signaling that my master's magic still held sway over me. Today, it seemed, I would be all on my own.

We turned and walked to our respective sides. I licked my lips, remembering how it had felt to kiss Mora. She was counting on me to come back to her. And I was counting on kissing her a few thousand times more.

"Begin!"

Cyrus didn't strike right away, perhaps waiting for me to make the first move. Maybe waiting to give me time to collect my wits.

"I believe she said begin, Gav," he called, his voice echoing across our little dome.

"I usually give you the first blow," I replied, resting my hands behind my back. One of the sections in Mora's book had been on body language, and I'd crafted a few ways to draw him into a false sense of security.

Cyrus took the bait, sending a barrage my way. I easily avoided all of them, although I allowed one to hit a magical barrier, just to make him think he was winning.

"I've never killed a man before," Cyrus called when the barrage was over. "I wonder what it's like?"

"You'll have to tell me after you do it." Another powerful fireball, but this time I couldn't avoid it completely, and had to use a bit of magic to bat it away. My magic thrummed in my veins, begging me to let it loose, but I resisted. As long as I kept those exertions to a minimum, my strategy would work. Mora's strategy—

An attack spell landed hard against my left cheek, sending me staggering backward. Duly noted; don't think about Mora until the match was over.

Another came at me, this time from the right. Then the left again. I barely had time to recover before the next one arrived. Cyrus truly intended to kill me; I could feel his hatred in every magical blow. In the moments between the pain, I accepted that this was a necessary evil. For even though he thought himself to be winning, he was still playing into my hand.

Finally, the barrage ended, and I fell to my hands and knees, spitting blood onto the ground. The raucous crowd had grown quiet, a deafening silence.

"Well? Why aren't you cheering?" Cyrus screamed to the crowd. "I'm about to kill a man? Isn't that what you came here for?"

"Actually," I said, using magic to help me to stand. "They came here to watch me beat you. They don't like you very much, Cyrus."

His wild eyes narrowed, and the color rose in his cheeks. A wall of gray exploded from his body, barreling toward me with a force I hadn't seen from him before. At the last moment, I threw up a barrier spell, gritting my teeth as the pressure mounted between my ears.

Only this time—this time, his magic was less concentrated. With the crowd's growing cheers in the back of my mind, and the vision of Mora's blue eyes in the front of it, I searched for the cracks in his magic, the places where I could dig my own in and break him apart.

His magic released, dissipating around me in harmless, dark gray magical bursts. I straightened, facing him head-on and pleased to see his stance less confident, his breathing a little heavier than before.

But had it been enough?

"If you win," he said, stepping forward with something of a limp, "it's only because I wasn't at my best."

I had to laugh.

"And you won't become Guildmaster," he snarled, as he procured another spell. "No matter what these idiots think. It's mine."

"Whatever you say, Cyrus," I replied, forming my own magical reply. My magic was eager, ready to move. Tired of being kept inside and ready to do what it was made for—fighting. Defending. Winning.

And it was time to win.

I released magic in droves, hitting him as hard—if not harder—than he'd been hitting me. I dredged up every ounce of anger I'd held onto since my youth—anger that he'd been closer to my mother than I'd been, anger that he'd been given something I wanted by virtue of his birth, anger at my lot in life. And then I thought about Mora, about the new love I'd found with her, and New Salem. The five hundred souls in the crowd who were counting on me to save them.

A burst of new energy came from somewhere deep inside me, and I knew before it slammed into his body that it was the one.

Cyrus tumbled head over feet, landing on his back at the edge of our dome. He blinked once, twice, then his eyes rolled back in his head.

A loud roar of applause echoed from the stands as I waited for him to get up. Waited for the match to continue.

Instead, Alexandra appeared, a proud smile on her face.

"The match is over," she announced, her voice echoing once more. "Please welcome the two newest members of our Guild. Gavon and…well, when he wakes, Cyrus."

I couldn't help the sigh of relief that rumbled out of me. I'd done it—I was free. I'd survived a match against Cyrus and I was still standing. There would be a healing potion to imbibe once I left the ring, that was for sure. But it was over.

"Come," Alexandra said, glancing behind her at Cyrus. "Let's bring him back and enjoy a celebratory drink."

To be honest, the last thing I wanted was to return to Alexandra's house. But I allowed her to transport me there—to the library, where I collapsed gracelessly onto a chair.

"Here." A vial of white liquid was thrust under my nose.

"T-thank you," I said, uncorking it and drinking. "Where did you get this?"

"You aren't the only one who knows how to brew a potion," she replied, tipping another vial into Cyrus's open mouth. He grunted, blinking again, then fell back asleep. "Alas, it doesn't work the same for those who don't share your blood."

I licked my lips, the foul taste still lingering. "Since when do you make potions?"

"There's a lot about me you don't know," she said, conjuring a bottle and two glasses. She tipped the bottle and a blood red liquid swirled into the glasses.

I took one and sniffed hesitantly. "What is this?"

"Wine," she said, swirling the liquid in her glass. "Jones shared a glass with me when I was inducted, and I thought I'd continue the tradition with you."

We both sipped at the same time, and shared looks of disgust, although I could tell this liquid hadn't been addled by magic. "Where did you get it?"

"When we were banished, several hundred bottles made their

way to this land," she said, picking up the bottle. "Sadly, I believe this is all that's left. The Guildmasters placed a charm on it to seal in the freshness."

"So why share it with me?"

She flicked her wrist, and Cyrus's comatose body disappeared, presumably to return to bed. "Because you're my son, Gavon. And I'm very proud of your performance today. To be fair, I wasn't convinced you'd be sitting here. But here you are." The corners of her mouth turned upward. "Very impressive how you exploited Cyrus's weaknesses."

I wished I could tell her it was Mora's idea, that she'd provided me with everything I'd needed, but now probably wasn't the time. "Thank you."

"We now have three Warriors in our Guild," she said. "Three members of the Council. You will have much more responsibility now, you know. I would like you to continue finding ways to improve our food supplies."

I nodded. "Yes, M—" I cleared my throat. "What shall I call you now that you are no longer my mistress?"

"Alexandra," she said, tilting her head to stare at me as though she'd never seen me before. "I've always seen a lot of myself in you. You were an observant child, and willing to discover answers for yourself rather than ask them. Not great qualities for a Warrior, and less so for an apprentice. But I think it gives you an advantage. You think of things that haven't yet been done. We'll need more of that thinking if we're going to survive."

A few sips of wine had warmed my cheeks considerably, and I wondered if Alexandra was simply rambling. But her clear brown eyes focused on me as she spoke next.

"Gavon, I want you to be my successor," she said quietly. "I no longer have confidence in Cyrus's ability to govern wisely or fairly. Not after his performance today. Not after the cruel things I've heard from the villagers."

"Have you told him this yourself?"

"No," she said. "I believe he would accuse me of nepotism, and of being a soft Guildmaster. Even if I offered all the reasons I've just shared with you, the Council would take his side. They value strength over intellect. Therefore, I must be cautious with how I voice my preferences."

"What can the Council do?" I asked. "You're Guildmaster. And a Warrior."

She chuckled. "You'll find as you grow older that being a Warrior weighs about as much as words do. The people respect us because we've always been in charge."

"And attack spells," I added.

"Even those...one Warrior against the entire village?" She quirked a brow.

I'd never considered those odds. "Perhaps."

"But there's no reason for them to revolt. We provide them with what they need, they adhere to their traditions and customs."

I swallowed. If I told Alexandra about the tear, our village would have fresh food, medicine, and the like. But if, as Alexandra said, they were averse to change, would they even accept it? I couldn't see them driving cars or any of the other things Mora did.

"These are your people, too," she said. "Your Warrior Magic

is a gift. If you turn your back on them, you will be wasting your talents."

"Are you planning on stepping down soon?" I asked.

"No, not soon," she said with a smile. "But one never knows when the grip of death will reach for them, do they?"

I nodded, putting down my glass. "I think...." I paused, smiling to myself. "I don't have to tell you where I'm going anymore, do I?"

"It would be nice to see you every once in a while," she replied with a knowing look. "I am still your—"

Whatever she said after that, I didn't hear, because I'd already transported to the tear.

# Nineteen

I landed on the other side of the tear and promptly fell to my knees. The healing potion might've taken care of my bruises and cuts, but I was still weak. The sun was setting over the ocean, and I took a moment to stare at it, relishing the fact that I'd survived. I was still alive.

Now, if only I could get my girl back.

I closed my eyes and searched for her, finding her signature almost immediately. The effort of transporting to her was too much, so I had to hope she still had that charm on the tear and would know when I crossed it.

I lay there for so long I must've fallen asleep, because the next thing I knew, disembodied hands were shaking me awake.

"Gavon! Oh my God, Gavon!"

"Wha...?" I said, blinking as her face came into focus. "Mora, I'm glad you came to see me."

"Are you dying?" she cried, her eyes filled with tears. "You're so weak! What happened?"

"Oh, no," I said, cupping her face. "I'm fine. Just…very tired. I won."

"You won?"

I nodded, pulling her down to lie on my chest. Sleep with her sounded so very nice. "I did. But it was very hard, so I'm very tired. I just wanted to see you." I opened my eyes. "Wait… what happened with your clan?"

"They voted last night to give the final say to Ashley," she said, her brow furrowing as she raised her head to look at me. I winced as she pressed on a spot on my forehead; perhaps the healing potion hadn't worked as well as I'd thought.

"And what did Ashley say?" I asked after an exceptionally long pause.

"He wants to talk to you," she said. "Are you up for that? Do you need…something? Advil? Coffee? Drugs?"

I shook my head. "I can speak with him now. I don't want to keep him waiting. I'll be fine, I promise. But…if you don't mind…could you do the transporting?"

"Oh, um…" She chewed her lip. "I kind of can't. But I can drive us there."

I was certainly awake by the time we'd finished "driving." I'd never been in a car before, and I was quite sure I would never be in one again. Not with the lights of machines driving toward us, the metal boxes swerving this way and that, and the speeds Mora was going.

"It's just like transporting," she said, unbuckling the restraint she'd pressed on me. "Oh, you poor baby."

I unclenched my fingers from around the seat and exhaled.

"That is nothing like transporting."

"Are you gonna be all right?" She leaned across the seat and kissed me on the cheek. "C'mon, let's get you inside before my mom finds out I drove you in her car."

She opened the door for me, as I was woefully confused how the mechanism worked, and held my hand as we walked up to a large gray house. There was an audience for my walk to the Clanmaster's house. Groups of people sat in chairs on green lawns next door, others leaned on fences, and still others were just walking down the street. All of them magical, and all of them, I assumed, part of Mora's clan. And I was hopelessly out of my element. Perhaps prostrating myself on the ground in front of her great-uncle would do the trick.

Irene sat in a chair in the front room, her lips pressed into a thin line as we walked through the door. Mora hesitated for a moment, as if she wanted to say something. Then she apparently thought better of it and instead she led me up a very loud, creaky staircase. We padded quietly down a long hallway filled with paintings of past magicals, including, surprisingly, a painting of John Chase, gazing down on me as if I'd done something wrong.

"Go wait in there," Mora said, adjusting my shirt nervously. "Just...be yourself."

"I will," I said, leaning down to kiss her once more. Then, knowing it might be the last time, I deepened the kiss. "I still want to marry you, by the way."

"And I still think I'm seventeen," she replied, but there was a smile in her eyes. "Go on, he'll be up in a second."

I nodded and wished she were coming in with me. But this

journey I'd have to take on my own.

I walked inside to an empty office. The sheer number of books took my breath away, and despite my better instincts, I pulled one off the shelf and opened it.

"You're a fan of reading, I take it," said an old, weathered voice. Mora's Uncle Ashley, I presumed, had transported into the center of the library. "I like that in a person. Kids these days just don't appreciate the knowledge people already have."

I smiled at him and he beamed back. I could already tell this was going to go better than with Mora's mother. He was much older than anyone in New Salem. Even Master Jones had been only in his mid-fifties, but this man had to be at least eighty. His power had diminished somewhat, like a dimming light, but it was still formidable—bolstered by the stronger members of his clan. Unlike Irene, Ashley didn't show off his power, or use it to intimidate me. He smiled at me almost quizzically, as if I were a curiosity to be unpacked.

"So, Gavon. My niece Irene tells me you're here to kill us all. My great niece Mora says she's in love with you. Which of them should I believe?"

I cleared my throat, trying not to look too pleased that Mora had said she was in love with me. "I would answer that question, but you'd think me biased."

He laughed, a sound that put me at ease. "Well, I will say one thing: you've helped her improve her grades. I spoke with Rosemary down at the library, and she was highly complimentary. Most of the boys Mora runs around with would rather study other things with her. That tells me you're a good man, or will be soon."

"I do love her," I said, a little hotly. "I don't know what I've done to earn Irene's hatred."

"Exist? Threaten her campaign to lead?" He sighed wearily, sitting down in his chair with a loud groan. "It's all for naught. I don't believe Irene will be taking over for Clan Carrigan. She's too authoritarian for us, too focused on traditional magic. That poor little girl of hers, Jeanie, isn't even allowed to study magical theory—I'm sure you noticed that she'll suffer from a lack of magic after her fifteenth birthday."

I smiled. "Even a magical without much can always grow a little with practice."

"Preaching to the choir, my boy." At my perplexed expression, he laughed. "Mora tells me you've had some trouble adjusting to the world here. It seems your village was stuck in the seventeenth century."

"Just a bit," I admitted sheepishly, but my gaze went to the books on the shelves.

"And I find myself curious about the world you come from." He leaned forward, piercing me with eyes similar to Mora's. "Tell me of our magical brethren in New Salem."

I told him what I could of the world I'd grown up in, of my mother the Guildmaster and the Council. About the frigid nights and the dark days when the wind blew hard. How everything I knew came from books dated nearly three hundred years in the past. But when it came time to talk about the tear, I stumbled over my words. I hated admitting that I'd simply thrown together a potion and it had worked, but it was the truth.

"And have you informed your Guildmaster of this tear?" He

chuckled. "I only assume not, as we haven't seen anyone cross through it."

"No, I haven't."

"Would you bring your clansmen into our world, then? Or would you abandon them to live here permanently?"

It had seemed such an easy answer a few days ago. But knowing my mother wanted me to take over for her, knowing she entrusted me with the livelihood of five hundred souls, knowing what Cyrus might do to them if he were in charge instead of me…

"No," I said with a firm shake of my head. "I suppose I'd try to balance both. I don't want to leave them to the mercy of Cyrus, but…somehow I don't think they'd be allowed to live here."

"I'll be honest with you, Gavon. If you brought them here, they would introduce a new magical element into our world. Or, I should say, an old element. You're clearly not bound by the rules of the Danvers Accord. The rest of New Salem wouldn't be as well. And while I don't really mind a few Enchanters or Charmers—and we could possibly use some healers—the Warriors are what concerns me. You, Gavon, don't concern me. You seem the kind of man who'd use his magic to protect. Others? I don't have that level of faith."

I nodded slowly. Cyrus immediately sprang to mind. "So you're saying to let them live as they are? Don't tell them about the tear?"

"Close the tear, Gavon," he said. "It will only lead to trouble."

I sat back in the chair. While I understood what he was

saying, part of me couldn't agree with it. Couldn't agree to condemn my people to a life of never seeing the sun, never hearing the ocean. Of dying from curable diseases like magical rot. And we numbered in the hundreds—what harm could that do?

"I don't really know what I did," I said, buying myself some time. "How I created the tear, how to mend it..."

"Then I suggest you spend some time in my library trying to figure it out." He rose. "In the meantime, I believe my great niece is dying to know whether I'll allow you to continue dating."

I couldn't help the excitement on my face. "And?"

"I believe we may have some trouble if you break her poor heart," he said. "Although her previous dating history suggests you might be in more danger than she is."

I grinned. "I plan to marry her."

"Well, when that time comes, I'll be the first in line to congratulate you both." He rose. "But in the meantime, as a condition of your continued presence in this clan, you must provide me regular updates on your progress to close the tear."

I nodded. "I will. Perhaps...you could help me know where to look?"

He beamed. "It would be my pleasure."

"How'd it go?" Mora asked, standing as I walked out of the office.

"I am not banished," I said with a grin.

"I figured, since you're standing here." She practically flew into my arms, and I crushed her to me as I transported us both to our private beach with the tear. For now, I wanted to celebrate, and I didn't want an audience.

174

# part 2
## devilry

# One

"And the brewers?"

"They're doing exceptionally well," Humbert said with a bright smile on her face. "Councilman McKinnon's latest concoction seems to be much better than the last batch."

Humbert smiled at me, but I offered nothing but a nod in response. Last week, I'd tried to introduce a higher-quality beverage than the watered-down, two-dollar beer I'd been supplying for several years. Sadly, the inhabitants of New Salem didn't seem to like the tartness of an IPA. So this week, I'd returned with a higher quality lager—still an improvement over what they were used to.

What had started as breadcrumbs had grown into an intricate lie about seeds, charms, enchantments, and more. As a result, the New Salem diet flourished into one rich in fruits, vegetables, and protein. The annual census reported steep declines in magical rots and stillborn children, furthering my conclusion that the cause of it was the lack of nutrition. The villagers seemed happier, their magic more potent, and I couldn't have been more pleased.

But today, my attention was elsewhere. The Council meeting was running a little long. Out of habit, I checked my empty wrist as Councilwoman Humbert wheezed on about the beer I'd brought her. But there was nothing to be done about my tardiness; I couldn't just walk out of the meeting room.

Cyrus, to my right, fidgeted just as badly as I did. Though he just hated when the attention wasn't on him. Although we were both thirty, he still hadn't lost his need to be the most important person in the room, even though he was nothing more than a councilman.

Finally, after another half-hour of dithering, Alexandra ended the meeting. I sprang to my feet, eager to get out the door before anyone could stop me. Unfortunately, Alexandra was quicker, appearing in my path with a curious look on her face. She now sported gray streaks in her brown hair, and a few extra wrinkles around her eyes, but she remained as powerful and formidable as ever.

"Somewhere to be?" she asked.

"Unfortunately," I said with a forced smile as I sidestepped her. "I'm in the middle of a time-sensitive experiment."

She sighed. "Very well."

I hid a smile as I transported away. No matter how many times I did so, it never failed to give me pleasure when I was able to leave the Guildmaster's attentions.

The tear crackled and sputtered as it always did, and I dove in, landing gracefully onto the sandy beach. Immediately, I transported myself into a house nearby, right onto the plush rug in the front hallway. I listened, knowing that, even if they hadn't felt me arrive, they would've heard me.

Two pairs of tiny feet scuffled against the floor—one much faster than the other. Around the corner, my precious daughters came into view. Nicole was three, with long brown hair that bounced as she ran, and Marie, fifteen months, whose running was more of a toddle.

I bent down as they leaped into my arms then stood, balancing the two of them on my hip. Nicole babbled on about her day, although I only understood about half of what she said. Marie simply squealed and giggled, desperately trying to keep up with her sister.

We ventured toward the delicious smells coming from the kitchen. There, my beautiful wife was pulling bread out of the oven. A pot of meat sauce and spaghetti sat on the stove as well.

*"Finally,"* Mora said with an exasperated sigh. Her golden hair swung from a high ponytail, and her shorts—the same ones she was wearing when I left that morning—were covered in all manner of sauces and paints, as was her shirt.

"Tough day?" Gently, I put Nicole in her chair (she'd decided last week that high chairs were for babies) and set Marie in her chair with the tray. I summoned a jar of baby food from the fridge and a spoon from the drawer, placing both out of reach of the baby until we were all ready to eat.

"You try chasing a pair of toddlers all day and tell me how much *you* like it," Mora said, blowing a strand of hair out of her face. "Nicole peed in the hallway again, by the way. Your charmed diaper didn't work."

"Maybe now she thinks it's a game?" I asked, patting Nicole

on the head as she grinned up at me.

"Game or not, I don't like cleaning up pee." She knelt down to look at Nicole in the eyes, her anger evaporating into a smile. "Especially baby pee. Do you hear me, munchkin? No more peeing in the hall. We go in the potty like a big girl."

"Pee in the hall!" Nicole chirped.

I stifled a laugh, and Mora sighed. "And how was your day back in the mothership?" she asked, walking to the stove.

"Same as ever." I went to the wine rack and chose a vintage, summoning a few glasses for the table. I uncorked the bottle magically and poured Mora a glass. "I'm sorry I was late. I tried to speed it along, but you know how they like to talk."

"I know." She crunched on a piece of bread. "Mom stopped by again."

I hid my annoyance as I spooned pasta and sauce onto Nicole's plate, magically slicing the noodles and meat into smaller pieces. "What did she want?"

"Mom's just…mom," Mora said. "She's freaking out because Marie already has magic and she doesn't know what to do about it."

Of that, I was well aware. There wasn't much I put my foot down about, but my children would *not* be magically bound until they were fifteen. It hadn't been as big of an issue with Nicole, whose magic was already contained to what she could do in a cauldron. But three weeks ago, I would've come to blows with Irene about Marie's burgeoning magic if not for my lovely wife.

"Then we'll be more careful," I said.

She reached across the table to take my hand, kissing it

softly. "Yeah, and take a look at your daughter over there."

I turned just as a spoon rose from the baby jar and arriving in Marie's mouth. She hummed with excitement as the spoon returned to the jar then traveled back to her mouth.

"Look at the bright side," I said to Mora's pursed lips. "Feeding oneself doesn't usually happen until two or three in New Salem, so…" I decided wisely to end the rest of my sentence at her narrowed gaze. "So…I love you?"

"Uh-huh. Love me so much you leave me here to take care of these two for *eight hours*?"

"I'm sorry, my love," I said, taking her hand and kissing it. "I don't have a Council meeting for a few days. Why don't you go take a day to yourself tomorrow? A facial or massage perhaps?"

Mora surveyed me with a mix of amusement and annoyance. "You're lucky you're cute, baby."

I gazed into her exhausted eyes and pressed my hand against her cheek. What had begun as an explosive and frantic lust eventually had settled into a deep bond. It had taken me several years to get her to marry me, and several more before we'd had any children. Marriage and fatherhood were the most difficult— and rewarding—phases in my life. But after twelve years of exploring the world and two little girls, I could honestly say she could still make my heart race with that one look.

A loud belch broke the moment, as my three-year-old dissolved into giggles, quickly joined by a squeal from her sister.

"We also need a date night," I said, stabbing my fork into the pasta. "Badly."

"Yeah, and who's gonna babysit our two magical kids, huh?" Mora asked with a laugh. She turned to Marie and wiped her mouth with a damp cloth. "Our two crazy, messy kiddos."

"Jeanie could come up from school," I offered.

"Jeanie? Yeah, right. She *hates* kids," Mora said. "She's got about as much maternal instinct as my mother."

"Nina would watch them." Irene's sister was much less strict than her sister, and always offered to watch the girls.

"Nina…eh." Mora frowned. "I don't like asking her for too many favors. She's always been kind of weird to me."

"But she loves the girls."

"And that's weird," Mora replied. "I mean, don't get me wrong, our girls are great. But everyone else in the clan thinks they're ticking time bombs."

"Your *mother* thinks they're ticking time bombs." I didn't want to talk about Irene so I changed the subject. "I'll talk to Nina next time I see her. I miss you."

"Maybe you could take the kids with you next time you go to work," Mora said. "While we're on the subject of *mothers*."

"I'll tell her eventually," I demurred. And by eventually, I meant never. My mother would be horrified to know her two grandchildren weren't Warriors, or at least Charmers. But I'd also never told Mora the truth about what happened to children like Nicole in New Salem. And I had no plans to.

"Also, Uncle Ashley wants an update," Mora said. "Mom hinted he's annoyed we haven't gone looking for tear stuff in a while."

"Well, have you informed him we have two toddlers?" I said, sitting back and magicking the mess off the high chair and the faces of my daughters. "It's not like we have a ton of time to just wander around the world, reading books."

"Yeah, and didn't that used to be your favorite thing in the world?"

"I have a new favorite thing. Hanging out with my wife and kids."

"Well, you are in *luck*, cowboy. Because it's your turn to give them a bath," Mora said, taking her glass. She paused and kissed me sweetly. "Have fun."

I sighed, praying my girls would be merciful, but knowing full well I'd need to charm my ears to keep the screaming from deafening me.

# Two

I awoke the next morning with a bed full of children and a note from my wife informing me she'd gone to visit a girlfriend in Montreal for the day, but she'd left us a pot of oatmeal warm on the stove. Soon after that, Nicole kicked her sister in the face and we were all awake.

As they made a giant mess of breakfast in the kitchen, I sorted through the mail and caught up on the morning paper. I'd become a voracious reader of current events, once I'd gotten up to speed on what was current. Out the corner of my eye, I watched Nicole try to poke the baby with her spoon and magically removed it. A loud wail was my reward.

"Don't poke the baby," I said to Nicole.

"The baby poked me!" came the high-pitched retort.

I lowered the paper, looking at the cherubic face of my blonde child. "Marie, did you poke Nicole?"

The baby, predictably, had no idea what I was saying, and just laughed.

"Daddy, why don't I have magic?" Nicole asked.

"You have magic, princess," I said, putting down the paper. "Just a different kind. You can heal people and transport places and do everything I can. You just have to do it a different way." I summoned a damp cloth and wiped the pasty mess off her face. "You're a very powerful little girl. Never forget that."

That seemed to satisfy her, because she declared she was finished and wanted to watch cartoons. Unfortunately, I had other business to attend to, so I dressed them in their thickest coats for the brutal January weather, and we headed out in the snow. Nicole waddled ahead as well as she could, and I followed behind with the baby, using magic to catch the toddler when she slipped on the ice.

Nina's house was about a block away, which took us much longer in the heavy snow. We walked by Irene's house, which neither Nicole nor I mentioned. Instead, we made a beeline for the house next door, a stately manor with dead vines running up the sides.

"My girls!" Nina cried, opening her door. "Come see your Auntie Nina."

Nicole's jacket and snow pants disappeared in a puff of purple smoke, and she squealed as she ran into the kitchen, where something delicious was baking.

"I shouldn't be very long," I said, setting the baby on the ground. "Just a few minutes."

"Take as long as you…" She blinked as Marie's clothes—not just her jacket and snow pants, but her shirt, regular pants, and the diaper—disappeared. Stark naked, my one-year-old toddled into the kitchen after sister.

"Sorry about that," I said, running a hand through my hair. "She doesn't like wearing clothes lately."

"She's fine," Nina said with a smile. "Now don't worry about a thing. We'll have fun today."

I summoned a diaper, shirt, and pants to Marie's small body. Remembering what Mora had said about the girls' reputation, I cast a containment spell on Marie to keep her out of trouble, although it pained me to do so.

"That should help," I said to Nina. "I apologize. She's becoming more opinionated on what she wants."

"Opinionated little girls make for strong women," she said. "I swear, she looks just like Mora. We would've had as much trouble with her had she had magic at that age."

I couldn't disagree. "I won't be more than a few minutes."

"Take your time, Gavon, sweetheart."

I left my girls and transported across the small subdivision to the oldest house. There, I landed by the front door, as was customary, and called up the stairwell.

"Uncle Ashley?"

"In the library, my boy," came the feeble response.

I ascended the creaky stairs, went down the hall of portraits that never ceased to make the hairs rise on the back of my neck, and walked into Ashley's office. The old man sat at his desk, his skin sagging against his cheeks and his hair now a bright white instead of gray. Irene had been campaigning hard for him to step down—so I'd heard. She'd banished me from clan meetings, although Mora was still permitted to attend. But even though he'd aged, he was still as smart and commanding as the day I'd met him.

"Ashley, good to see you," I said, helping him sit down.

"Thank you, my boy. How are those girls?"

"They're three and one," I said with a heavy sigh.

"And magical, that certainly complicates things."

"Certainly," I said with a small laugh. "But nothing we can't handle. Mora had them all day yesterday, so she's run off with a girlfriend to Montreal for the day."

"I heard a rumor that Marie used magic in front of a nonmagical last week," Ashley said.

I started. "She…did? Mora didn't say anything about that."

"I'd imagine she wouldn't. This report came outside of Irene's grapevine, so I'm sure Mora wanted to keep it quiet."

"What did she do?" I asked. She was fifteen months old; what harm could she do?

"Summoned a toy, I believe."

I swallowed, a nervous dread growing in my stomach. "I'll tell Mora to be more careful when she's out with them. And I'll be more vigilant as well."

He nodded. "I'm not here to discuss your children, although I do enjoy listening to Nicole tell me about her drawings." He smiled, but I didn't share it. "How's your progress on the tear?"

"About the same," I said.

"Did you follow up with my friend in London?"

"Not yet." I tried not to look guilty. "It's been a little hectic with the girls lately. Time's slipped away from me."

I was no closer to finding a solution to closing the tear than I'd been when I'd made it. But if I were being honest, I didn't feel it to be a complete necessity anymore. Cyrus and the rest of the Council, including Alexandra, remained blissfully unaware of its existence. The only people who seemed preoccupied with it were Ashley and Irene.

"Gavon, people are starting to talk," he said. "We have to show them progress or else..."

"Or else what?" I said, knowing this was Irene's doing.

"I'd prefer not to find out," he said. "I know you must have some loyalty to your Guild, and I understand how hard it must be—"

"I haven't found a solution yet."

"You haven't been trying very hard either."

"I have toddlers, what do you want me to do?" I said. "And why is it a big issue now?"

"Because we are starting to see what happens when a child born outside the Danvers Accord comes of age," he said.

A sliver of fear slipped through my body. "What does that have to do with closing the tear?"

He remained silent, and the sliver turned into a storm.

"I hope you aren't insinuating that I should close the tear and leave my children on the other side of it," I said. "Because if that's what you're saying—"

"Absolutely not," he said. "But it is something we have to think about with Marie."

"And, again, what does Marie's magic have to do with the tear?" I said, warm anger rising in my cheeks.

"Merely to point out that if *any*one from New Salem were to cross the tear, we would have a larger problem on our hands," he said. "I, and the rest of the clan, trust you, Gavon. Your girls are contained through their membership to Clan Carrigan. The rest of your Guild, however..."

We'd had this conversation a long time ago, when Mora was first pregnant with Nicole. "They don't know about it, though."

"Can you be confident that will remain the case? In fifty years, when you're as old as I am, can you be confident that no one will stumble across the tear if it remains open? A hundred years, when you're gone?"

"I take pains to hide it," I said. "Charms, that sort of thing. They'll live on long after I'm gone."

Ashley sighed, and I could tell he was growing tired of my delaying. "Gavon, I hate to have to be strict, but I will. You're simply married into Clan Carrigan, not a part of it. I need to see some concrete progress on the tear—and by that, I mean you have to do *something*—or I will have to recommend your banishment."

I sat back, stunned. "You would do that?"

"Only because being nice hasn't seemed to work," he said with a pitying look. "And because Irene is becoming more and more vocal as I grow older. She won't be as gentle or forgiving as I am, so you'll need the rest of the clan on your side if you want to overrule her."

I couldn't argue. "Very well. Maybe Mora would like to take a trip to London with the girls. Check on that lead."

"That's the spirit," he said, clasping his hands together. "I look forward to hearing what you find."

I did my best to hide my discomfort as the girls played on the playground I'd charmed to be a little warmer for them. Nicole was climbing the stairs, her little sister barely able to keep up. I hoped one day they'd get along and be best friends, but if

Mora and her sister were any indication, that might be a bridge too far.

Nicole laughed as she slid down the slide, guided by my magic on either side. I refused to be like Irene, pressuring my daughter into being more than she was. I wanted Nicole to love her magic and know how unique she really was. Nicole was the first of her kind in a very, very long time—the only Potion-maker in existence. And perhaps it was the combination of her mother's magic and my own, but she held within her a great deal of power that I hoped we could tap into when she was a little older.

But as a baby, when she'd wanted something, all Nicole could do was scream. Marie was starting to find her magical abilities, as babies did at her age. And now, summoning and transporting and levitating as she was…

Would it be better to put a containment spell on her? That, I didn't know. It seemed cruel to take away years of magical training just to appease the nonmagicals. But that was the world I'd chosen to live in. And bringing her to New Salem was out of the question.

Marie swayed on a step then fell backward. My magic caught her instantly, placing her back on the playlet.

"Baby. We've talked about this."

I looked up at my wife, wrapped in a black wool coat, her yellow tresses flying in the breeze.

"Yes, my love?" I said, feigning ignorance. "What have we talked about?"

"You're in the middle of a nonmagical park," she said, taking a seat on the bench next to me. "You can't be plucking children from thin air."

I wrapped my arm around her and kissed her forehead. "There's a Look Away charm on the playground."

"That only affects nonmagicals."

"If your mother is surprised by magic, I think we have a lot more to worry about. Perhaps she's developing dementia…"

"I'm serious, Gav," she said. "You didn't hear the earful I got from her the other day. She wants Marie under a containment spell pronto."

I sighed instead of responding. I'd had too many fights about Mora's mother to rehash it further. "How was Montreal?"

"Bitterly cold," she said with a shiver. "But fun. I haven't been ice skating in years." She rested her forehead against my cold cheek. "There was a handsome guy at the rink, too."

"Oh? Magical?"

"Not a drop," she said. "Still cute. I didn't have the heart to tell him I had two kids and a husband at home. Gave me free skates though."

"With more than a little bit of flirting, I'm sure."

"Just a bit, Gav. I am a married woman."

I chuckled, and she leaned further into me as we watched our two little girls chase each other around the park. Later, we carried them back home and cooked dinner together, tripping over each other in our small kitchen and sharing a glass of wine as the girls watched cartoons before we put them to bed. With the house to ourselves, Mora and I engaged in a little more marital bliss before finally calling it a night and going to bed.

As I lay there, my wife in my arms, Ashley's warning flitted in the back of my mind. Things were so perfect, it was easy to forget that I had obligations in New Salem and to Mora's clan. My agreement with Ashley so long ago was now more a formality, but still valid.

I kissed Mora's forehead and promised myself I'd worry about it tomorrow. But just as I was drifting off to sleep, I felt something odd that woke me right up. It was a small kernel of magic—similar to the one I'd felt when she'd been pregnant with Marie. But this was…

"Mora," I said, shaking her. "Wake up."

"Huh…what?" She blinked. "Baby, what is it? What's wrong?"

"Are you pregnant?"

Her eyes widened. "W…*what*? I'd better not be."

I concentrated, searching for that small kernel again. It was faint—barely there. But it still existed. The smallest indication that a Warrior was coming.

# Three

We confirmed Mora's pregnancy via nonmagical means three days later. She was less ecstatic than I was.

"*Three* kids, Gavon?" she said, pacing the bedroom. "What the hell am I supposed to do with *three* kids. I have two arms. And a Warrior? So she or he'll be tossing spells like you do?" She ran a hand through her hair. "This is insane. We can't have another kid."

"Baby, come here," I said, holding out my arms. With a frown, she trudged toward them, resting her head on my shoulder. "We'll figure it out. I promise."

"Mom's going to be livid."

"I dare her to say one thing in front of me," I said, unable to keep the venom from my voice. "I dare any of them to say one thing about my children in front of me."

She leaned back and smiled. "You know I like it when you get all feisty about our babies."

Some of my anger cooled, and I allowed myself to relax. "I

can't believe you're having a Warrior. It's...amazing."

"And why is it any more amazing than a Healer and Potion-maker?" she asked with a raised brow.

"Because..." How could I explain it to her? She had no idea the bond that came with specialties. Beyond that, I couldn't help but find this to be almost poetic. My mother had given me away as a child for someone else to raise. I would be there for my child—to show them that a Warrior could be powerful even trained by their parent.

"Because?"

"Do you know how your cousin Charlie takes his kids to the Red Sox games?" I said. "And how he was so excited when his daughter started softball so they could play it together?" She nodded. "It's kind of like that. I love the girls, but I can't spar with them. I can't show them how to block a spell. I can't—"

She pressed her finger to my lips. "I get it. You're such a dork."

I kissed her fingertip. "You know what else this means, don't you?"

"Hm?"

"Remember when you were pregnant with Marie, how you suddenly had all this healing magic?" I said, casually sliding my hands down the side of her body. It had been a curious oddity—presumably a byproduct of a magical under the Danvers agreement playing temporary host to a child not under it. "Well, I believe the same will happen here."

"So?"

"*So...*" I pulled her closer. "That means you and I might be able to spar."

Her eyes lit up. "For real? You'd let me into the ring. Me and my delicate sensibilities?"

"I have *never* called your sensibilities delicate," I said. "But yes, perhaps I can teach you a couple of things. But not for a few weeks, at least. The baby's magic is pretty weak right now, it needs to grow. But I can already tell, this one's going to be a powerhouse."

"Look at you," Mora said, taking my face in her hands. "You're really excited about this, aren't you?"

I nodded. "I know you're nervous about having three kids, but I promise you, it's going to be fine. We can handle it."

"Oh geez, what if it's a boy?" Mora said with a horrified look. "I can't deal with boys."

I honestly didn't care, although we'd be spending significantly less money on clothes and toys if it was another girl. "When do you want to tell the kids?"

"Nicole won't be able to keep it from Mom," Mora said. "And I don't want to tell Mom until…" She sighed. "Ever? Can I just keep this secret from her forever?"

"I think when you show up with a squealing baby with Warrior magic, she might have some questions."

"Ugh." Mora dropped her head in her hands.

"Hey," I said, gently removing them and holding her close. "Don't get upset. It's bad for the baby."

"Maybe we could just…I don't know, take the girls for a few days. Go somewhere."

"Well, Ashley did want me to follow up on his lead in London," I said with a grin. Might as well kill two birds with one stone. "Delay the inevitable a bit longer?"

"Sounds awesome." She stood. "I'll start packing."

Even with magic, getting two kids under four ready for a week-long trip was more complicated than it seemed. But soon, we'd transported into an alley in the middle of London, away from prying eyes. I'd perfected the art of casting a Look Away charm before I arrived anywhere new, just in case.

The girls always loved transporting. Nicole would scream excitedly as the world changed beneath our feet, and every time she'd ask me when she could transport.

"Soon," I promised her. First I'd have to find a Potion-making book that contained such a spell, but there had to be one out there. There seemed to be a potion for everything else.

"So you're going to follow up on Ashley's lead?" Mora asked. "How long are you going to be?"

"Uh…"

"Long," she said. After glancing around the alley, she magicked the baby's carrier from her back to my front—along with the baby. "You take her. I'll take Nicole and go sightseeing."

"Find us a good hotel too, will you?" I said, adjusting the baby on my front. She was fast asleep, a good sign. "And can you leave the diaper bag?"

"Have fun," Mora said, kissing me sweetly on the lips. "C'mon, munchkin. Let's go see what London looks like."

I pressed my hand to the baby's back and watched them go, offering a small wave when Nicole looked back at me. When they disappeared around the corner, I pulled the letter from Ashley from my pocket and read.

"Okay, Marie, for your first magical lesson," I said softly. "We're going to learn how to use magic to find an address."

The baby was a poor study, but as I'd seen with Nicole, even the simplest magical lessons seemed to stick. I let my magic guide me into the city, glad to be back once more. Shortly after I'd been allowed into the clan, Mora had taken me here to see a Shakespeare play performed live at the Globe Theater. Both had been thrilling, but didn't hold a candle to the moment we'd stopped by the bank and found a large sum of money in my name.

The account had been charmed—as was, I found out, most of the money in that section of the bank. The magical who'd taken me to it said that no one had been able to unlock the vaults for centuries. It was based on DNA, and when it opened and revealed a large sum of money…

Let's just say the clan was a little more eager to let me hang around.

Mora and I didn't take much—we didn't need a lot, either. Our house had been a gift from Ashley on our wedding day, as it had belonged to Ashley's father, and had been vacant for some time. But I was glad I could give the money to my girls one day, perhaps for college, or even for their own houses.

I looked down at the baby, marveling at how quickly time was passing. Just yesterday, she'd been born. Soon, I'd have a new baby to carry around and dote on.

"I'm so excited for your new sibling to get here," I said, as we continued down the street. "You two should be good friends. A Warrior and a Healer. And you share the same blood, so your powers will be extra helpful to her." I chuckled. "I hope you can spare some for your old man, too."

The baby, predictably, slept on.

After a long walk into the more magical part of London, I arrived at the address. I walked to the door and rapped on the knocker, also signaling my presence magically. It was an older practice—something the younger magicals didn't do—but Ashley had told me once it was still a sign of respect.

The door opened to reveal an Indian man with a bushy mustache and jet-black hair. He gave me a once over, then opened the door wider. "You must be the magical from the Carrigan Clan," he said in a thick London accent.

I held out my hand. "Very nice to meet you. Gavon McKinnon."

He introduced himself as Sahil Jha and welcomed me into his home, guiding me to his book-filled office. I stood in the doorway, admiring his stacks with glee.

"You're a fan of the written word?" he asked. "Or just the magical one?"

"All of them," I said, patting Marie on the head as she squirmed, but didn't wake up.

"You've got a strange sort of magic," he said, peering at me as if I were a curiosity. "As does your child."

"Yeah." I'd become used to this question over the years, having the explanation down to a short few sentences. The look of surprise when I mentioned the tear never ceased to make me feel uncomfortable.

"And that's why you're here, I suppose," he said with a knowing nod. "Ashley's letter said something about magical pockets."

"Anything you have on the subject, I am all ears." I took the seat he offered me.

"I'll put on some tea, then."

I had a fantastic talk with Sahil over a cup of strong brew, with only a short break to feed the baby who'd woken from her nap. His knowledge on magical pockets was limited, but his family had once been the world leaders in it, so he had plenty of books. Prior to the Danvers Accord, Sahil's clan had been a strong line of Charmers, and their magic still held an affinity for it.

"The old ways aren't practiced so much anymore," he said as I flipped through his book. The words were in a different language, but I magically charmed them into English. A cursory glance told me I would find nothing valuable in them, but I didn't think Ashley would be happy if I returned home empty handed.

"So tell me of this New Salem," he said. "And how you came to make the tear?"

"To be frank, I don't know," I said with a sigh. "It was something of a youthful tantrum. The only thing I recall ever showing promise was the infinity symbol and a mix of potion ingredients. I can't even remember what I threw in there."

"Have you tried recreating it?"

"Thousands of times," I said. "I even have a Potion-making daughter. Perhaps one day she'll be able to unlock the secret."

"Oh, that reminds me," he said, popping upright and scurrying to his stacks. He procured a book from the shelves and handed it to me. "Ashley's letter mentioned the Potion-maker. I thought she might like this book. I found it a few years ago in the trash heap."

I grinned as I read the title—*Potions and Potion-making.* "This is wonderful. Thank you for rescuing it. Nicole will love it. One day, perhaps, when she's old enough to read."

"Are there no Potion-making books in New Salem?"

"None," I said grimly. "Some old ways are better left unpracticed, if you get my meaning."

He nodded. "Then it is a wonderful thing your daughter was born here."

I felt my wife's gentle call on my magic, and I smiled. "I couldn't agree more."


I left Sahil with a promise to return one day to learn more about India's magical culture, and to tell him more about New Salem. He seemed of like mind to myself—a man curious about the world and everything in it.

I found my wife and daughter sitting in a cafe, Nicole sipping on a hot chocolate that had to have been magically charmed—otherwise, she would've spilled it all over herself.

"Weren't you just getting onto me about using magic in public?" I said, kissing Mora's forehead.

"This is not obvious," Mora said. "And there's a Look Away charm on her. Also, hooray, I can use magic in front of non-magicals again. Thanks, pregnancy."

"That baby is something else," I said with a grin, before turning to the toddler. "And how was your day, Nicole?"

She gave me a whipped cream grin and then went back to it.

"How was your meeting?" Mora asked.

"Fantastic." I pulled out the potion book Sahil had given me and put it on the table. "An actual Potion-making book for Potion-makers. Just what I was looking for."

She pursed her lips. "And how is that going to help you close the tear?"

I cleared my throat. "I mean…"

"Gavon. Ashley was *pretty* clear—"

"I talked to him about it and got some books, though I don't think they're what I need. But it's something."

She sat back and leveled one of those glares at me. "Sometimes, baby, I don't think you want that tear closed at all. I think you want it to remain open forever."

Luckily, Marie waking up and loudly wailing ended that conversation pretty quickly.

# Four

Our trip to London was short-lived, and soon we were back in our home, just in time for a massive January blizzard to overtake the neighborhood. And, unfortunately, just in time for me to have to return to New Salem for another Council meeting. But thanks to the blizzard, Mora would have another few days to hide from her mother.

"You'll have to tell her eventually," I said gently.

"Oh, that's rich," Mora said, putting her hand on her hip. "Mr. I haven't told *my* mother about either of my daughters."

"Touché." I kissed her forehead, but her gaze had changed. "What?"

"Are you going to tell her about this one?" Mora asked. "Since it's a Warrior?"

I opened and closed my mouth. "I...don't see how or why I would. I would have to tell her about you, and the tear, and this world. She'd want that child to grow up in New Salem. And she'd probably give the baby to..." I narrowed my eyes, hot anger crawling up my spine, "Cyrus to raise."

"Oh yeah, no," Mora said, pressing a hand on her lower abdomen. "Don't tell your mother about this."

"Not a chance." I wiped the anger from my face and kissed her forehead. "I'll be back later."

It was always jarring to return to New Salem after a few weeks at home. I'd become so used to seeing the sun and hearing the ocean nearby that the dark silence was unnerving. When I'd become a councilman, I'd been given Master Jones' old house to live in. It suited me well enough—there were no servants, no one to bother me. It was easier still to pretend like I was an eccentric old man (after all, thirty was old in New Salem), too focused on science experiments to leave my house. I would let the reputation continue as long as it needed to.

If possible, it was *colder* in New Salem than the blizzard I'd just left, although there was no snow on the ground. I charmed my cloak to warm me, but it didn't seem to do much as I strolled through the streets. The village was bustling even in the chill, for the inhabitants had no idea of any other life.

As customary, I stopped in at Mary's house first with a fresh batch of bread. She and I had become cordial over the years, though, thankfully, she'd fallen in love with another Enchanter. They had five children now (six, maybe), all Enchanters with rosy dimpled cheeks and long brown hair.

"Master Gavon," she said, ducking her head as I walked into her shop. "Always a pleasure to see you."

We exchanged more pleasantries, and she told me the latest with her children. Her second youngest little girl reminded me of Nicole in age and precociousness, and I wished I could bring her something sweet from the new world. Perhaps one day.

"Your experiments seem to be going very well," Mary said, taking the fresh roll from me and disintegrating it into small crumbs. From each crumb, she formed a full loaf, which she put to the side as she worked. The food that New Salem consumed was still mostly dirt, but at least it started from fresh food.

"I hope to be close to creating a new kind of beer," I said. "But so far, it hasn't done very well. The last batch I brought wasn't very well received."

"I wish you could share your secrets," she said with a sigh.

I patted one of the little girls on the head. "One day."

Alexandra and the Council were the only ones who "knew" I was using potions to improve food. They thought it might cause a stir if the villagers knew potion-making was suddenly legal— especially considering how many of their children had been killed for having the specialty. Nuance, Alexandra had said, wasn't something they'd understand.

I also thought it might be another way for her to consolidate power. Once I'd been accepted into the inner circle as a councilman, I'd seen a side to politics I didn't like. It was clear that Alexandra, Cyrus, and I were only on the Council, only living in the nicest houses in the village, only given such incredible say over the lives of everyone else, because of tradition. And keeping the rest of the village from questioning that tradition was the only way we remained in power.

The rest of the Council were already in their seats when I arrived, and I caught the look of annoyance from Cyrus as I sat in my chair next to him.

"We're so glad you could grace us with your presence," he muttered under his breath.

"Apologies for the delay," I said. "I had to stop by the Enchanters to deliver another batch of bread."

Rogers, the Enchanter, beamed. "Excellent work, my boy!"

Cyrus scoffed, rolling his eyes.

"Yes, well, please note the time of our meetings," Alexandra said with a glare. "We can't be sitting here all day waiting for you to arrive."

I nodded, picturing her face when I told her my wife had sent me on a mission to retrieve Ho-Ho's and other junk food. And also picturing what she'd say if I told her I had a Warrior on the way.

"…Warrior baby."

I jumped in my chair, coming back to the conversation at the tail end. Had I spoken aloud? No, I couldn't have. That was impossible.

"Something wrong, Gavon?" Alexandra asked.

"No, I must've nodded off," I said, hoping I didn't look too guilty. "I apologize. I stayed up too late experimenting."

"Have some tea," Alexandra said, magicking the brew in front of me. I ducked my head as I sipped, trying not to grimace at the watered-down taste. Perhaps I'd bring some more tea to the Enchanters next.

"What was the question?"

"No question," Alexandra said. "We were merely discussing the latest with Agatha, and her child."

Agatha… Agatha… My mind drew a blank.

"The Charmer having the Warrior baby," Alexandra said

with more than a little heat.

My eyebrows shot upward. "Are you serious? A Warrior? Is it certain?"

"It's clear you haven't been around the village lately," Cyrus chimed in. "As it's all anyone's talked about the past few days."

This was incredible news. Our village would have a Warrior —and it wouldn't be mine. Not that I would've volunteered my own, but knowing there was another absolved me of having to make that choice. Our village would have a steady hand for another generation.

"As I was saying," Alexandra continued. "The midwives are very pleased with Agatha's progress. The child is healthy and turned the right way, they believe. We will have a child in a few weeks."

Unlike Mora, who was probably four or five weeks along, the New Salem mothers could tell the strain of magic around six months.

"The question now becomes who will take the new Warrior as his apprentice," Alexandra said.

"You won't take him?" Cyrus asked. "You were an excellent teacher."

"I would prefer one of you take him. I'm too old to worry about it."

"Gav should," Cyrus said with a smirk. "It would do him some good to get out of that dark house he shuts himself up in. Nobody sees you for weeks. I can only imagine what sort of trouble you're getting into."

"But Cyrus," I replied with the same feigned civility. "Having an apprentice might humble you and bring your head down to a manageable size."

"Enough," Alexandra said. "I won't have squabbling in my Council. I will make the final decision when the baby is born."

But I caught her gaze on me and frowned. Mora was already freaking out about having three kids; imagine what she'd say when I came home with a fourth. And another Warrior.

I shivered. Better to nip this in the bud before Alexandra made her decision.

After another excruciatingly long meeting, I didn't disappear right away, instead choosing to loiter and wait for Alexandra to become free. She was having an extended conversation with Rogers, one I was sure she was stretching out just to get my goat. But I remained patient, standing with my hands clasped behind my back.

Finally, she left him and joined me at the front of the Council house.

"It's been a while since we've spoken," Alexandra said. "You usually run away to your manor and disappear until the next Council meeting."

"I could still," I said with a mysterious smile. "But I'd like to talk to you about this Warrior child. I don't think it would be wise to let Cyrus raise it."

"I agree. That's why I want you to."

I swallowed. "I don't think that would be wise either."

"And why not? You dote on the villagers. You currently aren't doing anything of import—"

"Except for devising potions to keep the villagers alive," I replied. That would be my angle. If I were busy training a

Warrior, I couldn't possibly have time to experiment.

"Ah, unfortunately, people have become accustomed to it, and no longer think it anything special."

I stopped in the middle of the street. "And what is that supposed to mean?"

"People talk, Gavon. They wonder what you're doing. Nobody sees you. They put up with you because you bring us food. But..." She shook her head. "But you're nearly thirty and you've yet to have any children."

"That you know of," I said.

She turned. "Oh? Have you been hiding things from me, son?"

"There have been a couple," I said. "Unfortunately, they haven't made it."

"I see."

Better to let her think there was something wrong with me. "It's not something I've been eager to share. Especially considering our lineage."

She nodded, but didn't look convinced. "Then it's a good thing we have a new Warrior on the way. And a better thing I have you to train them."

I frowned. "Yes, a good thing we have a new Warrior. But I don't think I'm the right one to raise them."

"We still have several months until the child is born, and several more until I have to make a decision about it." Alexandra quirked her brow. "It's not something you should concern yourself with right now."

# Five

My wife would certainly be concerned with it, but I returned home, filled with schemes for skirting my responsibilities and excited to see what trouble my kids had gotten into while I'd been gone.

"Baby, I'm..." I stopped short, finding Irene sitting in our living room, Marie nestled in her arms. She would've looked maternal, had it not been for the severely annoyed look on her face. Nicole was playing with her blocks on the floor, but even she wore a look of nervousness, as if she could sense the mood in the room.

"So I hear congratulations are in order," Irene said dully.

I glanced at my wife, whose eyes pleaded with me to make nice, so I swallowed whatever biting retort I had and forced a smile onto my face. "It's so wonderful. And *unexpected*."

"Is it?"

A terse remark was on the tip of my tongue, but I kept it at bay after another pleading look. It was the least I could do after leaving her alone with the girls all day. "Very unexpected. I don't believe we wanted more than two, did we, Mora?"

"Nope." Mora chewed on her nail, squirming under her mother's gaze.

"And how very convenient that this was a Warrior, too." Her eyes narrowed at me.

"If you're suggesting I had something to do with that, then please enlighten me to how the specialties work," I said, catching Mora's eye. "I've certainly not done enough research on how alleles work."

"You had something to do with it by your mere presence," Irene snapped.

"*Mom*," Mora barked before I could jump in again. "Gavon and I are married. We have kids. They've got specialties. Get over it already."

"And now you have one more child who'll be summoning toys and transporting all over the place," Irene said. "I heard about Marie's little magical escapade. Lucky it didn't require a memory charm on some nonmagicals."

"It's a toy, Mom," Mora said, again, catching my eye and warning me to stay quiet. "And we'll be more careful."

"What you need is a containment spell. On both of them. Until they're fifteen."

"That's not happening," I replied hotly. "I believe we've had this conversation, Irene. I'm not changing my mind."

"Of course you aren't," Irene said, rising and handing the baby back to Mora. "And that is precisely the problem."

"W…what is that supposed to mean?" I said, struggling now to keep the anger out of my voice.

Irene shrugged, the message more for my conflicted wife than for me. "We'll continue this conversation—"

"Never," I said. "If you can't be happy for us and our kids, we just won't have a conversation about them. Get the hell out of my house."

Irene rose and disappeared in a puff of dark gray smoke. My final words echoed in the air and promised some sort of retribution later. Probably toward my wife.

"I had it handled, Gav," she said softly. "You don't need to get involved. You know how she gets."

"I didn't say anything you didn't say," I snapped.

"Yes, but I'm her daughter, you're—"

"Her son-in-law." I folded my arms across my chest. "And the father of her grandchildren. Is that a problem for you now, Mora?"

"No, of course not. It's just…" She stood, tears in her eyes. "I'm just… Can you watch the girls for me?"

She dashed up the stairs.


I hated Irene—probably more than I hated Cyrus. She had a nasty habit of ruining everything good in our life with her judgment. With the way she treated my children and me, ready to betray the clan at the drop of a hat. I'd hoped the girls would've tempered her anger toward me—proven something to her—but if anything, it had made her more suspicious.

Even more, I hated how her visits always resulted in fights with Mora. I tried so hard not to let her get a rise out of me. To ignore the thinly veiled comments about me and the dangers I posed. But when it came to our kids, I had a short fuse. Family meant something to me, even if it meant nothing to Irene.

To calm down, I gave the girls a bath and read them a bedtime story. Once they were tucked in, I kissed them both and left them in their beds.

Then I went downstairs to watch TV and drink a beer.

When bedtime rolled around, and my wife still hadn't shown herself again, I steeled myself, climbed the stairs quietly, so as to not wake the girls, and opened the door. Our room was dark, but I could see her form outlined on the bed and hear her sniffling. What was left of my anger evaporated. I couldn't stand to hear her cry.

"Mora?" I called, softly closing the door behind me. "Baby, I'm sorry—"

"I gotta know," she whispered in the darkness. "I gotta know if you had anything to do with this."

I stopped in the middle of the room. "What?"

"Please don't be mad," she said, sitting up and wiping her face. "But Mom has a way of putting thoughts in my head, and I can't shake them. I just have to look at you in the eyes—"

"Mora." I knelt in front of her. "Do you think if I had any control over this, I would've had a Warrior third? If I were truly this genius master planner, I'd have had one Warrior and been done with it."

She sniffed. "Not helping."

I took her wet cheeks in my hand. "I have no idea how the roulette works with genes and specialties. Perhaps one day our children can study themselves and understand it. I'm sure there's a genetic marker or something..." She released a sob, and I kissed her forehead. "What other stupid thoughts did your mother put in your head?"

"Why don't you want the tear closed?"

"I want the tear closed," I said, a little too quickly.

"No, you don't. You *kind of* want it closed," she said. "You put it off and dance around it. And when Ashley gives you a lead, you only sort of follow it."

I didn't want to know, but I asked, "And what does your mother think?"

"Gavon, you know what she thinks. You're biding your time until you've created an army of magicals to take over the world." She wiped her cheeks. "I don't believe her, but I also don't believe you want the tear closed. If you did… you're brilliant. You would've done it by now."

I closed my eyes. "I went to London. I talked to the guy. What do they want from me?"

"I don't know, Gav. But Ashley isn't really happy right now either. And with a Warrior coming, it just looks like…"

"I don't care what it looks like," I snapped angrily.

She rested her cheek against my shirt. "But they do. And unfortunately, that's how it works around here. Image is everything. One small indication you aren't who you say you are…" She exhaled shakily. "But you have to tell me. Why haven't you closed the tear yet?"

"Because I don't know how."

"Baby."

I released a loud sigh. Perhaps I wasn't as good at hiding my intentions as I'd thought. In any case, I supposed I needed to come clean for my wife to trust me again. Damn that mother of hers.

"If I close the tear, I'm effectively sentencing everyone in that village to death.'

"What?" Mora said, wiping her cheeks. "How?"

"I've been bringing fresh food for years. If I stop, if the tear closes, they'll die."

"But you survived three hundred years without the stuff from this side?"

"And it was slowly killing them," I said. "Magical rot has all but disappeared since I started introducing real food into their diets. People are living longer, they're healthier. If I close the tear, they go back to what they had before."

"But Gavon…they were surviving before."

"Barely. If I hadn't made the tear, we would've dwindled to a few hundred within a generation. All the children were dying from malnourishment. Maybe they would've lived to adulthood, but…" I hung my head. "Despite what you might think, they're still my people. I still feel like I should protect them—should help them. I have a duty to you and the girls, but I also have a duty to them and… I'm sorry."

I expected her to go on, to rant and rave at me. Instead, she just exhaled. "I understand."

"Do you?"

She wiped her cheeks and shook her head. "I do, baby. I get where you're coming from, but…those people. You don't owe them anything."

"They're *my* people."

"They may be your people, but we're your *family*," she said. "What might happen if someone like Cyrus made it over here? What would he do? What could he do to our kids?"

It had been my fear for many years, but I'd balanced that with the knowledge that I'd been saving more lives in New Salem. A balance I'd been keeping for over a decade. "The tear is hidden," I said.

"Baby, listen to me. I know you feel responsible for New Salem. But you can't… They were banished for a reason."

"No, their *ancestors* were," I said. "Just as mine were. What gives me the right to enjoy you and our girls when they have to live in darkness?"

She worked her jaw, unsure what to say. "So what would you do? In an ideal world…"

"In an ideal world…" I sighed, closing my eyes and letting my true hopes come out. "In an ideal world, I would gather all the magicals in New Salem and bring them to our world."

"But they would—"

"Most of them are Charmers and Enchanters," I said with a sad shake of my head.

"But they could have kids like ours. What if they had a Warrior like we are?" She swallowed. "What are we gonna do with *our* Warrior?"

"Our kid will be a good kid. She or he'll only use their powers for good," I said with a smile. "But I can't say that for the others." I slumped against the bed. "The truth is, I know what I have to do. I have to close the tear, and I'll have to live with the guilt of knowing I've sentenced them to death, albeit a slow one, for the rest of my life. I just…want to delay the inevitable for as long as I can. It's not an issue right now, so…"

She wrapped her arms around me. "I wish there was an easier solution."

"Me too." I loosened a chuckle. "And since we're being honest with each other, there's another Warrior in the village."

"You mean Cyrus?"

"No, I mean…there's a woman pregnant with a Warrior," I said.

My wife's head rose off my shoulder. "And is it yours?"

"Oh, of course not," I said, with a laugh which evaporated under her stare. "And I don't think it's Cyrus' either. Most Warriors are flukes anyway."

"So…why are you telling me this?"

"Because if you'll recall, Warriors don't raise their own children. They give them to other Warriors to raise and train. You know, to make the best, strongest, and most ruthless children they can. And today, my mother hinted that she wanted me to train the child."

She was silent for a long moment. "I'm not raising another child. Three is my limit."

I laughed, and she tucked herself under my arm. "I agree. Three kids is all I want."

# Six

Irene left us alone for the next few weeks, especially as word spread of Mora's pregnancy. The rest of Clan Carrigan stopped by with well-wishes and toys for the girls, along with curious questions about what a Warrior meant and what they might do. Having gone through this twice before, Mora and I were old hat at deflecting interest and gossip.

"But how will you manage having *three* children with magic at such a young age?"

Mora shared a look with me. "We'll make it work. Luckily, Nicole's magic is much more controllable."

"Any luck on closing that tear, Gavon?"

"Absolutely," I said with a firm nod. "I feel we're close."

And that was the end of that—no mention that I'd been saying the same thing for the past five years. But Ashley's warning to me hung in the back of my mind like a storm cloud in the distance, as did the seed of doubt Irene had planted in Mora's mind. For her, and the sake of my marriage, I dove back into research with fervor.

I decided to spend some time back in London, re-reading the journals of John Chase and his associates. This magical library, a rarity in its own right, was the largest collection of letters and documents related to the Separation outside of Clan Carrigan. It would take me several hours, maybe even a few trips, to sort through all the boxes.

"You get to take a kid," Mora said, when I informed her of my plans. "I don't care which one."

I settled for the baby—much less prone to get into everything. With Marie strapped to my chest, I transported to London.

These days, magical libraries were few and far between. I'd heard rumor of one in Boston, but it had long since closed. The Separation had shattered the usual magical communication channels. Before, there had been more traditional guilds like those in New Salem, which had been collections of magicals of different specialties. Guildmasters would choose the best and brightest to be included, and they would stake their claim on villages and towns. But now, with everyone having more or less the same magic, clans had become the magical grouping of choice. But in that transition, they'd lost the need to collaborate across family lines.

That, in a nutshell, was the problem with my research on the tear. Guilds tended to pride themselves on things like history and conquests; clans focused mainly on the here and now. Much of the information about the Separation had been lost or destroyed as the clans separated. Magicals now had everything at their fingertips without their special powers. So a lot of the old knowledge had been lost.

I'd visited this particular archive a few times now. There was no card catalog, no librarian. It was a room simply filled with information, and those privileged enough to see inside were expected to keep it tidy. Therefore, it was a haphazard collection of papers, books, and journals.

I sat down at the table and put the baby on the ground with a toy to keep her occupied (and a charm to keep her out of trouble). Normal summoning was an easy task—barely worth a second thought. But in this case, I would have to think very specifically about what I wanted to find.

"Marie," I said to the quiet room. "The key to summoning something you don't know is to phrase it correctly in your mind."

The baby stared at me with her big blue eyes and summoned another toy from her bedroom.

"Well, see, that's easy," I said with a laugh. "But it's harder still to find something unknown. The first step is to clear your mind. Concentrate on the nebulous idea of what the thing might be. Your magic is smarter than you are, you know. Then you let it fly."

In my mind's eye, I could feel the books in the library, their crinkly pages, the darkness of the ink. My magic read them too quickly for me to process, but it knew what I was looking for. And when I next opened my eyes, the previously empty table was filled with boxes, stacks of papers, and books.

"And that, my love, is how we do that," I said with a grin.

It faltered as I got a whiff of something foul and grimaced at the telltale grin on my child's face.

After dealing with a messy diaper, I worked through what I'd assembled. Most of what had been stashed here were letters between magicals in Salem and the new world and magicals back in Europe. The letters were charmed to resist aging, but still delicate in my hands. They ranged from the mundane (crop harvest numbers, births, weddings) to the horrific, especially after the magical war broke out between Chase and the Separatists. I'd grown up on the stories, but it was always jarring to think about the numbers of magicals killed during that time. There had to be some middle ground between shutting off New Salem completely and letting my people walk freely in this world.

Among the documents and boxes, I found a small leather-bound notebook with a very familiar name inscribed on the front page. Johanna Chase, daughter of John. She'd been the brains behind the Separation in the first place, devising the plan to create a magical pocket that would become New Salem. Most of what I knew about her came from her father's journals, and the general accounting I'd found in Ashley's archives. Based on the first entry, this journal had been started years before the Separation took place.

**September 12, 1686**

**This journal contains the thoughts, tests, and results of Johanna Chase, daughter of John and Bridget. The intended result will be to resolve the conflict between the factions of magicals in Salem.**

1686—five years before the Two Years' War would begin. The first few pages were verbose with theories, ideas, predictions, and experimentations. Like me, Johanna methodically perfected her potions through slow trial and error, changing a piece of the puzzle a little at a time.

I skipped ahead a few pages.

**Nov 14. My sister Abigail, a Potion-maker, has a penchant for uncovering the issues I cannot see. She has recommended we try to use the frankincense in our next brew. She believes it has regenerative effects, which will be essential to building the world where we plan to imprison the Separatists.**

I skipped ahead more pages, minding the dates as they aligned with what I knew about when certain events had happened in the Separation, then I stopped on a page.

**May 1. They have killed Abigail. I am inconsolable. My work becomes even more important so no one else dies in this slaughter.**

I should've assumed that had happened. During the two years of war, thousands had died—many of those Potion-makers and nonmagicals. The bloodshed had been the primary reason for the Separation in the first place.

**Aug 3. I believe I have discovered a potion that will work. Made in my cauldron with my magic, it is a living organism. Abigail once theorized that adding additional magic, perhaps using the old coven count, might increase the potency. I wish she were here to help me test it.**

The potion listed was a complex one with ingredients I'd never even heard of. But the dates aligned—this must've been the final potion. And knowing it had taken a coven squared of magicals to complete, killing several in the process, Abigail the potion-maker had been right in her assumptions. It was incredible that a simple potion had that much power.

But what could I have done to break that? For the thousandth time, I returned to that day. I'd been so distraught over Alexandra telling me I couldn't be inducted, I'd been so *desperate* to create something that would work. I suppose I'd done the same as Johanna—adding magic to the potion to create the desired outcome.

Did that mean healing the tear would require the same sort of activity?

I flipped to the last page, where an intricate potion list was written out. Some of the ingredients I recognized, many I didn't. In the absence of any other leads, I could always just recreate Johanna's potion and see what answers it gave. But would it be enough to prove to Irene that I wasn't screwing around?

That, too, I had no answers for.

Recreating the potion, it seemed, was easier said than done. My potion-making skills were mostly self-taught, and it seemed the concoction I was to make was…well, more complex than merely adding ingredients. I'd made more than a few potions that hadn't turned out right because of improper mixing, and with this sort of power, I didn't want to play around.

What I needed was a Potion-maker, but since the only one I had was just getting the hang of potty training, I had to work through the ingredients piece by piece.

"I'm afraid I'm no help either," Ashley said, squinting through thick glasses at the journal when I showed him what I'd found. "I've never seen a potion like this before."

"I'd suppose it needed to be difficult in order to do what it did," I said, looking through the journal. "There's mention of a set of Potion-makers from Clan Vargas. Is that clan still around today? Maybe they have some information?"

"Hm," Ashley said, thumping his fingers on his desk. He rose slowly and walked to the table next to the window, where he had stacks of books and papers. After searching a moment, he procured a large, thick binder and walked it back to his desk.

"What's that?" I asked as he examined the pages.

"It's something of a compendium of Clanmasters around the world," he said. "I'm not quite sure how accurate it is, as it's all from memory. Many of these names I've never seen in person."

"It's pretty thick," I said, guessing it at three inches.

"Magicals are quite splintered now," he said, turning the page. "And not every magical belongs to a true clan anymore, which makes it tricky to keep track of them all." He smiled and turned the book toward me. "Lucky for us, Clan Vargas has kept themselves pretty robust in Spain. You should be able to contact the Clanmaster. I don't know if she'd be more helpful, as they're bound by the same accords as we are, but they may have some knowledge."

I'd sent a letter to the Clanmaster of the Vargas clan in Seville, Spain and, three days later, received an invitation to come for dinner and a chat. This time, I decided to take Nicole

—knowing that they weren't Potion-makers exactly, but it was still good to expose Nicole to other magicals like her. The toddler, of course, was just happy to be going with me on another excursion.

We arrived just as the sun was setting. Like Clan Carrigan, the family had purchased a large swath of land on the outside of the main city, surrounded by desert-like conditions. Because the clan had isolated themselves from the nonmagicals, and because I had an invitation, I was able to transport right into the center of their little village.

"Ah, you must be Gavon!" Josefa, the Clanmaster, greeted me almost immediately. I pegged her in her mid-fifties, thick-set and short, with wiry gray hair balled on top of her head. She kissed both my cheeks and turned her attention to Nicole, who'd hidden herself behind my legs. "And who is this?"

"This is my daughter, Nicole," I said, placing a hand on her head. "She's a Potion-maker."

"It is very nice to meet you," Josefa said, holding out her hand.

"Sorry, she's shy," I said, as Nicole hid herself further.

"She's quite a special girl, isn't she?" Josefa said. "Curious magic. Yours, as well."

"I would be happy to tell you the story," I said. "Shall we?"

Josefa was a marvelous hostess, providing an excellent rioja and a cheese plate, as I told her the story how I came to this world while Nicole hid her face in my shirt.

"So perhaps recreating Johanna's potion would close the tear," I said, pressing my hand to Nicole's head. "I hope, anyway."

"It's possible," Josefa said, reading through the potion with thick bifocals. "This is quite possibly the most difficult potion I've ever seen."

"Yes, I know," I said. "I'm sure I could work through it, given enough time, but neither Ashley nor I have ever heard of these ingredients before."

"Some of these may be older names for plants," Josefa said, summoning a few books and using magic to sort through them. "Ah, like this one, Sanguinaria? That's really just bloodroot."

She summoned the ingredient, a delicate white flower. Nicole, who'd been hesitantly getting more comfortable, poked her head up as more plants appeared.

"Oh, you like these?" Josefa said with a grandmotherly smile as she held up a long stem covered in lilac flowers. "Do you know what this is?"

She shook her head, casting me a wary glance before climbing down from the chair.

"This is called hyssop. It's said to be used for protection, but really, it's great for colds," she said, handing the beautiful flower to Nicole before turning back to me. "To be honest, Gavon, this potion is quite brilliant. It appears to be a combination of a magical pocket plus a touch of limb regrowth potion and a smattering of barrier spells. How Johanna Chase figured it all out, I have no idea."

"It was her sister, mostly," I said, smiling as Nicole climbed up on the empty seat next to Josefa and poked at the plants. "She was a Potion-maker. They killed her, though."

"You know, our clan lost a great deal of family members in the Two Years' War," Josefa said. "We had a strong line of

Potion-makers. Some of the best in the world. We were one of the last hold-outs for the Danvers Accord, because it meant an end to our family's pride." She smiled sadly at Nicole. "It's wonderful to see the magic reappear in the world."

"You're the only person to say that," I said with a sad sigh. "My wife's clan thinks they're an abomination, to put it lightly."

Josefa tutted and shook her head. "She's just precious. How could anyone say that?"

I smiled, casting Nicole a long look. "You don't know the half of it."

"You know, I don't know what these last two ingredients are. The way it's written, it seems to be a plant of some kind." She handed the journal back to me. "I'm sorry, that's all I have for you, Gavon."

"Well, you've been incredibly helpful otherwise," I said. "I'll keep looking. Are there any other families out there who might have the Potion-making line?"

"None as good as the Vargas clan," she said with a proud smirk. "But perhaps I'll send a few letters."

"And…" I eyed the bookcase behind her. "I'm afraid my entire library of potion-making books is comprised of one book. Do you have any you wouldn't mind letting us borrow?"

"Absolutely," she said. "After all, if Nicole will be the only Potion-maker, we must make sure she knows what she's doing."

# Seven

Josefa sent me the names of a few other clans in Singapore and Zambia, but when I visited them, they didn't know the ingredients either. Still, I was showing progress, and Mora was pleased to report that Irene's complaints had died down. Which I considered to be victory in and of itself.

At the end of March, I came to New Salem for a Council meeting only to find no one in the council room. I walked out into the village square to a bustle of activity—men and women spilling into the streets and drinking beer, openly clapping me on the back, and wearing smiling faces I hadn't seen since…ever.

"What's going on?" I asked Mary, one of the onlookers. She had two of her children hanging off her dress in curious anticipation.

"The new Warrior is being born," she replied with a smile. "It's a most wonderful day!"

Curious to see the new Warrior baby, I made my way toward Agatha's house. Her family was inside, plus the Warrior's father, who boasted to everyone with an ear that it was his input that had resulted in the miracle. I was sure he'd be using that line for years to come, as my father had. Even Cyrus had lowered himself to be present. He stood off in the corner, away from the rest of the villagers and councilmen. My mother was presumably inside the room.

"It's stifling," Cyrus said with a scowl. "Why are all these vermin in here?"

"Then perhaps you should wait outside," I offered lightly. "I know how it pains you to be amongst the rabble."

He glared at me then winced as another loud scream echoed through the house. "How much longer is this going to last?"

"How long has she been laboring?" I asked.

"I haven't the faintest…"

"Six hours," a woman nearby replied.

"Is she close?"

"What do you know of childbearing?" Cyrus asked. "You've never even fathered one."

I shrugged rather than let him goad me into divulging that I'd been the best student at the birthing classes Mora and I had taken.

The screaming from inside the room ended, and a short while later, Alexandra walked out with a squalling child in her arms. A shock of black hair on his head, a pink face. And power —so much power in such a little body. A hush descended over the room as the little pair of lungs wailed and wailed. I smiled, thinking about my own little Warrior coming in a few months.

"It's a boy," she announced. "James Malcolm Riley is his name."

I looked up. A bit presumptuous to name her child after the leader who'd had us all banished. But it wouldn't be the first James Riley in the village.

"He will make a fine Guildmaster," I said.

"Who will be training him?" Cyrus asked, with something of a disgusted look.

"Still to be decided," Alexandra said, smiling down at the boy with motherly affection. Had she worn the same look when I'd been born?

"Are we done fawning over him?" Cyrus drawled.

Alexandra's soft gaze grew hard. "Be careful. He might just take my position from me instead of from you."

Cyrus's eyes narrowed and he turned on his heel, marching out of the small room. Alexandra loosened a breath, returning to the baby and cooing at him quietly.

"And you want Cyrus to raise him?" she said, turning to walk back into the birthing room.

With everyone busy at Agatha's house, I could slip fresh ingredients into the Enchanters' stores and bring fresh hay and grass to the Charmers' cows. All the while, I thought about how I might broach the subject of the boy with Alexandra. If I let it linger too much longer, she might solidify her decision and I would have a fourth child. So I waited until she was finished with the new babe—which meant I was in the village until well after nightfall.

Alexandra wearily left the house, continuing to receive congratulations and handshakes even until she reached her house. She turned to find me there on her doorstep and offered me a tired look.

"It's unlike you to hover on my doorstep like this," she said, exhaustion evident in her voice. "You must really want to speak with me about something."

"I thought we might share a drink," I said. "To celebrate."

She nodded, seeing right through my ruse. "Very well."

I followed her into the library, where she procured the same bottle of red wine we'd had the night I'd been inducted. I thought of the hundreds of bottles I'd sampled since, the vintages from Chile, Spain, California, even as far as Australia and New Zealand.

"To our future," she said, raising her glass to me.

"To the future," I replied then took a sip. It was surprisingly good. "Which brings me to what I wanted to talk about."

She sighed heavily. "The boy's apprenticeship can wait. Tonight, we should just celebrate."

"I don't want to train the boy," I said firmly. "I don't think I would be the best for it. I think you should do it."

"And why is that?"

*Because my wife would kill me.* "Because you're a better Warrior. You said yourself that Jones had been lax in my tutelage. How am I supposed to create a strong Warrior when I'm not one myself..." The amused smile on her face ended my self-depreciation. "What?"

"I'm just trying to figure you out, son," she said gently. "I would think you would've jumped at the chance to mentor the boy. Since you've been unable to have any children of your own."

"Exactly," I said, scrambling. I hadn't expected her to be so attentive. "I don't know the first thing about being a parent—"

"Then it's a good thing the boy needs a master, not a father," she said, tilting her head. The amused smile hadn't left her face. "My question is: what aren't you telling me? Because none of what you've said so far is aligned with the man I know you to be."

I was at a loss for words, finally saying, "You know me so well?"

"You are my son, of course I know you," she said softly. "It's why I couldn't raise you. I am soft where you're concerned, because I see myself in you."

"I'm soft," I spat out. "That's why I can't train the boy."

"If given the choice between a soft master and Cyrus, I would choose you every time." She sipped her wine again. "He wants me to step down, you know."

I nodded. "Will you?"

"Not a chance. He'll have to wrest the Guildmaster's position from my lifeless corpse," she said examining the glass closer. "And I'm sure he'll challenge me soon, once he tires of hearing from me."

Another responsibility I was hoping to avoid. Why was I so intent on keeping the tear open again? "I'm surprised he hasn't already."

"One of the many things I've learned about Cyrus is that no matter how slighted he feels, he won't move unless he's certain of victory. He's not a rash man. He bides his time until the opportune moment, and only then strikes. It's what makes him so volatile—and so dangerous."

"Is there any way to contain him?" I asked.

"Of course," she said, putting her glass down. "As Guildmaster, I've been able to contain him for years. But only until he feels he's ready to challenge me for this position. That day is coming soon."

And that was a day I'd been dreading. "What will you do?"

She stared off in the distance, looking younger and at the same time, wearier. "If I have to kill him, I will, but…once he challenges me and loses, I could spare him."

"Would you, though?"

"Depends," she said. "He wouldn't be able to challenge me again as Guildmaster. And…perhaps I'm a little more attached to him than I've let on." She shook her head. "It's not like me to be sentimental, but when I saw that child today, I thought about the day you were born. You looked so little, but you held within you so much power. I only wish…" She smiled. "I only wish you could experience that joy."

"Joy?" Oh, joy was an apt description of the day my girls had been born, but I was surprised to hear it coming from her.

"Yes, Gavon. The day you were born was the best day of my life," she said. "Something you might understand if you take the boy."

I had a feeling I wasn't going to make any headway, so I bade her adieu and went home.


One thing was for sure: I needed better excuses where Alexandra was concerned. I didn't want to be Guildmaster, and I certainly didn't want to have a fourth child to raise. Not to mention all the complications therein. Irene would have a field day.

I arrived home to find a scene of paint, toys, and tantrums, and one wife at her wit's end. I shuffled her up to the bedroom, drawing a bath and leaving a silencing charm on the room so she could relax in peace. I tended to the fussy girls and made dinner. Mora joined us as soon as I pulled the chicken out of the oven, refreshed from a long bath, and we dug in.

"So what the hell kept you?" Mora asked, clearly still salty about my prolonged absence.

"Oh," I said, nearly forgetting in the chaos. "Agatha had the baby. A Warrior boy. Alexandra was over the moon."

"And did she say who's going to train him?"

I swallowed a particularly large bite. "Not yet. I'm still lobbying for it to be her. Trying my best to appear irresponsible and unconcerned."

"What are you gonna do if she shoves him off on you anyway?"

I sighed. I didn't want to think about it. "She also still wants me to take over the Guildmaster spot."

"And again, I ask, why haven't you closed that tear yet?" she said, but it was mostly under her breath.

"I asked myself that very question today," I said, reaching across the table and taking her hand. "I did promise you I'd have it closed by the time the baby came."

"I'll believe that when I see it."

I looked up at her, shock evident on my face. "Mora, are you really that upset with me for being gone so long?"

"I just...I had something important to show you," she said with something of a pout. Then, to my surprise, she formed a bright purple attack spell in the palm of her hand. "What do you think?"

"I think…" Tears sprang to my eyes. Sure, it was my wife wielding it, but it was the first time I'd seen my little one's magic. "I think that's beautiful. I think you're beautiful."

"It's purple," she said. "Does that mean it's Warrior magic?"

I shook my head. "The color of magic varies from person to person, just as it does here. Purple means…well, it means she comes from my blood. My mother has purple magic, too."

"Cool," she said. "By the way, don't throw it at a wall."

I started. "Yes, please don't do that. Which wall did you destroy?"

"I fixed it but…" She grinned sheepishly. "I scared the kids."

"We'll have to find a better outlet for you," I said, taking her other hand. "Perhaps a beach nearby where I can teach you a few things. But only if you promise not to overdo it. This is uncharted territory."

"With you, it always is," Mora said, as she pulled together another bright purple ball. "I can't believe this kind of magic exists. I can't believe our little girl is going to have this."

"Girl?" I said, blinking. "I thought your appointment wasn't until next week?"

She grinned. "I have to have *some* mystery in the marriage, you know." She summoned a small ultrasound and handed it to me. "You're three for three in little girls, McKinnon."

I took the photo, still completely unable to read the black and white blob, but trusting that those smarter than me had read it and found a little girl in there. "A little girl. And a Warrior, too."

"So you're okay with that?" she asked. "Cause I'm not having a fourth. That other Warrior baby is on his own."

I smiled. "I wouldn't want it any other way."

# Eight

Three little girls. Could any man be so lucky? I was on cloud nine for the next few weeks, even as I toiled through more journals, more trips to far-flung places with either Nicole or Marie (or sometimes both) by my side. Mora was starting to enjoy her newfound powers as well, although she wanted me to join her in the ring, and I still wasn't ready.

The weather had turned bright and warm with spring's arrival. All the gardens were growing once again. And with it, Nicole had begun to offer some unusual conversation.

"The flowers are singing to me," she said, twirling down the sidewalk as the family went on a late afternoon walk.

Mora turned to me with a quirked brow. "That's new."

"What do you mean, the flowers are singing to you?" I asked, bending down to Nicole's level.

"They sing!" she said.

This became a refrain she would repeat over and over—whether it was while Mora was chopping spinach for a salad or whether Nicole was digging in the dirt. But it told me one thing.

"I think it's time we started potion-training with her. For real."

"We should probably get *potty* training figured out first." She frowned. "Besides that, she's too young. She can't even read yet."

Reading didn't seem to be a prerequisite for sparring, so I assumed it wasn't for potion-making either. To that end, I decided to take Nicole over to her Aunt Nina's house to wander through her garden, as it was the best in the neighborhood.

"Oh, of course, of course," Nina said, clapping her hands together. "I love seeing you two stop by."

We joined her in the backyard, the large green rectangle growing quickly in the early spring weather. Nicole stomped her way toward it, singularly focused.

"She's magnificent, isn't she?" Nina said with a grin. "Children are fascinating creatures. They're so untainted by thoughts. They just do."

"Nicole has plenty of thoughts," I replied as she yanked a bushel of flowers from the ground—roots and all. "She tells me about her opinions all day long."

"She's very lucky to have a father like you," Nina said.

"Okay, kiddo, tell me what this is," I said, pointing to a patch of lavender.

"Purple!" Nicole chirped.

"Lavender," I said gently. "Can you say lavender?"

"Purple!"

"Yes, it's purple," I said. "But it's called lavender."

We wandered through the garden, taking each species slowly

until she made a word that sounded something like the actual name. Nina followed behind, helping out as she saw fit, but Nicole wouldn't parrot back the words when she did.

"She does the same thing to her mother," I said, by way of an apology when Nicole ignored another overture from Nina. "She's three."

"Ah, speaking of girls who don't like their mothers," Nina said, glancing to the front of the garden. "Jeanie's arrived for her weekly session."

"What session?"

"Magical training," Nina said. "Irene's insistence, of course."

"I thought she was attending school in D.C.?" She was twenty now, a junior at a college as far away from her mother as she could possibly get. The girls barely knew her, as she only came around during holidays and big events. Even when she'd received her magic at fifteen, there wasn't much. It was something Irene was working hard to change.

"Oh, well, Irene felt they weren't teaching her well enough," Nina said with a sad sigh.

I looked at Nicole and frowned. "Jeanie may have other talents. Maybe she got a strain of Potion-maker?"

"Or perhaps just an overbearing mother who won't leave her alone long enough to get past her mental block," Nina said with a snort as Jeanie walked into the garden. She took one look at me and I saw the urge to bolt.

But Nina intervened. "Hello, Jeanie, dear."

"'Lo," she said.

Nicole hid behind my legs, peeking out from behind them with a shy look.

"Nicole, do you remember your Aunt Jeanie?" I asked.

She shook her head.

"She's Mommy's sister," I said. "Like Marie is your sister. Can you say Jeanie?"

She shook her head and hid.

"We'll get there," I said with what I hoped was a disarming grin. Jeanie didn't look terrified to be there anymore, but she didn't exactly look comfortable.

"She's getting big," Jeanie said.

"She'll be four in a few months, and Marie will be two. Happened overnight, it seems." I cocked my head to the side. "We'd love to see you more often. Nicole should get to know her aunt."

"Yeah, well, school keeps me busy," Jeanie said, running a hand through her short hair. "I hear you guys are having another baby."

"Yeah," I said. "We're really excited."

"I don't know what I'd do with three kids," she said, an obvious attempt at a conversation she didn't want any part of. "You guys are crazy."

"This one wasn't exactly planned," I said.

She nodded, looking more uncomfortable the longer we stood there. "So, can we get started, Nina?"

"Of course, my love," Nina said with a look at me. "Gavon, why don't you join us today?"

"Oh, does he..." Jeanie's cheeks reddened. "I mean, it's not necessary to..."

"Gavon knows your magic already, my dear," Nina said gently. "And I'm sure Nicole would love to pick up a few magical tips."

No matter how many times I explained that Nicole's magic was limited to potions, Nina just didn't get it. But it was a chance for me to build the relationship Jeanie didn't want with me—but that I wanted her to have with Nicole.

The four of us settled in Nina's small kitchen, Nicole perched on my lap as she watched Jeanie ready herself. Nina was a proponent of more New Age techniques, so their practice had begun with a five-minute meditation. From Jeanie's fidgeting, I could tell it wasn't helping.

"Today, we'll work on summoning," Nina said with a bright grin.

Jeanie nodded and cast a nervous look in my direction. "A-all right."

"Now, let's start easy. Summon the phone book from the other room."

Jeanie held out her hand and concentrated. After a moment, the phone book appeared in her hand in a puff of yellow. She furrowed her brow again, and the book disappeared.

Nicole clapped and giggled. "Again! Again!"

Jeanie half-smiled. "Okay...."

She performed the trick once, twice, then three times, and Nicole was absolutely enamored.

"I don't get it. Why is she so excited?" Jeanie asked, her cheeks red. "Don't you guys use magic around her?"

"Oh, of course," I said, gently brushing Nicole's hair off her shoulder. "I think she just enjoys watching you do it."

"Well, now that we know you can summon something here," Nina said. "Let's try expanding our reach. Why don't you try to summon something from your dorm at school?"

Jeanie closed her eyes and concentrated. But nothing arrived.

"I don't know what I want to bring," she said, opening her eyes. "I can't think of anything I own."

"Try…" I began then quieted down. I was sure Jeanie didn't want to get lessons from me.

Nina smiled at me, though. "What do you suggest, Gavon?"

"I thought maybe she could try using her magic to see her room then pick a pencil or something like that." I cleared my throat. "It's the technique I read about in a book."

"I don't understand how that works," Jeanie said with a glare. "How am I supposed to use magic to see something?"

"You've got to let go of your magic," I said gently. "Don't keep such a tight grip on it. It can do so much more than you can physically." As her scowl grew more pronounced, I wisely decided to cease sharing my opinions.

"Gavon is right, my love. Your magic may not be the strongest, but it's still capable of quite a lot," Nina said. "Why don't you—"

"I don't even understand why I'm doing this in the first place!" Jeanie barked, jumping to her feet. "Who cares if I don't have magic? None of my friends have it, or even know it exists!"

"Your mother—"

"Screw her," Jeanie said, tears in her eyes as she sank back down. "All she cares about is whether we make her look good for the clan. As if Mora hasn't already ruined everything by marrying *him*."

Nina looked at me for support or apology, I wasn't sure which, but I held up my hands. "No arguments here. I think

Jeanie should be free to do whatever she wants."

"Thank you," Jeanie said, sniffing and wiping her eyes. "Thank you."

"I'll see if I can't get your mother to change her mind about our sessions," Nina said after a moment. "I understand you may think you don't have magic, but I assure you that you do."

Jeanie just wiped her eyes again.

Nicole slipped off my lap and wandered over to Jeanie, climbing up into hers. She pressed a kiss on Jeanie's cheek and smiled.

"Don't cry," she said. "Can you bring book?"

"Yeah, kiddo," Jeanie said, holding out her hand and making the phone book appear and disappear, much to the delight of my toddler.

"See?" I said gently. "You can do the important stuff."

"What? Amuse kids?" She chuckled, but it was less desolate.

"Why don't you come over for dinner?" I said. "See the kids and Mora. No magical lessons, I promise."

"Mom would throw a fit," Jeanie said then smiled evilly. "Sounds great."


"Jeanie!" Mora said as the three of us walked in the door. "Oh my God, is it Mom? Is she hurt? Did someone die? Did she die?"

"N…no?" Jeanie blinked, confused. "Gavon just invited me over for dinner."

Her eyes widened. "He…did? And you accepted?"

I kissed Mora on the cheek and whispered, "Just roll with it, baby. She's had a hard day."

I left the four girls in the living room and went to the kitchen to start dinner. Nicole had been eating nothing but chicken nuggets lately, so I charmed a few of those on the pan while I defrosted some actual food for the adults. Every so often, I'd hear a loud burst of laughter from the living room, especially after I sent in a bottle of chilled wine. Despite her frosty opinion of me, I'd always liked Jeanie, and I wanted her to be in my girls' lives.

About an hour later, we sat down to dinner, and Jeanie, plied with a few glasses of wine, was a little more eager to divulge the secrets of her life.

"She's really cute," she said, her cheeks reddening. "But like…I've never asked out another girl before."

"I'd assume it's the same as asking out a boy," Mora said with a grin to me.

"I've never done that either…" Jeanie mumbled.

"I usually just walked up to the boys I liked and told them to take me to a movie," Mora said. "Or they just appeared and asked me to take them around the world."

I reached across the table to take Mora's hand. "I have no insight to offer," I said. "But I wish you the best."

Just then, a giant beach ball appeared on top of the baby's high chair. Marie squealed and grabbed it, kicking her feet against the leg rest.

"Holy crap," Jeanie said, her eyes wide. "She can already… do that?"

"Yeah," Mora said with a sigh. "She's going to be trouble, I think."

"No more trouble than her mother," I said, taking the beach

ball away from Marie and sending it back where it had come from. "No, ma'am. Not at the dinner table."

"Daddy, I want a ball," Nicole said.

"You can play with it after dinner," I said.

"No, I want to make ball appear." She held out her hands like Jeanie had, and furrowed her brow. "Ball!"

Mora shared a pained look with me and Jeanie looked at her food as an awkward silence descended around the table, punctuated by Nicole asking for the ball to appear.

"Baby," Mora said gently. "You won't be able to summon a ball."

"You could, with a potion," I added quickly. "We could—"

"I don't want a potion. I want the ball. Like Marie."

Mora caught my gaze, and I swallowed hard. "Nicole, your magic is different from Marie's," I began slowly. "You can't summon a ball, but you can do—"

"I want the *ball!*" Tears were now starting to fall as she made her way toward a full-blown tantrum.

I rose from my seat and knelt beside her chair. "Nicole, listen. You are a unique and special little girl. The only Potion-maker in existence. And just because you can't levitate or summon doesn't mean you can't do other amazing things. You'll just have to do them a little bit differently."

"But it's not fair."

"I know, sweetheart." Mora knelt on the other side of her. "Sometimes life just…isn't really fair. But we have to make the best of what we've been given."

"I-I w-want the b-b-ball," she said, thick tears dripping down her cheeks. "I w-w-want magic like Mommy and Daddy and

Nene and Marie."

Mora looked at me for help, and I swept Nicole into my arms, carrying her out of the kitchen while she cried.

"Just because you're a little different doesn't mean you aren't perfect in every way," I said, rubbing her back. "You've got a power I haven't even begun to understand. I wish I had…I wish there was some way to get you to see how wonderful you are." I stopped by the window, spotting our neighbor's garden in the moonlight. "Do you remember when you told me the flowers were singing to you?"

She nodded against my shoulder.

"I don't hear the flowers singing," I said. "Mommy and Jeanie don't either. That's something only *you* can do." She peeled her head off my shoulder. "And Mommy and I love you *exactly* as you are. We love that you can hear flowers and love cartoons. We love you even when all you want is ketchup for dinner."

She wiped her face clumsily, her bottom lip jutted out.

"And I promise you that you will be the *most* powerful Potion-maker out there," Mora said, appearing in the living room. "Daddy's going to show you how to make all the potions, right?"

"As soon as Mommy lets you near a cauldron," I said.

"Can we make a potion now?" Nicole asked.

Mora's eyes widened. "Um…"

"Why don't we go upstairs and read more from our book?" I said, giving my wife an out. "And we'll pick out the potion you want to brew first." I put her down on the ground. "Go get it, huh?"

As Nicole disappeared up the stairs, Mora released a breath. "That was hard, Gav."

"So…she really doesn't have any magic?" Jeanie asked. "I mean, like…our kind of magic."

"No," I said. "But she's perfect just the way she is. Don't you think?"

Jeanie smiled. "Yeah, I agree. She's a great kid."

# Nine

It wouldn't be the last Potion-maker conversation I'd have with Nicole. As she grew up and realized her talents differed from her sisters, she might resent them for it. I never wanted her to feel like Jeanie had—a second-class magical with nothing to offer. Especially with two younger, more powerful sisters.

The next night, Mora tended to the baby upstairs and Nicole and I descended to the basement with my old cauldron and an assortment of ingredients. I thought I might start her off with a healing potion, since I was quite familiar with it, and could better guide her in the instructions.

I propped open my old potions book, the only one I'd owned until recently, feeling something like pride that I was sharing something from my childhood with my daughter. Also, grateful that I'd thought ahead to charm the pages as she angrily flipped them.

"Careful," I said, guiding her hand. "This is very old. And very special to Daddy. You see here? This is a healing potion.

Can you say healing potion?"

"Healing potion."

"Very good," I said. "You see that it says we have to brew it at night, right? That's why we're down here now. I've tried to brew the potion in the day and it doesn't work as well."

She nodded and squirmed in front of the pot. With a laugh, she stuck her head inside the empty pot and giggled as her voice echoed around her.

I gently pulled her upright. "Now, a healing potion usually begins with a liquid like water, or sometimes vinegar. This one calls for apple cider vinegar. Can you pour it in?"

She took the bottle from me and dumped it into the cauldron as I lit a magical fire underneath.

"Now, I want you to take this aloe leaf and dump it in—no, not three," I said as she plucked three from my hands. "One. It's important that you make the potion exactly as it's written."

"No, Daddy," she said, grabbing the other two from my left hand and throwing them into the pot. "It needs them."

I chuckled. "And how do you know that?"

"The potion told me."

"Tell me what else the potion says," I said. "Does it speak words?"

"No," she said, dropping another handful of flowers into the pot. "It's music."

I smiled. "Like a lullaby?"

"It's so pretty," she said in a singsong voice as she stirred the silvery concoction with the spoon. "It tells me it also wants some pretty yellow flowers."

Well, perhaps we wouldn't drink this one, especially as she

decided the marigold flowers were much better for the potion than the echinacea buds. And she took extra care to dump spider legs into the mix, wearing an adorable look of concentration.

"Too hot, Daddy," she said, pointing to the fire.

"As you say," I said, lowering the temperature. "Now, we'll need to let this brew sit for two days. Why don't we run upstairs and see what Mommy and Marie are doing?"

Nicole, prouder than I'd ever seen her before, marched up the stairs to tell her mother about what she'd done before we tucked her into bed.


"Are you going to drink it?" Mora asked, staring at me from the bathroom mirror.

"I don't know. Maybe?" I said, leaning back on my hands. "She seemed pretty determined about it."

"She's also determined when she wants to eat ketchup for dinner," Mora said. "She's three, honey. She's a brilliant kid, but she's not…that brilliant."

"You don't know that," I said. "I don't know that either. There are no Potion-makers out there I could talk to. Sparring is pretty innate…"

"Yeah, speaking of that," Mora said, walking out of the bathroom with a bright purple attack spell in hand. "This is getting pretty potent, wouldn't you say?"

I whistled. Something about the sight of her, five months pregnant, holding an attack spell was so incredibly beautiful. It was like falling in love with her all over again.

"Oh what?" she said, absorbing the magic back into her body. "You think I'm hot or something?"

"Always," I said, holding my arms out for her.

"When are you gonna let me take this magic for a spin, then?" she asked, walking over. "I only get it for so long, and I want to see what it can do."

"Baby, I want to spar with you, but I don't want to hurt you," I said, running my hands over her bump. "Or the baby. Most mothers don't inherit the magic of their kids' magic while they're pregnant so I don't know how much we can push it."

"What if I promise to go really, really slowly," she whispered, kissing my neck. "Please?"

Well, when she phrased it like that…

We began with the basics of duels, sparring, and the mechanics behind the magic itself. She was as attentive as a student now as she had been at seventeen and it wasn't long before she was ignoring my attempts at taking things slow and egging me on.

"Mora, if you zap my ass one more time, I will retaliate, and you won't like it," I snapped as I nearly dropped Marie.

She giggled and disappeared around the corner.

"Mommy's silly," Nicole said with a frown.

"Mommy is very silly," I said with a sigh.

Finally, I could put it off no longer. With the pretense to Nina that we were going out on a long-awaited date night, Mora and I left the girls in her charge and headed out to a desolate beach nearby. It was early May, so a light chill still hung in the Massachusetts air. The days were getting longer, and the sunset cast a beautiful orange glow over my wife.

"You ready for this?" she asked, punching her other hand.

"I'm ready to knock your ass out."

"Just take it easy, okay?" I said, second-guessing this plan as she tossed the magical spell from one hand to another. "Warriors lack the natural control on their magic that prevents them from overdoing it. And you could really hurt the baby—and yourself."

"I promise I'll be careful," she said with a tone that told me she wouldn't. Against every instinct I had, I formed a spell and gently sent it over.

Mora easily deflected it with her own and pursed her lips at me. "What the hell was that?"

"Just a test," I replied. "I wanted to see how you'd react."

"By soft balling it in like that?" She scoffed. "I can take a punch."

At that, I had to laugh. There she was, five months pregnant, our child distending her belly out over her maternity pants, with her hands on her hips. "Then maybe I just don't want to hurt you. I love you too much."

"Pssh. You're just a wimp," she said, taking a stance much like a football player. "C'mon, baby. Let's take this magic for a spin."

And so we did, back and forth, the softball hits growing steadily more powerful as I determined she could handle them. Her instincts were fairly good, and she wielded the new powers with ease. Having only been the recipient of training, it was strange to parrot the same words that Jones and Alexandra had once said to me.

"You're thinking too much," I said. "Just let your magic work for you. It's faster than you are."

"This is some powerful stuff here, Gav," she said, holding aloft a spell. "Our kid is going to come out of the womb with this kind of firepower?"

"I suppose," I said. "But it'll be some time before she can really use it like you are."

Mora released a ball so powerful it singed the side of my head as it whizzed by. "Be careful. Remember what I said about not having limits. You've been using your magic for years. The baby needs time to develop hers."

"I feel fine, baby," she said. "I feel…" Her eyes crossed and she fell to her knees. "Wait, maybe not."

I sighed and transported to her side. "See? What did I tell you?"

"But I barely did anything," she said as I helped her to her feet.

"You did more than you think," I said.

Mora allowed me to take her back home, setting her on the couch with her feet up while I retrieved the girls. They were, of course, all wound up from making chocolate cupcakes with Aunt Nina, which I thanked her oh so much for.

The girls bounded into the house, climbing up on the couch next to Mora, who listened gingerly.

"Mommy owwie?" Marie asked, climbing onto her lap.

"No, baby," Mora said, kissing her forehead. "Just tired."

"Mommy owwie," she said, pointing to her stomach.

"Mommy doesn't have an owwie," she said, stroking Marie's hair. "She's just tired. Come lie here with me while Daddy gets us a glass of water."

Marie snuggled up against her mother and rested her small

hand on Mora's stomach. I turned to go retrieve water when I heard Mora gasp. Marie's hands were glowing white, as were her open eyes.

"Gavon, what the hell is she doing?" Mora cried. "Baby, stop —"

Marie's eyes returned to normal and she smiled. "Mommy no owwie!"

"Did she just…heal you?" I said, cocking my head.

"I…guess so," Mora said as Marie yawned and tucked herself back in. "I feel better, a little. That was weird."

"Well, Mom had an owwie," I said with a chuckle. "She wanted to help."

"This isn't funny. She looked possessed," Mora said, sitting back against the couch. "Not funny at all, McKinnon."

Nicole tugged at my pants. "Daddy, Daddy. I want to help Mommy."

"Oh, sweetie," I said, kneeling down. "You know how you've got special magic to hear the plants? Marie's got special magic to heal Mommy."

"But the potion!"

I winced. That healing potion. I supposed she'd remembered it after all. "I don't know if that's…"

"Potion, Daddy!" She took off toward the basement.

Torn between not wanting to give my wife something untested and not wanting to disappoint my daughter, I followed her into the basement where the cauldron was happily bubbling. It had taken on a bright silvery tone, which was different from the greenish gray it normally was.

"It's done!" Nicole announced happily.

I joined her at the cauldron, summoning a ladle and a mug and pouring a little into it. Childhood memories of drinking potions that resulted in days of vomiting came back to me, and I swallowed a little bile that had risen up.

"Baby, maybe we need to redo it," I said, dropping the mug from my lips.

"Drink! Drink!" she said, taking the potion from me.

"No, no." I pulled the mug back. "You can't drink it. It's dangerous."

Her bottom lip stuck out and her eyes filled with tears.

"Nicole," I said with a heavy sigh. "Fine."

I swallowed my pride and took a gulp, promising myself that making my daughter feel good about her magic was more important than maintaining stomach integrity. The taste was horrific, like eating grass and bleach. And then, where I expected the concoction to come right back up, it settled happily in my stomach. A warmth spread from my midsection to my fingers and toes, clearing out the few cobwebs from using the magic.

"Daddy no owwie," Nicole said proudly.

I stared into the cup, at a loss for words. I'd made this potion hundreds of times, and it had never been so…fast-acting or potent.

"*Gavon*!"

"Coming," I said, ladling more into the cup and bringing it back up the stairs. "Mora, you have to try this."

"What, the potion?" she said with a disgusted look. "The one you said your daughter…" She glanced at Nicole, who was climbing up on the other side of her. "…made."

"Just…try it. I did, and it's safe." I handed her the cup.

"Trust me."

Mora took a hesitant sip then grimaced. "Oh my God, Gavon, this smells like feet," she said, pushing the cup away from her. "Is this safe?"

"Absolutely."

"Mommy, drink it." Nicole's wide, brown eyes were trained on her mother. And with that same look of guilt mixed with apprehension that I'd probably worn, Mora took a long sip. She swallowed, the crease between her brow prominent, but forced a smile onto her face. "It's a good potion, baby. Why don't you run up to your room and get your blanket? Then we can watch cartoons."

She dashed away, and Mora's dissolved into retching.

"I'm going to vomit," she said, handing me the glass. "How can you drink that shit?"

"Do you feel better?" I asked with a laugh.

"Well…yeah, except I feel like I'm going to vomit," Mora said, rubbing her stomach. "Are you sure that was safe to drink?"

I nodded. "She's got good instincts. She might be able to make that potion even better. She won't ever get it not to taste like feet, though. That's just the way it is. But your magic…?"

"I don't feel as tired as I did," she said, belching and making a face. "But at what cost, baby? At what cost?"

I kissed her forehead and covered her with a nearby blanket. "That's why you need to listen to me and not overdo it."

"Can we spar again tomorrow?"

"Only if you promise to take it easy."

# Ten

Nicole made several other potions over the next few days, all of which far surpassed anything I could've made. Her transporting potion was so powerful that a mere drop of it sent me to the edge of town. I was completely out of my depth when it came to helping her; all we had was the book that I'd found, which seemed to take advantage of her innate powers.

Back in New Salem, the village was still celebrating the arrival of James. Every visit seemed tinged with more beer and celebration, and less work. It was helpful for me, because I was better able to sneak in fresh supplies. But I was growing tired of his mother, whose new celebrity status was getting on my nerves.

Especially when I saw her sitting in the Council room, having taken over Humbert's usual seat.

"Why is she here?" I asked.

"Because she's the mother of our future Guildmaster," Alexandra said with something of an annoyed tone. "And she will keep the position until such time as he takes her place."

"Really?" I couldn't see a reason she'd want to sit in on the Council meetings, except for her inflated sense of self.

"And she's also going to help me decide who will teach her son how to wield magic," Alexandra finished.

"Oh yes," Agatha said, rocking the child in her arms. I didn't miss how her gaze landed on me. Perhaps she hadn't heard the rumors I was putting out in the village.

"We're just waiting on Cyrus," Alexandra said with a frown. "It's not like him to be late."

The doors to the Council room opened, and an Enchanter ran in, her face pale and horrified. "Guildmaster, there's been a discovery in the village. It's Mary, she..."

I jumped to my feet and followed Alexandra and the Enchanter out into the village. We didn't have to walk for very long. Cyrus stood in the city center, ranting and raving at Mary, who had a small child in her arms. I'd never seen the child before—it wasn't one of Mary's.

Except, she resembled Mary's children. The same nose, the same eyes.

"Cyrus, what's going on here?" Alexandra said. "Why are you frightening this—"

She turned to the child, just as I realized I was getting no magical signature from her. This child was...a Potion-maker. A living, breathing Potion-maker who'd lived past her first day in this village.

Alexandra's face was a mask, but Cyrus's was full of delighted glee. "Guildmaster, she's been hiding this abomination in her grain cellar. As if we wouldn't know—as if we wouldn't be able to find her. It's an affront to your leadership and our—"

"Enough," Alexandra said softly. "That's enough, Cyrus. Mary, please explain yourself."

Mary said nothing, holding her child for dear life. The child was three—the same age as Nicole. She looked at me with big brown eyes, and I felt sick to my stomach.

"Very well," Alexandra said with a heavy sigh. "You know the rules of the village, Mary. There will be no Potion-makers."

She sobbed and held the child tighter.

"Think of your other children," Alexandra said, walking toward her. "They need their mother."

"I need my daughter," Mary snarled. "You can't take her."

"Mary." Alexandra closed her eyes. "I order you, by command of the Guild and my place as Guildmaster, to relinquish your child."

Mary wailed, but her arms detached from the child. Without thinking, I took the child's hand, stepping away from her mother as she collapsed to the ground.

"Please, Alexandra, please," Mary sobbed. "Please don't take my child from me."

"I don't have a choice," Alexandra replied.

"I'll take care of her," I announced. "It will be quick and painless."

Alexandra gave me a look of surprise, but it was quickly drowned out by Mary throwing herself at my feet.

"No, please! Please Gavon, I beg of you. Don't take my daughter from me. She's a babe—she's innocent! Please, Gavon—"

I knelt beside her, wishing with every fiber I could tell her I would be taking her daughter somewhere safe. I'd find her a family in Salem—Irene would have to understand if I told her. And if she didn't, I didn't care. I wasn't going to let anything happen to this little girl.

But for her mother, in front of this crowd of magicals, I could do nothing but stroke her head, listening to her hysterical sobs as she contemplated the sanctioned murder of her baby.

"She won't feel it," I whispered. "I promise."

"Gavon, you can't let them do this." Her eyes, bloodshot, begged for relief. "You're so much kinder than the rest of them. Don't let them take my baby. Don't take my baby."

"Enough of this."

A flash of magic whizzed by my hand and Mary fell backward. I knew before I heard the screaming what Cyrus had done.

Mary scrambled to her knees, clutching the little girl in her arms. But the girl was gone, with open, unseeing eyes.

I swallowed the bile that rose in my throat. It was hard not to picture my daughter's face. Hard not to imagine what might happen if Cyrus were to find out about my own child. Hard not to strangle him right then and there.

Cyrus straightened, a cruel smile on his face. "It's taken care of, Gav. No need to shelter this woman from it." He adjusted his shirtsleeves, impervious to the heartrending wails echoing up from the ground. "Let that be a lesson to all of you. Lawbreaking will not be tolerated. *Vermin* will not be tolerated."

"This child wasn't *vermin*," I snarled, letting my anger rise. "This child was a *child*, no different than any of the creatures you've sired in the past few years."

Cyrus lifted his chin. "Are you saying we should let Potion-makers live? For what purpose?"

I was treading on dangerous ground, and felt the gaze of the gathered on the back of my neck. "You could've at least let the mother look away before you killed her child. That was inhumane."

"She chose to ignore the rules of the village."

"Cyrus." Alexandra stood in the middle of the fracas. "You've done enough. Return to your home and leave them be."

"You don't get to order me around," Cyrus replied with a sneer. "You aren't my mistress anymore."

"True, but I remain your Guildmaster," she replied with icy certainty. "Now go."

That he couldn't argue with, so he swished his cloak and wandered off, giving no second look to Mary, who cradled her child through body-wracking sobs. My heart broke for her, but I couldn't show too much sympathy. Not with an audience.

"All of you," Alexandra bellowed. "Be gone. There's nothing more to see here."

The villagers, who, like Cyrus, couldn't disobey a direct order, turned and disappeared into their homes.

"Come," Alexandra said quietly. "Let's take care of your child."

It was an interesting procession, Alexandra carrying the small baby, and her grief-stricken parents following behind. I held the rear, making sure no curious onlookers were following us.

With a gentle wave, Alexandra magically dug a small grave at the end of our cemetery. She stood, her hands clasped behind her back, giving Mary the time she needed to grieve. A cold wind blew right through my shirt, but I seemed to be the only one who noticed it.

Mary's husband rose with the child in his arms and handed her to Alexandra without looking at my mother. Carefully, Alexandra laid the child in the ground and re-covered her with dirt. Then she magicked a small white stone at the head of the grave—similar to the small stones dotting this part of the cemetery. All the Potion-makers. There were more than I could count, almost like the innumerable stars in the sky.

So much death.

"I am sorry," Alexandra said. "Come, Gavon. Let's leave them to grieve."

I followed her, still torn between shock and anger. Still picturing that little girl who resembled my own, and hating this ridiculous tradition that had no reason for existence. I was now torn between wanting the tear closed to keep Cyrus away from my girls, but also wanting to keep it open so I might save more Potion-makers. It wasn't just the Charmers and Enchanters I was sending to their deaths if I closed it; I would be condemning every Potion-maker born.

"Thoughts, Gavon?" Alexandra said over her shoulder.

"Many."

"Feel free to share them. I can hear you seething from all the way back there."

I stopped mid-stride. "The killing of Potion-makers is an absurd tradition that we should've done away with a long time ago," I said hotly. "That we continue to do it is barbaric."

"I don't disagree," Alexandra said softly. "But change comes slow—"

"Change comes as quickly as the Guildmaster decrees it," I responded hotly. "You made an entire village turn around and go back to their houses today."

"I look forward to hearing your opinions of what the Guildmaster is capable of when it is yours to hold."

I swallowed. "I told you, I don't want it."

"Still?" she tutted. "You'd give Cyrus that kind of power? After what you witnessed today?"

"You'll live long enough for James to grow into a man, and then give it to him," I said.

"You know, I had a Potion-maker," she said, looking at the dark gray sky above. "My first child. I miss her every single day."

I stood back, aghast. "You let them kill your child?"

"I had no choice in the matter," she said, her face somber. "I barely got a chance to look at her face before they took her away from me." She continued walking. "I don't blame Mary for what she did. I only wish there was another way. If I'd let that child live, others…would wonder why not theirs? Why not my daughter?" She sighed. "It's a tradition I don't know how to break."

"Easy. Just stop killing the children," I asked.

She sighed. "I would have petitioned strongly for it. Especially considering your work in changing minds about potions in general. But I would've been overruled by the Council."

"And you would've abided by it?"

"It's a small village, Gavon. There's not much to hide here," Alexandra said, turning to look out the window. "As poor Mary found out."

I couldn't stomach returning to the village, so I came home. Nicole met me at the door, and the very sight of her was like a kick in the gut. If things had been different—if I'd never made the tear—she wouldn't even be here. She would have been taken from me, killed at birth. A powerful little magical who could make a healing potion to rival even the strongest healers…

I held my little girl tightly to me, thanking my lucky stars that things had turned out the way they had.

"Baby, what is it?" Mora said when I walked into the kitchen. "You look like a wreck. Did something happen over there?"

In the twelve years we'd been together, I'd never told Mora about what happened to Potion-makers. She'd never understood why I'd been so happy to have Nicole, so eager to show her just how perfect she really was. I suppose I'd never wanted her to see the people of New Salem for the barbarians they were. Perhaps I was afraid she'd blame me for partaking in it.

But today, I needed her to know.

"We found another little Potion-maker today," I began, my voice cracking. "Potion-makers aren't…well, they aren't valued in New Salem. In fact they're…" I looked down at Nicole and cast a charm around her ears so she wouldn't hear. "They're put to death at birth."

"Oh my God," Mora said, inhaling sharply. "Are you serious?"

I nodded as Nicole looked up at me, obviously confused why she could no longer hear. "This little girl, her mother had hidden her. I don't know how. She was Nicole's age. Just…just a baby."

"Don't tell me someone…"

I nodded. "Cyrus. He killed her in one strike. It was…" A tear fell down my cheek. "Mora, I couldn't stop it. I was going to save that little girl. Bring her here, give her to a family who would show her love and…"

"And my mother would've had a cow," Mora said, coming to sit next to me. "But I would've let her stay here. There are some things worth fighting with my mother for."

"My mother had a Potion-maker before me," I said, letting Nicole slide off my lap and walk away, poking her still-charmed ears. "A sister. So I suppose it runs in my blood."

"Your mother let them take her child and kill her?" Mora said with a gasp.

I averted my gaze to our joined hands. "She didn't have a choice. Mary didn't have a choice. It's…it's just how it is there."

"And you still have a loyalty to those people?" Mora said. "You still want to let them loose in our world?"

"They can't help that they're ignorant," I said, but I didn't feel it. It was hard to justify what I'd seen on pure culture alone. Not when Cyrus had been so gleefully unrepentant about murdering a child.

# Eleven

I thought a lot about that little Potion-maker over the next few days, especially as Nicole and I worked through her book more. I also thought about all the other Potion-makers who'd died since I'd had the tear open. How many could I have saved by removing them from New Salem?

"You should be focused on closing the tear, not trying to save hypothetical children," Mora said, as we discussed it, lying in bed. "I know…I know that it's hard, and you feel responsible, but there's nothing we can do."

"I mean, there's nothing really *preventing* me from bringing them over," I said.

"Other than my mother threatening to banish you—and me and our girls—from the clan."

Damn that Irene. "She wouldn't do that. The clan wouldn't agree to that. Not if we were saving lives."

"I don't know. You aren't at these clan meetings," she said, rolling onto her side and walking to the bathroom. "I swear this kid is right on my bladder."

"What are they saying?" I called to her.

"Oh, you know." She reappeared in the doorway, holding a bright purple attack spell in her hand. "Curious to know how we're going to handle this lovely miracle."

"Oh, she'll be fine—"

"No, not just her, Gav. They want to know about our kids' kids. We've disrupted the peace amongst the magical community here." She absorbed the magic back into her body and climbed into bed. "Imagine what'll happen in a hundred years when there's a whole brood of Warriors and Healers and Potion-makers…"

I kissed the side of her head. "Have I mentioned how beautiful it is when you use magic like that?"

"Uh-huh." She moved away from me. "Don't change the subject. It's a problem people are starting to consider. Especially some of the younger people—the ones who always ask why they don't get to use more of their magic."

"Oh? And see, from what I hear from Irene, everyone's just ecstatic about the Danvers Accord."

She rolled her eyes at me. "Jeanie was telling me about a group she fell into. Some secret society or some crap like that. It's part of the reason Mom pulled her out of that Arlington School for Magicals down in D.C. Too many rich magicals with too much time on their hands." She let out a sigh. "God, when did I become such a mother?"

"You're a great mom," I said. "Maybe one of the other clans would absorb the magicals. The Vargas Clan in Spain might."

"You've got to get this idea out of your head. The only thing you should be focusing on is *closing the damn tear,* not trying to bring all the unwanted Potion-makers to this side. If they decide to do what they do—no matter how barbaric—that's not your problem."

But it was my problem, and it gnawed at me when I returned to New Salem for a Council meeting, and I walked by Mary's house, which had draped black sheets over all the windows. Her children, who would've normally been outside playing, were nowhere to be found. The village itself had become despondent —even the tavern was less busy than it had been.

The only person who seemed to be in good spirits was Cyrus.

"Oh, why do we look so glum?" he said with a laugh. "Our village is strong. Our magicals are happy."

"The Enchanters are not happy," Rogers said. "They would like the Council to formally censure Master Cyrus for his role in the death of Mary's child."

"The only role I played was administering justice," Cyrus said. "Had she followed the rules in the first place, we never would've had that spectacle. Don't the midwives have some blame here? Who let the woman give birth and didn't take the child immediately—"

"Cyrus, that is enough," Alexandra said. "Have you no sense of decency?"

He quieted, but the look of superiority remained.

"What's done is done," Alexandra said after a moment. "How is…how is Mary?"

"She has declined to make bread for the past three weeks. She's sworn she will never make again," Rogers said. "The other Enchanters are…asking that they not be asked to make bread."

"They're revolting," I said under my breath.

"I will deal with Mary," Alexandra said wearily.

"Good. It's about time we restore some order in this town," Cyrus said. "Shall we make a spectacle of her or simply send her to the gallows?"

"Maybe we'll send you to the gallows instead," I said with an acidic look. "Or would you prefer to starve when all the Enchanters and Charmers decide to stop making food for us? Do you know how to make bread from crumbs? Milk a cow? I suggest that you quiet down before you get us all killed."

"We'll make them make it. This isn't complicated," Cyrus said. "We have power. They don't. If they fall out of line, we'll merely start destroying them one by one until they're docile again."

"If this is how you plan to lead us when you become Guildmaster, Cyrus, I'm afraid I must strongly object," Rogers said, his face growing pale.

"And I'm afraid it's not up to you, is it, Rogers?" Cyrus said.

"No, it's up to me," Alexandra said. "And I happen to agree with him. Until you decide to challenge me for this seat, you will quiet down and not speak of such horrible things. Am I clear, Cyrus?"

The look she gave me wasn't lost on me.


When the meeting was over, I disappeared from the council room, but didn't return home. I was too angry, and I could already predict what my wife would say: Close the tear, Gavon.

And leave the inhabitants of New Salem to Cyrus and his unique brand of justice.

I needed to cool off, so I returned to the manor I was supposed to be inhabiting and walked into the library. I took a moment to breathe in the dusty air, quiet my mind, and let the events from the past few days disappear. But I couldn't. All I could see was that tiny little girl.

I paced in the library, feeling trapped between two very bad outcomes. Close the tear, doom the village. Keep it open...

And what? Bring them over? Let an entire population of magicals not bound by the Danvers Accord loose in the world?

Then again, that was already a problem. My own children were that problem. And any children they had, and so on. The only solution to this problem, the solution someone like Irene wanted, was for me and them to be locked up in here with the rest of New Salem.

Or...

I stopped pacing, standing in the middle of the library. There was a rather elegant, albeit challenging solution—update the Danvers Accord. I knew little about pacts, having made precious few in my life. But Alexandra kept a tome about them. As I didn't trust myself to be nice, I summoned the book from the library, plopping down in the seat where I'd spent so many days of my childhood, and started reading.

Traditionally, pacts were designed to have loopholes and double-meanings, which was why they should never be entered into lightly. Much as Alexandra's decrees were enforced by the collective magic of the guildmembers, a pact would use the magic of both individuals—or however many members of the pact there were—to force them to adhere to it. The book was full of details on the different kinds of pacts, how to word them so one didn't get hoodwinked, and there, at the end, was a long chapter on changes with one very important passage:

**If a pact must be updated, it requires the original signatories or their descendants.**

Well, that complicated things a little. In the case of the Danvers Accord, there were over two hundred signatories, each representing a clan or guild around the world. That amount of magic had been the only way such monumental changes could be enforced. The original Danvers Accord was signed in 1714—twenty-two years after the Separation. It had taken Johanna Chase that long to track down Clanmasters and have them agree to the details. And as Josefa had said—it was either sign or be eliminated.

Tucking the book under my arm, I returned to Salem and made one final detour to Ashley's house.

"Ah, Gavon, so nice to see you," he said, opening his front door. "Come in, come in. You look troubled."

"Very much so," I said, following him inside.

"I hope you haven't come to a dead end with the tear research?" he said. "Did you visit Clan Vargas?"

"I did, thank you. Josefa helped with a few ingredients, but I'm still searching for the final two."

"Is that what you've come to talk about?" he said.

"Ah...no, actually," I said, momentarily second-guessing myself. Mary's child reappeared in my mind, strengthening my resolve. "I wanted to ask to see your binder full of Clanmasters. I was...hoping to contact them."

He sank into his desk, a puzzled look on his face. "For what purpose?"

"I…" I exhaled, shaking my head.

Ashley smiled. "I hear you've been thinking about bringing more magicals from New Salem."

"How did you know?" I said.

"Mora stopped by the other day with those lovely children of hers," Ashley said. "She wanted to know if it was feasible to update the Danvers Accord, or if there was any way the clan would allow more magicals over here. She mentioned there was an incident with a Potion-making child."

I sat back. "Yes, there was. And yes… I guess that's what I wanted to talk to you about. I have this book about pacts, and it says that a pact *can* be updated, as long as it has the approval of all the original signatories. Hence why I was hoping to get your list of Clanmasters, perhaps send them a letter. I know it's a long shot, but I thought it might be…worth trying."

"To what end?"

"To…amend the Danvers Accord so the magicals from New Salem would be bound by it—or at least, their future children would be. My children's children would be included in that. Then, when all the danger has passed, they can live freely in this world. Without the fear of…" I shrugged. "Cyrus."

Ashley leaned back in his chair. "Do you believe your mother would sign such a thing? Give up specialties?"

"If it was a choice between closing the tear with everyone in it or being allowed to see the sun, to live a free life…I believe she'd take it," I said, though I wasn't actually sure that was true. Alexandra remained an enigma to me most days, our recent bonding over Potion-makers aside. "But it would assuage my guilt, in any case. The people of New Salem aren't evil." Except Cyrus. He could remain there for all I cared.

"As noble as your goals are, I'm afraid, my boy, that updating the Danvers Accord might be a bridge too far. It would be best to continue our original effort to close the tear with the inhabitants inside."

"I refuse to believe that," I said. "It may take some time, but I could find them all. Even if the signatories don't have any direct descendent, that might not be an issue. They wouldn't be able to *protest*—"

"I know members of Clan Carrigan who would."

I blinked. "So you're saying Irene would prevent this from happening?"

"I'm saying Irene isn't the only one with concerns. We've had three hundred years of peace since the tear's been closed. What box would we be opening if we changed things?"

I sank into the chair. I'd always thought Ashley to be my ally, but now I wasn't so sure.

"Perhaps," Ashley said thoughtfully. "If we were able to close the tear, Clan Carrigan would be more willing to listen. After all, what are we going to do with them if we give them this opportunity to leave New Salem and they opt not to sign it? We'd have no recourse—and they are far more powerful than we are."

I forced a scowl off my face. "You want me to find a way to close the tear before you'll even bring it up for discussion?"

"I'm merely trying to give you the best chance possible." He folded his hands on the desk. "You said you were close, didn't you?"

I nodded. "I suppose I'll keep looking."

# Twelve

I didn't mention to Mora that I'd gone to see Ashley, or what he'd told me. To be honest, I was getting a little annoyed with their entire clan. There were good people in New Salem—people like Mary and her children. But until I had a key to the cage, they wouldn't trust my judgment.

To that end, I redoubled my efforts to find the final two ingredients of Johanna's potion. I spent hours in libraries, looking for the words Void Lily and Domdafosie. I asked magicals from Norway to the bottom of South America if they'd heard of this ingredient, but none had. I was beginning to suspect maybe Johanna had made a spelling error—or that I was looking for ingredients that no longer existed. And if that was the case, I would be back to where I'd started.

Summer arrived with fireworks and barbecues with all of Mora's cousins—and two little birthdays to plan. We'd started doing a joint party to celebrate summer and the girls at the same time, since their birthdays were two weeks apart. This year,

Mora decided to throw in her baby shower at the same time, just to get all the celebrations out of the way at once.

"But now we'll have a fall birthday," Mora said with a frown. "I guess we'll have to break them up."

"I bet we only have one joint party left with Nicole before she starts to protest," I said. "Besides that, she'll be going into kindergarten for the next birthday."

"Shut your mouth," she said with a stricken face. "Don't remind me."

"We should probably come up with a name, then, hm?" I said. "For the new baby."

"Uh, maybe," Mora said, plopping down on the bed. "Are we terrible parents that we haven't even thought about it?"

"Not at all." I rubbed her back. "We've just been busy."

"So…what are you thinking?" Mora asked.

"What are you thinking?"

"I asked you first."

I thought for a moment. "Well, she is going to be a Warrior. So it should be a strong name. Something that strikes fear into the hearts of people."

"For real, Gav?" She snorted. "You want to call her Joan of Arc or something? Xena?"

I laughed. "Well, okay, what are you thinking?"

"Ashley could work," Mora said.

"Like, after your uncle?" She nodded, and I made a face. "I don't know. Don't you have a cousin named Ashley?"

"I'm sure," she said. "But I don't know. I was thinking we could do a family name."

"What do you think about Alexandra?"

She lifted her brows. "As in…after your mother?"

"Yeah," I said, averting my gaze.

"The mother who still doesn't know about your daughters."

"The mother who is a fierce Warrior and powerful Guildmaster," I said. "She can't help how she was raised."

"I hate the name Alexandra, and I hate your mother. No way." She pursed her lips. "And why do *you* want to name her after your mother?"

I shrugged. "It's a tradition in our village. Name Warrior children after someone you admire. I was named after my mother's master's master."

"And why do you admire your mother? She's horrible."

"She…is just a product of her environment," I said. "But she's also powerful, formidable. Her name strikes fear into the names of everyone in the village." I grinned at her. "And I rather like the name, too."

"Our little girl isn't going to be some bitch warrior like your mother," Mora said. "She's going to use her powers for good."

"If she's anything like you…" I wisely tempered my words at the dangerous look on my wife's face. "She'll be the most well-behaved, easy-going child ever."

"Uh-huh," Mora said. "Are you serious about this? Like, does it mean a lot to you?"

I nodded. "It's kind of like that Warrior thing. Hard to explain but…"

She held up her hands. "I'll consider it. I still hate the name Alexandra." Her eyes lit up. "Oh, what about Torie?"

The day of the party dawned bright and warm, and right on

the nose, familiar faces began appearing in our front yard, along with their children, who made beelines for the play set I'd conjured for them to play on while the adults caught up and enjoyed beer and finger foods. Mora had really outdone herself, cooking the spread herself and using a warming charm (and one of my freshening charms) to keep it all together before the day of the party. She'd even baked a triple-layer cake and cupcakes for the kids.

"This is too much," I said, eyeing the spread. "Mora, you really need to take it easy. Please make sure you sit down."

"I will, I will," she said, whizzing by me with another plate of food. "Promise."

"Mister Gavon! Mister Gavon!" A redheaded child with bright blue eyes ran over to me, wiping her nose on the back of her hand. "Your baby is using magic! She's not allowed to do that."

"Marie is a very special girl," I said, bending over. "You'll have magic too, when you're fifteen. She just has it early."

"Oh." The girl turned and ran back into the fray. I scanned the magical signatures for my girls', and found Nicole swinging on the playset with a little boy close to her age, and Marie was…

Levitating herself. To what end, I had no idea, but she was enjoying herself.

"Gavon," Mora called. "Take care of your daughter please."

With a wave of my hand, I surrounded Marie with magic and gently placed her back on the ground. Happily, she turned and climbed back up the playset the nonmagical way.

"I don't know how you put up with that."

Jeanie was behind me—a sight for sore eyes. "Hey, I'm glad

you could make it."

"Of course," she said, thrusting two bags at me. "For the girls."

"Oh, wow," I said, genuinely surprised that she'd shown up and even more surprised that she'd brought the girls a present. "Thank you. The girls will love them, I'm sure."

She nodded, tucking a lock of hair behind her ear.

"I'm really glad you came," I sent a little magical call to my kids to get their attention. "Hey, girls, come say hi to your aunt."

Twin squeals echoed amongst the crowd of kids as Nicole and Marie came barreling over and slammed into Jeanie's legs.

"Oh wow," she said with a laugh. "You two are huge!"

"Why don't you take Jeanie to the playset and show her your slide?" I said.

They dragged her toward the gaggle of kids and she disappeared amongst them. It was nice to see her let her hair down, so to speak. I worked the party, talking with cousins and aunts and uncles, who all inquired about the girls, myself, and Mora's pregnancy. It was easy to forget that someone like Irene thought we were weren't worthy of inclusion when the rest of the Carrigans seemed so welcoming.

"Gavon, my boy! How's that blasted tear research going?" I wasn't sure which of Mora's cousins or second cousins Gary was, but he lived four doors down and always had a smile and a wave.

"It's going," I said with a grim smile.

"Those girls of yours are trouble, aren't they? Not even five and already wielding magic. How are you going to handle a third?"

"We'll manage, I suppose," I said.

"Gavon!" Mora called, blessedly saving me from more of this conversation. "I need you!"

We sang a raucous birthday song while both girls beamed happily then dug into their cake. Marie just licked off the frosting one fingertip at a time, while Nicole picked up the whole slice, getting it all over her face and hair. Mora wandered around snapping photos of every moment and going through two different film cartridges.

Once the cake had been demolished, the party started to dwindle. I spotted Jeanie sitting with Nicole on the front steps of our house, reading her one of the books Jeanie had bought her. Nicole was pointing to the words, and Jeanie was nodding and smiling. It might've been the first genuine smile I'd ever seen on her face.

"You guys having fun?" I asked.

"I want to spend the night with Nene," Nicole announced.

"Oh, I think that's up to your Aunt Jeanie," I said with an apologetic look to Jeanie. I doubted she'd want to bring a four-year-old to the dorms. "But maybe she can come by and play with you some more? Why don't you go get your sister?"

"I can't believe how much they've grown," Jeanie said. "I mean, Nicole's sitting here having a conversation with me. Marie's talking, too. They're so...big."

"I turned around and they were little humans," I said with a frown. "I can't imagine how quickly the little one is going to grow up. I'm sure before I know it, she'll be off to college."

"Slow down. She hasn't even been born yet," Mora said, waddling over to us. She ungracefully plopped down next to her sister. "I'm glad you came, Jeanie. Really."

Jeanie shrugged, watching the girls chase each other around. "They are my nieces. I guess I should get to know them a little more."

"Yeah, you should. And you should come home more. I miss you." She rubbed her belly. "And these babies need you."

"You just want me to babysit."

"Well, duh." Mora nudged her sister. "But maybe we'll leave the kids with Gav and go on a date. Just us two."

"Y-yeah, I'd like that," Jeanie said.

"Are you quite sure that she's capable?"

A noticeable chill descended on me, even though it was the dead of summer. Irene stood with two small bags in her hand, looking about as pleased to be there as we were to have her. Nina was next to her, nervously looking between Irene and myself. It was clear she'd been the one to goad her sister into coming—albeit two hours late.

Mora pushed herself to stand and placed a calming hand on my shoulder. "Be nice. I invited her under the condition that she not say or do anything to antagonize you." She turned to Irene with a smile. "Hi Mom. Glad you could make it."

"Mora, you're looking lovelier every time I see you," Nina said. "How far along are you?"

"Eight months," she answered with a smile. "October twentieth is my due date."

"That's just a few weeks away, isn't it?" Nina said to her sister, who didn't share her smile. "Have you decided on a name yet?"

"In debate," I answered.

"We'd already exhausted all our girls names with the first two," Mora said with a nervous laugh. "I still like Torie, but Gav likes Alexandra."

Irene's hawkish gaze slid to me. "As in the name of your mother?"

"It's a family name, yes," I said, careful to keep my tone even. "But as I said, we're still discussing it."

"You'd better come to a decision soon," Nina said with an overly cheery smile. "That baby will be here before you know it."

"Yes, and with all that unbound power," Irene said. "I hear you two have been practicing. Already planning on turning your baby into an expert, are we?"

"*Mother*," Mora said. "You promised."

"Did I say something offensive?"

"You certainly implied it," I snapped. "What my wife and I do with our kids, and how we choose to raise them, is none of your concern."

"It certainly is," Irene said. "Every day their powers grow stronger, and you two encourage it. All the while, the tear between the worlds sits wide open for anyone to cross through."

"And yet, it's been only me," I said.

"For now. But how long until you change your mind? I've heard you wanted to bring more of your kin here. For what purpose—"

"To save their lives, Irene. Unlike you, I happen to have a little thing called empathy." Mora's hand tightened on my shoulder, and I swallowed hard, eating the rest of my angry words. I would not let Irene cause another fight, not on such a happy day. I wouldn't give her that satisfaction.

"I've asked the clan to reconsider their original decision about you," Irene said, lifting her head. "It's clear Ashley has lost his ability to lead effectively. Having you here, and letting you drag your feet on everything you've promised, all the while growing your brood of potential problems—"

"Those are your *grandchildren*," Mora said, rising to her feet. "They aren't problems. They're kids."

"Mommy?" Nicole said, hiding her face behind Mora's legs. "Why is Gram yelling at us?"

"She's not," Mora said, pressing a hand to her head. "She was just leaving."

"The next meeting, I'm calling for a reconsideration of your placement here," Irene said, turning on her heel. "I suggest you make progress by then."

# Thirteen

Despite my best efforts, Mora and I did have something of a fight, but it was less words and more Mora's unsaid annoyance. Also the locked door when I tried to go to bed.

So I sat in the basement, staring at the confounded journal that I'd read cover to cover more times than I could count, with a six pack of beer beside me and no good answers. I fully believed Irene would make good on her promise, and I also believed the clan members who'd just dined and had cake in my backyard might be inclined to permanently remove me from it, if they listened to her. Updating the Danvers Accord was a pipe dream at this point; I first needed to make sure *I* could stay. But just as it had been the last time I'd picked up this journal, I had no idea where to find the last two ingredients of Johanna's potion.

"Daddy?"

"Nicole?" I looked up. "Nicole, go back to bed. It's late."

"I had a bad dream." She padded down the stairs in her

white nightgown, her brown hair hanging around her shoulders. "Can I stay down here with you? Mommy's door is closed."

"Of course, baby, come on." I held open my arms, and she crawled into them, resting her small head on my shoulder. "Did you have a scary dream?"

She nodded. "Gram is scary."

"Gram is very scary," I said, grabbing my half-empty bottle of beer and taking a swig. "But deep down, she does love you. She just…doesn't know how to express it very well."

"What are you reading?" she asked.

"Just a journal," I said, showing her the potion. "This was a potion made by a Potion-maker over three hundred years ago."

"Like me?" she said, leaning forward.

"Yes, baby, just like you." I smiled. "She made this potion to keep all the bad people in a faraway place. And that's where Daddy came from."

"So are you a bad people?" Nicole asked.

"No, all the bad people died hundreds of years ago. Now it's just…people there. But your Gram wants me to fix the hole I made. That's what she's so mad about." I ran my fingers along the page. "But Daddy can't figure it out, and that's why Mommy is mad at Daddy tonight."

She twisted in my arms and took my face in her hands. "Mommy shouldn't be mad at you for that."

"No arguments from me, kiddo." I rose with her in my arms. "But she will be mad at me if I keep you up. Let's go to bed."

I ended up contorted in an odd position on my daughter's bed, while she snuggled up next to me. I didn't sleep, watching the lights pass on the ceiling until dawn broke. I heard the door open down the hall, followed by quiet footsteps. My wife appeared in the doorframe, surprise turning into amusement as she took me in.

"You look uncomfortable," she said, leaning on the doorframe.

"So do you," I said, turning on the pillow.

"Well, that goes without saying." She rested her hand on her stomach. "I'm sorry."

"I am too."

"Come to bed?"

"I don't think that's possible," I said, gesturing to Nicole who was lying on my arm.

"I think…" She sighed. "Gavon, I think you have to make a choice now. It's either your family or New Salem. You can't have both."

"I know, Mora… I know."

"And I…Gavon, I don't want to have to say this but…" She sniffed and a tear fell down her face. "Gav, if they make me choose, I'm gonna choose our girls. I don't want to make that choice. Please don't make me make that choice."

"Do you really think if Irene kicks me out, she won't also kick our girls out?" I said, trying to keep my voice low. "She's had it in for them."

"Fix it, Gavon," Mora said, standing up. "Please, I'm begging you. This has gone on long enough."

Domdafosie and Void Lily.

I wore a hole in my basement floor thinking and re-thinking and searching through every piece of material I'd found on the tear. I was spinning my wheels, but with the clan meeting in the next three weeks, and my new daughter coming in the next two months, the pressure was on. I wrote letters to every magical I knew, went to London to beg Sahil to ask his contacts if they knew anything. I even spent days searching through Alexandra's library, just looking for a *mention* of the ingredients.

Finally, like an angel descending from heaven, on a September afternoon, my savior arrived.

"Gavon?"

"Sahil!" I blinked, jumping to my feet as the man in question walked downstairs. I was fairly sure I was hallucinating. "This is a surprise. What are you doing on this side of the Atlantic?"

"Couldn't wait to share what I'd found with you," he said. "Adorable family, by the way."

"Thank you," I said. "What did you find?"

"I was in contact with Josefa Vargas, from Seville. She'd mentioned you'd come by to see her, looking for a few potions ingredients. So I set to my various tomes, looking for it."

I held my breath. "And?"

"It's an obscure reference," Sahil said, handing me an old journal, not unlike the one I'd been staring a hole into. "But I was able to find another journal mentioning it from a man named Frederico Fages, from Clan Vargas. I put in a call to Josefa, and she sent me a box of his old affects. It took me a few weeks, but I was able to find a hand-written note." He procured another, thicker book and opened it to a page.


**Void Lily — Cypripedium reginae is known as the Lady's Slipper, the Queen's Lady's-slipper, and other names, is a rare orchid native to North**

**America. The plant is rare, and neither magical nor nonmagical have been able to successfully grow it from seed.**

**However, it's prevalent in the bogs of Prince Edward Island and other northern climbs, if one searches long enough.**

"This is brilliant," I said, unable to bring myself to smile fully. "One down, one to go."

"Ah, well, that's not the best news," Sahil said as the book disappeared and another appeared in its place. "Josefa and I were talking about the potion, and she mentioned that I might look into ingredients that increase potency. After all, it was a fairly complex potion already, but nothing in it was particularly powerful. So I spent a few days searching through my library, and I found this."

**D. Cinnabari, sometimes known as Domdafosie, is a tree resin used since ancient times as a cure-all, dye, and varnish for musical instruments. It's used in potion-making to increase the potency of magic within the cauldron, and also as a cure for skin conditions.**

"Sahil, I could kiss you. And Josefa," I said, grinning ear-to-ear. "Seriously, if I wasn't married—"

"I'm just glad I could be of assistance," he said. "I have to say, it's one of the more complex research projects. Hunting and cross-referencing and—"

"And please, tell me all about it over a large cup of tea, and soon," I said, grasping him by the shoulders. "But for now, I have a potion to brew."

The Domdafosie was the easiest to summon, as it was used fairly prevalently, albeit under its pseudonym. But the Void Lily was a bit harder to find, and I spent several hours scouring bogs and marches in the northern climes of North America until I found one.

With those two ingredients in hand, I assembled the rest of my ingredients, which were much easier to find. I laid them out on the basement floor, checking and double-checking my amounts to make sure I had enough.

I made no mention of this breakthrough to Mora or the girls, and I kept the basement locked. I wasn't quite sure what this concoction would bring forth, and I didn't want the littles in the house when I did. This potion could be the answer I was looking for, or it could be a deadly concoction that destroyed the house. Or it could be absolutely nothing at all, and I'd wasted eight months on yet another dead end.

Finally, on a stormy night in September, I'd finished what I'd started out to do. I had gathered all the ingredients to remake Johanna's potion.

And there I sat for several hours, staring at the plants and minerals and my cauldron, not making a move. Perhaps Mora was right. I'd been putting off this effort as long as possible. Perhaps in my gut, I knew this was the solution I'd been searching for, and it would require me to make decisions I didn't want to make.

*"It's either your family or New Salem."*

I rose from my seat and summoned a small table to rest the cauldron on. I followed the directions with the utmost care, pausing between each step to make sure the colors were changing as they'd been written. As the mixture frothed and bubbled, the hairs on my arm began to stand up. I was truly making something potent—and dangerous. Energy crackled in the room, filling my lungs with an ionic-smelling fume, and I glanced at the ceiling, wondering if I should tell Mora and the girls to leave. I risked an even bigger catastrophe if I moved it—magically or otherwise.

Finally, I was at the end of the potion, with the final two ingredients—the very special, very strange pieces that Sahil had helped me find. Hands shaking, I said a prayer that my new friend had been as careful as I'd hoped.

I placed the Domdafosie and waited for the potion to shimmer orange.

"Daddy?"

"Nicole, get out of here," I barked. "It's too dangerous."

"Baby? What are you doing down here? It stinks."

"Mora, take the girls and go visit Nina," I said, watching the color of the potion. It had shifted from a dark green to a reddish color, but was that orange? Was it ready?

"Gavon, what the hell are you doing down here? Are you…" She took a step back, pressing her hand to her stomach. "Are you brewing the potion?"

"Y…no," I said, not sure why I was lying to her. "No, this is something else. Another potion I'm trying. It's a long shot, but…"

"Oh." The disappointment was clear in her voice. "It creeps me out. How can a potion creep me out?"

"Because it's…well, it is," I said, hoping she'd take the hint and leave.

"Do potions always feel this way?" Mora said with a little shiver. "It's like it's alive."

All the more reason it was dangerous. "Sometimes they do. This is old, deep magic powerful enough to sustain life after the magical who created it was gone. You can only do that in a potion. I'm almost finished, and I'm a little worried it's volatile."

"So you want us to get out of here?"

"Just in case," I said, forcing a smile onto my face. "I don't know what this will do."

"All right. Girls, let's go get some pizza while Daddy…does whatever he's doing."

I waited for the door to close above, and a few extra minutes for good measure. And it was a good thing, too, for the potion had turned the color of a satsuma. I held the last ingredient in my hands, shaking with nerves—hoping it would work and that it wouldn't.

With my girls in my mind, I dropped it in and waited.

The potion steamed, growing white hot and releasing a flash of bright, white light. Then, as if someone had opened a hole in the cauldron, the mixture spun and circled, though it didn't drain out the bottom. And there it sat, swirling in an unending vortex, changing from orange to black to white to green to blue. And finally, it ended on a pleasant silver color, stabilizing and settling in the cauldron.

I exhaled a breath. This was it—the potion that had created New Salem. The genesis for everything I'd ever known up until I'd made the tear. And it could be the answer I'd been searching for.

Carefully, I ladled a bit into a vial, the liquid cool to the touch. The rest of the cauldron, I safely hid in another magical pocket, far away from my house and my girls. And the vial... well, I sent that to a pocket, too. Using it was inevitable, but I wasn't ready to face reality.

Not just yet.

# Fourteen

I told Mora that the potion I'd brewed had been a failure, but I was close to finding the final two ingredients for Johanna's potion. I just hoped Sahil and Josefa didn't spill the beans. Irene wouldn't have the opportunity to banish me from the clan for three more weeks. And Ashley had been pleased the last time we'd spoken. So I had some breathing room. Besides that, if push came to shove, I would use the potion and that would be that.

It was time to return to New Salem for another Council meeting (although Mora was told it was another potion fact-finding mission). Alexandra would probably deliver a lecture about the importance of being on time to Council meetings. Today, I arrived a few hours early, just so Alexandra would be able to berate me privately before the rest of the council got a shot.

I walked into her house, finding her magical signature in her library, as usual. Patting the vial of potion in my pocket, which

I'd brought with me just in case, I strode through the house with all the confidence I didn't feel.

"Well, good to know you aren't dead," Alexandra said, lifting her gaze from the book she was reading. "I had half a mind to search the house for your rotting corpse."

"I'll consider it a sign of affection that you haven't yet," I said, taking a seat. "Obviously, you weren't that worried."

"You missed two meetings. That is unacceptable, even for a Councilman."

"Understandable," I said, feeling the vial shift in my pocket as I adjusted my legs. "And I apologize."

"I look forward to the masterful lie you'll tell."

I raised my brows. "I'm sorry?"

"You wear your emotions on your face," she said, returning to the book. "I know when you lie. It's not your best feature."

"I do apologize for my inadequacy."

"I suppose you've heard the news then. Come to argue?"

I tried to school my features, but since she was reading me like a book anyway, I let them go. "What are you talking about?"

"Since you neglected to come to our last Council meeting, I made the decision about the boy, James. I've decided *you* will train him."

Not wholly unexpected, but also not going to happen. "I can't."

"Tell me, son, why are you so averse to becoming a master?" Alexandra said, leaning her chin on her joined hands. "And please spare me your usual excuses. I would prefer the truth for once."

I'd spoken precious little truth these past few weeks. And yet, I did want to tell her the whole truth. About Mora, my girls. The potion sitting in my pocket. How I'd been able to bring fresh food into the village, staving off magical rot and other illnesses. I wanted to tell her that another Warrior was coming, even if that child would never adhere to our customs and traditions.

"Please don't make me compel you to speak the truth," she said quietly. "I have yet to use that power on any in this village, and I don't want you to be the first."

"Then…will you promise that what I tell you won't leave this room?"

She sat back, crossing her hands over the desk. "Is it so dangerous that the Council can't know?"

"Yes," I said. "Do I have your word?"

"I'm not promising you anything," she said, sitting back. "But I will do my best to adhere to your wishes."

"If you ever felt any motherly affection toward me, you will honor my wishes and keep this between us."

"It is my motherly affection that has prevented me from using a compulsion spell. But it's currently running thin, so I suggest you speak the truth now."

I exhaled, gathering my thoughts. "I cannot take the boy because…I already have a child. Or I will, very soon."

"Are you telling me you've succeeded in fathering a child? Finally?" The look on her face was nothing affectionate.

"Mother—"

"And, pray tell, is it a Healer? Or," she chuckled, "are you cursed with a brood of bastard Potion-makers? Are you here to beg me to allow them to live?"

The corner of my mouth twitched, and I forced myself not to look enraged.

"Even if this child turns out to be a Warrior, which is not guaranteed, you won't be able to raise it," she said. "The child would go to Cyrus—"

"The child is a Warrior," I said, keeping my tone even.

Alexandra's indifferent mask finally slipped away. "Are you certain?"

I nodded.

"This is… Gavon, this is *wonderful!*" she said, standing. "You've saved our Guild! Two Warriors! It is a blessing."

"There's…more," I said. "She won't be inducted into the Guild. She belongs to a Clan. Clan Carrigan."

For the first time in my life, Alexandra looked shocked— truly shocked. "I don't… I don't understand what you're saying."

So I told her everything—except, of course, about my two other children. I told her about the tear, and how I met Mora and we'd fallen in love and gotten married. I told her about exploring the world, about Clan Carrigan, and everything therein. I told her about the Danvers Accord and specialties. I spoke until my voice was scratching in my throat, and I had no more I wanted to tell.

"All this time," she began slowly, "you've been living in the new world? That's where you've been disappearing to? And where you've been getting all this fresh food?" I nodded. "Why haven't you told me before?"

I scrambled for an excuse that wasn't the truth. "I've been

researching. Learning what I can. The world is very different than ours. The nonmagicals have become quite adept in their… weaponry." Yes, better to make her think the world was dangerous. "They have bombs—nonmagical attack spells—that can obliterate entire cities in a single blast. I thought it best to be cautious."

She stroked her chin as if she didn't believe me. "And you're telling me this now so I won't give you another child to raise?"

I nodded. "My daughter will be here soon, so I won't be able to take care of the boy. Give him to Cyrus or take him yourself."

"Gavon, that's not how it works," Alexandra said. "Your child will go to Cyrus."

"My child will stay in my world, with her mother and me. By virtue of her birth, she's bound to Clan Carrigan, and therefore must adhere to their rules." I swallowed, ready to level the final blow. "And I must also inform you that I'm working to close the tear I made."

I didn't think it was possible for her to look surprised again, but she managed it. "So you'll go off into this new world and leave your people behind?"

"No. That isn't my preference, but…it's also not my choice." I considered my words, wondering how much to share. "Clan Carrigan wishes to close the tear with all of us still inside. If my mother-in-law had her way, I would be included in that number. But there are others who might be willing to allow us our freedom, if we were to agree to some parameters."

"Whatever assurances they need, I will give," Alexandra said with a wave of her hand. "Whatever agreements they will ask of us, I, and the clan, will gladly approve. My first priority is and always will be the health and wellbeing of the clan."

"Even...if it means giving up our specialties?" I said slowly. "The Danvers Accord, it was made to prevent magicals like us— Warriors. But there are no more Charmers, no more Enchanters. No more Healers and Potion-makers. Just...a very basic kind of magic."

"Then how are you having a child with Warrior magic?"

"Because while my wife is bound by the accord, I am not. And that, is...well, a loophole, I guess. And one they'd like to close."

"By updating this accord with signatures from the New Salem Warrior's Guild."

"Yes. I don't know how that would work, if it would be my future children or if we'd be under the spell immediately. I also...well, I don't have the original signatories. It will take me months—perhaps years to find them all. Even longer to convince them that updating the agreement is a good idea."

"Perhaps a signed letter from the Guildmaster might convince them otherwise." She procured a quill, ink, and paper and wrote hastily, signing with a flourish.

*I, Alexandra McKinnon, do hereby agree to sign the Danvers Accord in its entirety on behalf of the New Salem Warrior's Guild.*

"Will that be enough?" she asked.

I took the letter from her and tucked it into my front coat pocket. "I will bring it to them."

She smiled, and some of the lines on her face disappeared. "What does the sun feel like?"

If only I could tell her about the blistering sunburns, the taste of a cool ice cream cone on a hot day. The smell of salt water and the laughter of little girls playing on the beach.

"I look forward to showing it all to you very soon."

My mother's letter and the vial of potion sat heavily in my pocket as I walked up to Ashley's house. All I wanted was a vote of confidence—the ability to move forward with updating the Danvers Accord to include the inhabitants of New Salem. Alexandra's signature on this letter was as binding as any—as long as she was Guildmaster, the guild would do as she said.

"Gavon, come in, come in," Ashley said, waving me weakly into his office. "I apologize for not getting up, but the old body doesn't move as well as it used to."

I smiled, but the reminder of Ashley's age didn't sit well in my stomach. Did I have years to update the Danvers Accord? Or would Clan Carrigan's change of leadership veto it immediately?

"Tell me, how are those girls?"

"They're wonderful," I said. "Our new little girl should be here in a couple of weeks. We're very excited."

"Do you have a name yet?"

"Not…yet. Mora and I have a difference of opinion on what makes a strong name."

"I hear you want to name her after your mother," Ashley said, chuckling then coughing weakly into a handkerchief. "Dangerous waters, there."

"We could always call her Alexandra Irene, just to make it fair."

"Oh, that poor child," Ashley said with another laugh

punctuated by a wet cough. "I hope it's something less formal."

"We're still working on it," I said. "But I wanted to talk to you about…something else."

"I hear Sahil paid you a visit."

"Yes, he did. He was very helpful." With a deep breath of courage, I reached into my pocket and procured the vial. "This is…well, this is it."

"You've done it," Ashley said, leaning forward. "Are you sure it will work?"

"It is the potion Johanna brewed," I said, evasively. "But there's more. Alexandra knows about the tear."

Ashley sat back, concern etched on his old face. "Does she, now?"

"She was concerned about my absence, compelled me to speak about where I've been," I said, hoping Ashley wasn't as good at seeing through a lie as Alexandra was. "But there's good news. She's agreed to join the Danvers Accord." I slid the letter across his desk.

He picked it up gingerly, unfolding and scanning the page. "It doesn't surprise me that she would agree to our terms."

"I hope that this might…help Clan Carrigan come to a decision about updating the Danvers Accord. And others, as well. I know Clan Vargas would be on board."

Ashley gently placed the letter on his desk. "My concern, Gavon, isn't adding your guild. It's opening the can of worms to the rest of the world. There are those who believe we should return to a full breadth of specialties. Remove the restrictions around even speaking of magic around the nonmagicals. I fear if we bring this up for a vote, it would quickly devolve into something neither of us want."

My heart sank. "But what about New Salem? What about all this work I've been doing to close the tear?"

"What about it? You have the potion. Perhaps it's time to use it."

I rose to my feet. "Ashley, listen to me. These people don't deserve to live in the world they do. They're innocent. Alexandra is willing to do whatever's necessary to free them from that cage. They'll give up specialties, they'll sign on to the accord lock, stock, and barrel. You have her word."

He sighed and picked up the letter again, saying nothing.

"You have mine, too," I said, straightening. "That if you don't allow them freedom, I'll just bring them over here. We'll find a place for them to live and you'll have a community of magicals who won't adhere to your accord. Is that better?"

"That sounds like a threat, Gavon."

I swallowed. "It's a reality. We already have the problems we do. We might as well solve them."

After a long pause, Ashley held up his hands in surrender. "Fine. I will bring it up for discussion. If the clan agrees that this is a good route to take, I will call on my fellow Clanmasters. I'm not saying it's going to happen, so wipe that grin off your face."

I hadn't even realized I was smiling.

"But…you're right. We have this problem to deal with, and we should resolve it before it gets any worse."

# Fifteen

I didn't go home after that—I couldn't. I wouldn't be able to hide my glee from Mora, and I was sure she would be *very* angry with me for what I'd said to Ashley. But for the first time, I finally felt like I had some control. That things were moving forward in my life. I could see a light at the end of the tunnel.

I returned to New Salem for the second time that day, very rare for me. Only this time, I brought with me one of Mora's old high school history books. A gift for my mother, and what I hoped would be the beginning of a long journey toward educating her on the finer points of the new world. Perhaps I could invite her to meet with Ashley, or vice versa. His health concerned me, but—

All thoughts went out the window when loud cheering erupted in the village at my arrival. They rushed to me, grasping my shirtsleeves and thanking me for saving them, for being their hero. For saving them and the village. For releasing them from this sunless world into the real one.

My heart sank into my stomach.

I hurriedly detangled myself from the crowd and transported to Alexandra's house.

"What did you *do*?" I bellowed, slamming open the door to her study. There, Rogers, Humbert, Agatha, and Cyrus sat around her large desk, each with a glass of wine in hand.

"Ah, the man of the hour," Alexandra said, beckoning me inside.

"We had a deal, Alexandra," I snapped. "You weren't supposed to share this news."

"And why not, my boy?" Rogers said with a heavy cough as he sipped the wine. "You've found a way out of this frozen hellscape. You've ensured our Guild's survival for centuries to come. And I hear…you're bringing us another Warrior!"

I glared daggers at my mother, fury overtaking my words. "May I have a word in private?"

"No, you may not," she said. "This news is welcome indeed. And therefore, it's as good a time as any to announce my decision." She smiled at me. "I will be renouncing my Guildmastership at the end of the year. Gavon will be our new leader."

Rogers, Agatha, and Humbert roared in their approval, clapping and cheering each other with their wine glasses. Cyrus wore a look of horrified shock—not even noticing the wine pouring from his tilted glass. I couldn't think about what he might do to punish me now.

This was all happening too fast—I didn't want any of this. "A *word*, Alexandra."

"Fine, fine," she said, transporting to the other side of her desk and walking past me to the door. "Let's have it."

I was barely out of the office before I let her have it. *"What the fuck is wrong with you?"*

Her eyes widened. "Gavon, I've never heard such language from you."

"Because you lied to me. You told me you wouldn't share, and now I arrive and the whole village is applauding me. And now you give me Guildmaster? How many damned times do I have to tell you *I don't want it.*"

"You will become Guildmaster so you can shepherd us through this transition," she said softly. "I know nothing of this world, of the practices. You've married into Clan Carrigan, and will soon have a daughter by them. Who better to lead it than you? Cyrus?"

"You, Alexandra. I'm not ready to become leader."

"Neither was I at eighteen. Neither am I at present. But it's something we have to deal with." She rested her hand on my shoulder. "If what I understood of what you told me yesterday is true, the Guild as we know it will cease to be. But would you leave these people in the hands of Cyrus?"

Wearily, I shook my head. "I suppose not. But I still haven't secured your removal yet. Clan Carrigan hasn't given their blessing, and we have to find the original signatories of the Danvers Accord and—"

She waved her hand. "You forget, son, that as Guildmaster, you can compel the members to do whatever you please, as a temporary measure. So if you'd like them to adhere to the tenants of the agreement, you can do that."

"As long as I have the Council's blessing."

"Rogers, Humbert, and Agatha are in agreement," she said then added, "I don't believe Agatha knows what's going on anyway, but she'd agree with anything I tell her to."

"And Cyrus?"

"Can be overruled," she said.

"Oh, can I?" Cyrus stood on the other end of the hallway, his face a mask. Something like fear crawled down my spine—a feeling I hadn't had since I was a boy. Suddenly, I was eighteen and worried my fellow apprentice would retaliate after I'd received praise. And as much as I tried to shake off that fear, it remained firmly in the back of my mind, like a speeding train careening toward me.

And when he spoke, I was both unsurprised and terrified.

"I challenge you, Alexandra," Cyrus announced. "For Guildmaster."

"Very well," she said, glancing in my direction. "At dusk. Gavon shall officiate."

It was like a storm cloud had descended over the village. Where raucous laughter and excitement had been, now was silence. A nervousness of what was to come.

Alexandra walked through the village with her head held high, impervious to the cries and pleas of the villagers around her. They begged her to reconsider, to decline the challenge, but there was nothing she could do. Cyrus was well within his rights, and once uttered, a challenge couldn't be undone.

My heart thudded in my chest as I considered the match. It seemed improbable that she would lose, but Alexandra hadn't been in the ring with either of us since we were boys. We had the benefit of age; she was in her fifties now, and Cyrus was still a young man at thirty.

Worst of all, I was powerless to stop any of it.

Alexandra and the rest of the Council peeled off toward the underground catacombs where I'd prepared for my two matches as a boy. I couldn't be inside; it was already hard to breathe. So I ascended the staircase to the observation box where I would see the fate of my life and the lives of everyone in the village determined.

I leaned against the stone railing. From here, the arena seemed rather small and unremarkable. Just an open field with sand. Maybe it was age and distance, but it no longer held the fear it once had.

I sat down on the large center chair—the Guildmaster's chair —and rested my hands on the arms. I prayed this chair would become mine without any additional bloodshed. I prayed Alexandra would win, and perhaps might find some mercy for Cyrus. After all, she *could* decide not to kill him. Then he would be permanently barred from seeking the Guildmaster spot again.

What an elegant solution.

"Ah, Gavon, that's not yet yours."

Cyrus stood behind me, his hands clasped behind his back. He walked to the edge of the box and placed his hands on the ledge, gazing down at the sparring ring.

"It's rather strange to see it from up here isn't it?"

Stranger that he'd had the same thought as I had. I didn't take him for someone so insightful. "You don't have to do this, you know."

"Oh, but I do," he said. "We will duel today, and Alexandra

will die. I hope you've said your goodbyes."

"Are you so eager to kill the woman who raised you?" I asked softly. I'd mourned when Jones had died, and so had Alexandra.

"I'm more eager to see this new world you've discovered," he said, turning. "And how very exciting that I will be the one to lead us to victory over the magicals who enslaved us."

I sat back, wishing I was surprised. "I think you'll find that task a little more difficult than you anticipate."

He shrugged and turned back to the ring. "We shall see, Gav. We shall see."

The crowd had gathered, none of them looking pleased to be there. A few paused below the observation deck, watching me and perhaps seeking some kind of assurance that everything would be all right. I hated that I couldn't give it to them.

When the light dimmed in the sky, Alexandra appeared on one side of the ring and Cyrus the other. It was time for my very small part in this play. I appeared between them, taking a moment to steady my voice before I enchanted it.

"Today's duel will be for the Guildmaster," I began, my voice echoing around the arena. "Alexandra McKinnon versus Cyrus Fairchild. There will be one winner and survivor. The match will continue until death, or one party concedes."

"I will never concede," Cyrus snarled. "The Guildmaster position is mine."

"If you can win it," Alexandra countered. "Your pride will be your downfall, Cyrus."

"Shake hands," I said, if only to end their verbal bantering.

Alexandra took Cyrus's hand and shook it, erupting a large dome of magic around the ring. My mother's was a vibrant purple, the same color as my magic, and that of my daughter's. Cyrus's was a dark gray.

"I'm sorry it had to come down to this, Cyrus," Alexandra said quietly. "It will not be a pleasure to kill you."

"No, the pleasure will be all mine."

I inhaled deeply. "Begin!"

I transported out of the ring, arriving back in the Council box as the fireworks flew. Unlike for my induction match, the audience today was somber and quiet. This wasn't a celebration —and although no one wanted a death, we were all hoping it would be Cyrus.

I had no idea how long the match went on; it was much less terrifying sitting in the stands versus being the one fighting for his life. The activity inside the dome was nothing but purple and gray blurs, with the occasional errant attack spell landing against the side of the dome.

Eventually, the crowd began to dwindle. As the light disappeared from the sky, and the howling wind picked up, the inhabitants of New Salem left to their homes and hearths. Then, it was just Roberts and I, watching with silent reverence, and knowing that the combatants were probably exhausted.

Just as I was sure the fight would last all night, the dome collapsed, revealing two bodies on the ground. My heart sank into my stomach as Cyrus slowly rose to his feet.

"It is done, then," Rogers said, looking at me. "Unless you'd like to challenge him, my boy?"

But I wasn't listening. I transported myself to the center of the ring, slowly walking to my mother's body. Her eyes were open, and she blinked once, but her breath was light. She was dying.

"Mother," I said. "I—"

"Hush, Gavon," she said. "I won't have the last thing I hear be sentimental nonsense."

"I have to say this." I took her hands in mine. They were cold and weak. "Mother, I have two other little girls. Their names are Nicole and Marie, and they're a Potion-maker and Healer. You would be so proud of them—they're so…perfect. Nicole can create healing potions so powerful they're stronger than anything I've ever made. And Mother, she can hear the ingredients. She's a bright, brilliant child. I wish you could've met her. And Marie, precocious little princess. She's two and can already heal me. And my little baby—the one not yet born. If you could only see the power she has. Mother, it's…" I sighed. "I wish things were different and you could've met them. And my wife. You would've loved Mora. She's…"

Alexandra squeezed my hand. "Are you happy, son?"

"What?"

"Are you…happy?"

I nodded. "Very much so."

She closed her hand around mine and nodded once then the final breath left her body. Alexandra was gone.

"I…I did it," Cyrus said, shakily coming to his feet before falling back to his knees. "She's dead. I killed her. I am Guildmaster."

I rose with my mother's body and transported out of the sparring arena. I wasn't in the mood to hear him gloat.

# Sixteen

As customary for New Salem, I gave my mother a proper burial in our cemetery, next to the previous Guildmasters and Master Jones. It would've made her proud to be in such good company, and as I magically dug her a plot and rested her body in it, I hoped she would be the last one I buried there.

I remained at the gravesite for a while, thinking about the last words we'd spoken. I wasn't even sure what I felt—sadness, shock, relief? Worry for what Cyrus was going to do now that he was in charge?

But oddly, all that worry seemed far away. I was consumed by the thoughts of all the things I never to to share with her. The grandchildren she didn't get to meet, the Warrior she never got to train. The conversations we'd never had because she was too preoccupied with staying aloof and neutral for the rest of the Guild. How might I have turned out if things had been different? What might I have learned from her?

In that moment, all I wanted was my wife's warm embrace.

I transported myself to her side, appearing on the couch next to her without a word.

"Gavon, what—"

"She's dead," I said, hoping I wouldn't have to explain in detail. "My mother's dead and Cyrus is Guildmaster. I know that you might not feel anything for her, but—"

She rested her hands on my wet cheeks and tilted my head to look at her. "Come here."

She laid my head on her chest and stroked my hair, cooing quietly as my tears stained her shirt. I'd never felt this way before —not even when Mary's child had been killed. This overwhelming sadness was a new sensation.

"I was so worried when you didn't come home," she said, kissing my forehead. "Ashley said you came by to see him—said you had a letter of some kind?"

"I don't want to talk about that right now," I said, exhausted. "I just..."

Mora stroked my hair, shushing me. "We'll worry about all that later."

"I told her about Nicole and Marie," I said, after a moment of silence. "I wanted her to know about them, and about you."

"What did she say?"

"She asked if I was...happy." I'd scarcely registered the question at the time, but now it struck me as odd. My mother had seemingly never cared if I was happy. Healthy, yes. Alive, yes. But happy?

Mora chuckled, the sound rumbling in her chest. "That's all any mother wants for their kid. I'm glad you were able to tell her."

It was strange, how much I mourned her. How much I missed someone who I could go weeks without speaking to. Perhaps it was all raw sensation, to go from anger to worry to grief in the span of a few hours. Maybe I was in shock. Or, more likely, I was going through the very particular process of losing one's mother. But Alexandra had been more than just a mother. She'd been the Guildmaster, the protector of the village. A steady hand who remained above the fray. A judicious leader. Someone…I truly admired.

"Can we name the baby Alexandra?" I asked, lifting my head off my wife's chest. "Please?"

"I don't know," Mora said. "I mean, I know you're upset about your mom and all, but…"

"Please, Mora," I whispered. "I…I need this."

"I *suppose* I'm willing to compromise," Mora said with a small smile. "How about something like Alex or Alexis?"

"Alexis could work," I said, rolling the name around in my mind. It wasn't Alexandra, but it would be a fitting honor. "Do you think your mother will object?"

"We could call her Alexis Reneé, that's kind of like Irene," Mora said, looking at the ceiling. "Not that she'll care, probably."

"Daddy?" Nicole and Marie stood at the top of the stairwell, rubbing their eyes. "Daddy?"

I shared a look with Mora as I pushed myself upright. "I'm home. Why aren't you two asleep?"

Marie let out a mournful sigh. "Daddy sad."

"She's been saying that for hours," Nicole said, dragging her blanket down the stairs. "She woke me up."

"Daddy sad."

"Come on, girls," Mora said. "Let's all cuddle."

They barreled down the stairs (guided by a charm to keep them from slipping) and crawled under the blanket with Mora and myself. Marie pressed her cheek to my chest, watching me with big, blue eyes. I covered her little hand with mine, kissing her forehead.

"Why is Daddy sad?" Nicole asked.

"Daddy…" Mora looked at me. "Daddy's mom just died."

Nicole calculated that in her mind. "Gram?"

"No, Daddy's mom. You never met her," Mora said. "But she would've loved you. Her name was Alexandra, and she was a very powerful woman. Daddy's sad because he misses her."

I wrapped my arm around Mora, grateful for her. "But we have good news. We picked a name for your sister."

Nicole, who was now very interested in anything related to the baby, squealed with excitement.

"Alexis," Mora said with a laugh. "Alexis Reneé McKinnon. What do you think?"

"Wexie!" Marie chirped.

"Ah-lex-is," I said.

"Wexie!"

"Close enough, Gav," Mora said with a smile.

"It's all perfect," I said, sitting back. "Who wants to watch cartoons until we fall asleep?"

And so we did, the four of us nestled into the couch under a blanket. My two little girls fighting sleep on either side of me, and my wife, nearly nine months pregnant, resting her head on my shoulders. And even though my heart was broken, it was filled with love.

Perhaps Alexandra had wanted the best for me, and that was why she'd sent me to live with Jones. Or perhaps it was just the last breath of a dying woman, too weak to get up and berate me for having abominations. I chose to believe the former, and keep that one final memory of my mother alive in my mind.

I returned to the village early—before Mora and the girls were even awake. There was a noticeable unease in the air, as if everyone wasn't quite sure what the day would bring. Mary waved in relief when she saw me out and about, but I wasn't eager to talk. I had an unpleasant conversation ahead of me.

I arrived at my former home—the one I'd shared with Cyrus for the last three years of my apprenticeship. The one Alexandra had lived in. The one that Cyrus now called home.

I found him in bed, weak and groggy. "Here to kill me?"

"Why would I do that?" I said, softly closing the door.

"I've taken your precious Alexandra away from you," he replied, staring at the ceiling. His voice lacked any of its usual swagger. Instead, there was a noticeable sadness there. Perhaps killing Alexandra—the woman who'd raised him—had been much harder on him than it was on me.

"You did what you needed to," I replied, summoning and then sitting in a chair next to his bedside. "And now you're the Guildmaster."

He smiled. "Does it burn you up inside, Gav? Knowing I finally bested you and that traitorous mother of yours."

"Not particularly. You've always been more preoccupied with status than I have."

He grunted and pushed himself upright. "Well, now I have the status, and you will bow to me. It is as it should be."

"I'm a Councilman," I said.

"Not for long," he replied. "I'll replace you with someone more amenable. And then you'll take me to the new world."

My mother's words echoed in my mind. "I think you'll find things don't exactly work as easily when you're Guildmaster."

He chuckled. "And how would you know?"

"A guess," I replied, looking out the window. "You will be good to the villagers, won't you?"

"They're no longer my concern. When I triumphantly make my reappearance into the new world, they can rot in here for all I care."

I pulled out the letter in my pocket. "I had spoken with Alexandra about this prior to your match. There's much you don't know about the new world—"

"She told us everything," Cyrus said. "About the restrictions on magic, about how weak and vulnerable they are."

"I'm sure she didn't use those terms."

"It shall be so easy to return triumphantly to our rightful place," Cyrus said with a smile on his face.

"Unless I close the tear."

His eyes flew open. "What?"

"It was part of the deal I made with Alexandra. I would agree to leave the tear open as long as she agreed to become a signatory to the Danvers Accord. If you decide against signing it, I'll have no choice but to close the tear and leave you and the rest of New Salem in here."

"You wouldn't *dare*."

"Sign this, then." I handed him the sheet of paper.

Cyrus scanned the paper then sat back on his pillows. "No. I don't believe you'd close the tear. Not you, Gavon. You wouldn't leave us to that fate."

I exhaled through my nose.

"If you did, you would leave poor Mary and her children to suffer at my hand." He smirked, settling deeper into the pillow. "And I know you wouldn't ever leave an innocent to suffer. You're too soft."

"You...wouldn't." But he would. Cyrus would have no qualms about destroying an entire village just to get his way. And based on the self-satisfied smirk on his face, he had me pegged.

"There it is, Gav," he said softly. "Either you take me to this new world, unfettered by your silly restrictions and accords, or I will slowly torture every villager here."

I rose from my chair. "They won't let you. There are more of them than you."

"Oh, but I'm sure I'll take more than a few of them out with me. Maybe I'll start with your precious Mary. Perhaps she has another Potion-maker I can slaughter."

"Or..." I exhaled, trying not to second-guess myself and this decision I was making. "I can challenge you."

"For what?" He snorted. "Guildmaster?"

"Yes." This was a very bold decision, and even as I spoke, the magic danced along my tongue. If I spoke the words together, it would be official. No backing down.

"Gavon, my good man. Think about what you're saying. I slaughtered your mother without a second thought, and I would have no problem destroying you. And before you die, I'll *still* compel you to tell me the location of the tear." He smiled. "And I'll have so much fun training your daughter to be just like me."

That was enough for me. "Cyrus, I challenge you for the Guildmastership."

Magic burned my tongue, cementing my intention to the match. Cyrus exhaled, bewildered and shocked, and knowing that he would have to set the date. But would he be smart enough to push it out, or cocky, and make it soon? Based on his current health, and his blatant disregard for healing potions, I placed him back at full strength in a month.

I would have to push him a little. "You are, of course, welcome to heal first. You seem to have taken a beating—"

"Three weeks from today," he snarled. "I hope you get your fill of the new world before your death."

# Seventeen

"You look tense, baby."

I smiled, but I couldn't force the worry off my face. I'd gone from sure I was making a colossal mistake to confidence that I could beat him, back and forth every few seconds since the challenge had been uttered. The date on the calendar was a bright spot—the fifteenth of October.

"You keep looking at that thing," Mora said, wrapping her arms around me. "Baby's not going to come any sooner if you burn a hole in the calendar."

I kissed her hand. "I'm just excited. That's all."

"Me too. I'm tired of being pregnant." She waddled to the fridge and stretched her back while she looked. "I still think she'll be early."

"That would be nice." Prior to the fifteenth would be even better. That way I could see my daughter before—

No, I wasn't going to think about that.

"Hey." I stood and walked over to her. "I love you."

"I love you, too. What—" I kissed her soundly. "What's wrong with you? Is everything okay? You've been acting weird lately."

"Just feeling paternal," I said.

"Well, go feel paternal while you get your kids for dinner," she said with a smile.

I walked upstairs, listening for the sounds of playing. Nicole was ordering Marie around, as she did, and Marie was happily not listening. By the time I reached the room, Nicole was stomping her foot with a red face, and Marie was rocking one of Nicole's stuffed animals and singing to herself. I stood in the doorway, taking in the sight of them in the little pink room, the stuffed animals, the pink rug. The sound of Nicole's little voice, as angry as it was. The way Marie's blonde curls bounced as she moved.

I shook myself out of my stupor. "C'mon, girls, dinner's ready."

It was hard not to fall into the self-defeating thoughts, harder still to consider what might happen if I lost. Cyrus still wouldn't know the location of the tear, but for how long? It wasn't exactly unobvious, even though it was on the extreme end of our small world. Would he come for my girls, or would he be content with merely killing me?

More than once, I considered telling my wife. I'd mentioned that Cyrus was Guildmaster, but I wasn't sure she fully understood what that meant. Or how cruel Cyrus really was, and why it was important that I prevent him from causing any further damage.

But I didn't want her to worry. She was already fretting

enough about the nursery and how we were going to handle the girls at the hospital. Adding to her stress so close to her due date wouldn't be good.

"I suppose Jeanie could come up," she said, placing a pink blanket on the crib, then replacing it with a white one covered in ducks then the pink one. "Do you think?"

"If that makes you feel better."

"Just in case something goes wrong, you know."

"I don't think anything's going to go wrong, Mora. You've had an easy pregnancy."

"Yeah, but..." She held up a ball of magic. "What's gonna happen when all this magic disappears?"

"You'll just go back to the way you were."

She spun around and faced me. "Are you sure you're all right, Gav? You've been distracted lately. Everything okay?"

I nodded and held out my arms for her to sit in my lap. What could I even tell her? If things went well, she would have no cause for concern. If they didn't...well... She might wonder where her husband had run off to. I couldn't do that to her.

On the eve of the fifteenth, I sat down at my desk and penned a letter. I would charm it to appear only if I didn't arrive at a certain time.

*Mora,*

*If you're reading this letter, then I've failed. When Alexandra died three weeks ago, Cyrus ascended to Guildmaster. I'd hoped to extract the same agreements from him, but he, unsurprisingly, was uninterested. He would've compelled me to bring him to this world, unfettered by the Danvers Accord, and do what he wanted. I couldn't let that happen,*

*So, to protect my girls and you, I challenged him for Guildmaster. If I'm successful, I will become Guildmaster and can continue to push for the full update of the Danvers Accord, so my people can be freed. If I'm unsuccessful, there's a vial of potion attached to this letter. Take it to the tear and use it. It's the potion Johanna used to create New Salem.*

*I hope that this letter never reaches you, but if it does, I want you to know I've loved every moment of our twelve years together. I tried my hardest to be a good father to our girls and I love them more than life itself.*

*I love you,*

*Gavon*

I sat back, wiping tears from my eyes. The charm would wear off at six in the morning—plenty of time for me to return. The vial of potion I rested on top of the envelope. I heard footsteps behind me, and looked down to see Marie.

"Daddy sad."

I pulled her into my lap and held her. "Yeah, baby. Daddy's very sad."

Marie placed her head against my chest along with her hand. A warmth spread from my fingers to my toes—healing magic. Her magic was growing quite strong, even for such a little girl.

"Daddy not sad."

"Thanks," I said, hugging her. "Daddy has to go to work for a bit. Can you be a good girl for Mommy? Go play with

Nicole?"

She giggled, as if she completely understood. But she was only two, so I wasn't sure how much she got. She disappeared to her toy box and returned with a small figurine.

"Is this for me?" I asked. I slipped it into my pocket. "Thank you Marie."

I picked up the enchanted envelope and carried it downstairs, a sense of dread and foreboding descending on me. I laid it on the counter and cast the charm with a small prayer.

"Mora," I called, staring at the space where the envelope had been. "I've got to run over to New Salem for a bit."

"What?" She appeared in the doorway. "What if I go into labor while you're gone?"

"Har har," I said, kissing her. "I won't be long. Do you want me to pick up dinner on the way home?"

"Mm. Thai food would be great," Mora said. "Super spicy. Induce labor. Don't be long, okay?"

I smiled, hoping I'd become a better liar. "I won't, I promise."


The streets of New Salem were empty. Curtains drawn, doors shut. Everyone seemed to be hunkering down for the impending storm. But as I passed their houses, the coverings fluttered. Eyes peered out from the darkness within. Each one sending me a message of hope—and fear.

As I passed by Mary's house, the door opened and the woman herself walked out. She was still pale and haunted, her eyes bloodshot. But she greeted me warmly, taking my hand and kissing it.

"Master Gavon, we were afraid you might not show," she said.

"Of course I would," I replied, not mentioning that I was magically bound to this match. "How are you doing?"

"As well as can be expected," she said quietly. "I'm scared for my children. He cannot be our Guildmaster."

"Has he threatened you?" I asked. "Or anyone?"

"No one's seen him these past three weeks," she said, glancing toward the house that used to be Alexandra's. "He's been resting for this challenge. Only Rogers and Humbert have been to him."

I didn't know if that was a good or bad thing.

"People have been talking. Is it true that you've found a way into the other world?"

I nodded. "There's much we'll have to do before I can bring us there, but…yes. I have."

"That explains where that bread came from," she said with a small laugh that faded as soon as it left her lips. "Were you going to take Abigail with you? To this new world?"

I nodded. "I would've found her a good home…until I figured a way to bring you to her."

She smiled, her eyes filled with tears. "I hope in this new world, things will be different. Little girls like Abigail will be allowed to live."

I thought of my wife, and the potion I'd given her to close the tear. Then I summoned an entire roomful of fresh bread from the nearby grocery store—and anywhere else I could find it. I left it all inside Mary's house.

"It will be."

I continued toward the arena, feeling the eyes of every soul in New Salem on me. If I failed to defeat Cyrus, they would suffer. My daughters and wife would suffer. Humanity would suffer.

*"You have raw power and the mental discipline. What you lack is the training and the will."*

My mother's voice floated toward me from some long-ago memory. I had been able to win once, when I was a boy. And not by sheer power alone—by using my strengths. Cyrus was proud, cocky, and hadn't really been in the sparring ring much. He was also still recovering from his match with my mother. Whereas I'd been training with my wife, albeit on a limited basis.

And besides that, I wanted it more than he did.

I ascended the stone staircase, searching my mind for any other memories of my mother's training. But there was nothing except the sound of my footsteps. The dark hallway was familiar and yet not, and the spot of light at the end was ominous. Yet I continued walking, not because I had to, but because it was what needed to be done. I came to the end of the tunnel and stopped. Cyrus was already there.

"Gavon, my good man," he said, betraying nothing of how he felt. "So good of you to join me today."

"Are we not waiting for them?" I said, gesturing to the empty stands.

"I've ordered them to stay in their houses," he said with a sneer. "This isn't something to be witnessed by the vermin."

"I'm sure they appreciated being called that," I said, slowly walking out to the middle of the arena. "We should at least wait for the Council."

"I've dissolved the Council," he said. "The only one in charge of this place is me. And once you tell me where your portal to the other land is, I will subjugate those magicals as well."

I gauged his magic at maybe eighty percent. That boded well for me at one hundred percent. My goal was simple: tire him out before I lost too much of my own magic. Cyrus was easy to play, just stroke his ego, then needle it. Just as I had as a boy.

"The duel today will be to the death or to the surrender," I said.

"I don't plan on letting you surrender," Cyrus replied. "So to the death will suffice."

I shrugged. "So confident that I haven't been growing stronger in the new world?"

He hesitated, and I knew I'd won this round. "Fine. To the death or to the surrender. There will be no additional tricks outside of attack magic."

"Deal." I didn't have any worth bringing to the fight anyway.

I stuck out my hand, and he shook it, our magic exploding into a dome extending above our heads. It seemed superfluous; there was no audience that needed protection from our magic. But this was an old art, and the rules had been laid in stone for thousands of years.

"I'll give you the first move," Cyrus said.

I smiled. "No, please…after you."

"I insist."

So he'd learned that much from our first bout twelve years ago. I would have to be less obvious, I supposed.

I moved quickly, and he moved with me, deflecting my three spells with four of his own, the last one missing me by mere inches.

"Spry, aren't we?" he said. "Just like our childhood. You, standing there trying to defeat me. Me, pitying your attempts."

I swallowed my retort—better to let him think I was nervous. It wasn't hard, because I was, but it all played into it.

"This has been your game for a long time, hasn't it, Gav?" Cyrus said. "You let me do your dirty work, killing Alexandra because you lacked the stomach for it. Then, when you think I'm weak, you come to take my throne?"

"Is that how you think it is?" I said, dodging his spells with ease. "That I've wanted to be Guildmaster?"

"Isn't it? You couldn't stand that Alexandra doted on *me*, wanted *me* to follow in her footsteps." His eyes had grown wild with anger as he worked himself into a frenzy. "And so you bided your time until the moment was right."

"Right, I bided my time." I couldn't help myself; I laughed.

"What's so funny?"

"You," I said with a sad shake of my head. "You have no idea what my life has been like since I made the tear. I didn't want to be Guildmaster, Cyrus. You forced this when you challenged Alexandra."

"Because she was going to give it to you. You haven't earned it. You don't deserve to be Guildmaster."

I deflected one of his spells. "Neither do you."

The spells came fast and furious, and it was all I could do to keep him from knocking me into next week. My instincts, which had been dormant for so long, struggled to keep pace. But Cyrus hadn't learned his lesson, intending to use all his magic in a show of force and not reserving any for later.

I threw up a barrier so I could take a breath, but his attack spell shredded it, sending me backward.

"No rest for the weary, Gav," he said, although I heard a note of windedness in his voice as well. "Get up and fight me."

And again, we moved, parrying and blocking each other's strikes, the magic slamming against the dome barrier like booming thunder. A light sheen of sweat had broken out on my forehead as I moved, and fatigue crept into the back of my mind.

A spell that sounded more like a freight train came toward me, and I couldn't react fast enough to get out of the way. I tumbled head over feet until I hit the edge of the dome. My head spun and blackness circled my vision. If I collapsed, Cyrus would most assuredly kill me. But it was so hard to keep the darkness at bay.

Something was digging into my pants pocket, so I pulled it out—Marie's little plastic toy. It seemed so ridiculous in this world of darkness and cold to see something so bright and cheery. It was supposed to be a horse, but was cartoonish and humanoid.

Closing my eyes, I thought about her little hand against my chest and the healing magic. If I concentrated, I could imagine her healing me. It wasn't real, but it got me upright.

Cyrus growled as I got to my feet; he was tired, too.

"Can't you just *die*?" he said, wiping his forehead.

"Unfortunately, I have something to live for."

With most of the energy I had left, I released one final spell. Cyrus tried to block, but it tore right through his barrier, hitting him in the chest and sending him back to the edge of our dome.

And there he lay, panting, miserable. Ready to quit, but too proud to.

And that was when I knew I'd beaten him. Because although I had four very large reasons to continue living, he only had one.

I limped toward him, sensing his magic hanging on by a thread. "Surrender."

"No."

"Please," I said. "I don't want to kill you."

He looked up at me, squinting through a trail of blood that dripped down his face. "What?"

"If you continue fighting, you'll die. And I'd hate to lose my brother so soon after I've lost my mother."

He blinked at me. "Are you…serious? You'd let me live?"

"You would not be Guildmaster," I said. "But I'd let you remain on the Council. You will have to curb your selfishness, treat the villagers with respect. If you can stomach that, I'll let you live."

"Why?"

Why indeed? Cyrus was a narcissistic juvenile, but for some reason, I couldn't bring myself to kill him. Perhaps I just didn't like the idea of losing another Warrior so soon. Perhaps I just couldn't stomach the idea of killing. Or maybe it was that I wasn't sure I could take that final step without forfeiting my life as well.

"I…surrender," Cyrus said, staring at the sky before he fell into unconsciousness.

A swell of magic burst from within me.

Knowing that I was the Guildmaster was the last thought I had before I keeled over.

# Eighteen

Sometime later, I heard voices around me. Someone lifted my head and ladled dirty water into my mouth, which I sputtered and spat out.

"Guildmaster, you must drink."

"M-Mary?" I cracked open an eye. "What am I doing here?"

"You collapsed," she said. "Both of you. Cyrus is…well, he's alive. We don't understand. How can you be Guildmaster, and he be alive?"

"I spared him," I whispered, my throat raw. It would've been so nice to fall back asleep, but there was something keeping me in this world. Something digging into my leg from my pocket.

My eyes flew open.

"How long have I been asleep?"

"Several hours, Master Gavon. It's the afternoon—"

I sprang from the bed, barely acknowledging the spinning room. Transporting was out of the question, so I limped from Mary's house, coming to a village full of cheering people. They patted me on the back, clapped my shoulders, tried to hug and kiss me. But I pushed through them all, running as well as I could on a swollen ankle and bruised kneecaps. I couldn't go straight to the tear—they would follow me. So I pushed my way toward Alexandra's house, swinging open the door and slamming it shut behind me.

Transporting was still not an option, but Alexandra usually had a spare vial of healing potion somewhere in her office. So I limped inside, falling down at her desk and using what limited magic I had left to scour her drawers.

"Why did you let me live?"

Cyrus was sitting on the chaise, his face black and blue and pale.

"I told you," I said, finding the vial at the bottom of one of the drawers. I ripped open the cap and drank it, feeling the immediate effects. "I didn't want to kill you."

"But you could have."

I leaned against the desk. "I'm not sure. It doesn't matter now, you surrendered."

"You tricked me," he said.

"Believe what you want." I straightened and tossed him the second vial of potion. "There's nothing to be done about it now."

I transported out of the office, ignoring whatever else Cyrus had to say. He should've been grateful I'd let him live, not blaming me for trickery. I'd done nothing to force him to surrender, merely played on the idea that he loved himself over everything else.

But more importantly, it had been several hours since the

charmed envelope I'd left my wife had reappeared on the kitchen counter. Had she read it—and had she used the potion?

I arrived at the tear and heaved a sigh of relief. The tear was still there.

With a smile, I dove head-first into the tear and landed on the other side. My magic was still weak, but I used a little to get me back home. I landed in a heap against the front door, wishing I'd saved that second potion for myself.

"Mora?"

"Gavon? Oh my God, Gavon!" Mora came skidding into the front hall. "Gavon, what the hell? Where have you been? I got this weird letter from you and—"

"So you read it?" I said, cracking open an eye.

"Yeah, I read it," she said, her voice changing from worried to angry. "And you have some serious explaining to do."

"Daddy! Daddy's home!" Nicole announced at the top of the stairs. She and Marie took them two-by-two, barreling into me with hugs and kisses. Marie, ever the astute baby, surveyed me with those piercing blue eyes and touched the bruise on my cheek. A warmth spread from there, all the way down to my fingers and toes.

"Thank you, Marie," I said. "But you don't have to do that."

"What's she doing?" Nicole asked. "Is she healing you? I want to heal you! Can you get my potion for me?"

"Enough," Mora said. "Nicole, take your sister upstairs. Daddy and Mommy need to have a talk."

"But—"

"You can give Daddy your potion later," she said with a forced smile. "Take your sister upstairs."

Nicole took Marie's hand and did as she was told, casting worried looks over her shoulder. I gave her a thumbs-up, feeling much better than I had before Marie's healing, but also nursing a sick feeling in the bottom of my stomach.

"In the kitchen," Mora said, turning and walking inside.

I followed her, wincing as I put pressure on my ankle and summoning some of Nicole's potion that I'd stored away. It healed my ankle, but I would still need a few days of rest to fully recover.

"So," Mora said, sliding the opened envelope and vial of potion across the counter, "care to share what the fuck is going on?"

"I told Alexandra about the tear," I said, taking a seat at the counter. "She said I would become Guildmaster. Cyrus didn't like that, so he challenged her. He won, obviously."

"I know that."

"Yes, well…" I sighed. "Cyrus was going to compel me to tell him where the tear was. He could, as Guildmaster. So I told him I'd close the tear if he did. And he said he'd…well, he said he'd kill every last person in New Salem if I did that. So the only thing I had left was to…challenge him."

"The only thing?" She shook her head. "Gavon, you *have the potion to close the tear.* Instead, you decided to become *Guildmaster?*"

"Mora, he was going to kill people—"

"I don't care about *them,* Gavon. What I care about is my husband choosing to put himself in danger when he's got a wife and kids here who need him. You don't owe those people anything! And now…now you're their leader. Well, isn't that just *perfect*."

"I had no choice, Mora! Cyrus could've forced me to divulge the location of the tear—"

"You made the choice when you decided to keep the tear open," she said. "You could've closed it twelve years ago and you just didn't."

My mouth hung open. "I don't *know* how to close it, *darling*. We've gone over this a thousand times—"

"You say that. But I don't believe it. Not when every time I talk to you, you're trying to get around it. Trying some other experiment on potions or whatever. You've been half-assing this the whole time, because you don't want to close the tear. You'd rather put your mother and everyone else above your own family. Above me and your daughters."

"That's not true, and it's unfair," I said. "I challenged Cyrus *precisely* to keep you safe!"

"If you wanted to keep us safe, you would have used that potion," she said. "You could have stopped this once and for all."

"Then why didn't you use it?" I said, nodding to the vial.

"Maybe I should have," she said. "Then at least I would've known you'd made your choice."

"Mora…"

She placed her hand on her stomach. "You know what? I can't look at you right now. Just go back to New Salem or whatever. Go lead your guild. Maybe I'll use that potion and lock you in there."

"Fine," I snapped. I marched to the door when I heard sniffling at the top of the stairs. Nicole sat at the top holding onto Marie, whose bright blue eyes were wide and fearful. Our fighting must've been louder than I'd thought.

"Daddy, where are you going?" Nicole whispered. "Why are you and Mommy yelling?"

I climbed the stairs slowly and knelt in front of them both. "Sometimes Mommy and I disagree. I'm sorry if it scared you."

"Are you leaving forever?" Nicole asked.

I chuckled, holding her cheek. "Of course not. Daddy's just gonna run up to the store for a bit. Get Mommy some ice cream or something. I promise I'll be home soon. Can you be a good girl and take care of your sister? Make sure Mommy doesn't get too upset?"

Nicole nodded. "Can you bring me flowers so we can make a potion?"

"Of course," I said, rising once more. "Anything else?"

She screwed up her face. "Don't go too long."

"I won't," I said.

I stopped once more to give the baby a kiss on the forehead and waited in the foyer for my wife to appear and tell me not to go. But she was angry with me, and she would be for a while. Perhaps I deserved it. Before I left, I summoned a giant bouquet of flowers and left it on the dining room table.


I walked down the sidewalk, glowering at anyone and everything. I knew I was being unreasonable, and on some level, I understood why Mora was angry with me. But I'd just survived a deadly match with my mortal enemy. Would it kill her to be a little more supportive?

I rubbed the stabbing pain above my eyebrow. I could've

used some more potion, or some more healing. But I kept walking, knowing that Mora and I would go for round two if I returned right now. She needed space, I needed space, and tonight we'd make up. I'd promise her nothing would change, and I'd make her understand that I'd done what I did to keep her safe. Cyrus would now be permanently under my control through the Council, which I'd have to reinstate.

Another pain joined the first. I was Guildmaster. That…was its own challenge. I would seek out Ashley, get some pointers…

*"You'd rather put your mother and everyone else above your own family. Above me and your daughters."*

As I walked, I relived each moment of our fight. And as much as I hated to admit it, Mora was right.

I found myself at the water's edge, the very place where Mora and I had first met twelve years before. It was a lifetime ago. I'd been an ignorant idiot and she'd been a wild hellion. Together, we'd changed. Grown. I'd become smarter and she'd become tamer. I wouldn't trade her for anything.

And yet, I had. I'd bargained that I would be able to defeat Cyrus. I'd put the lives of my family on the line just to…what? Prove a point? No, I had a little more reason than that. I couldn't choose between them and the people in New Salem.

But perhaps it was time to.

The tear stood before me, crackling and furious as ever. I summoned the cauldron of Johanna's potion, levitating it to my side. It was time that I ended this once and for all.

I'd left Mary with plenty of bread, enough to last them for years to come. And into Humbert's house, I sent cases of milk and beer. I would find a way to undo what I was about to do, once I had the original signatories of the Danvers Accord onboard with updating it. And then, the people of New Salem would be free.

Using magic, I tipped the cauldron and poured an infinity symbol, the liquid silver lighting up with magic as it hit the sand in front of the tear. I held my breath, apologizing silently to those who would be stuck with Cyrus. I hoped my position as Guildmaster would remain, even though I was separate. That would keep Cyrus at bay for a little bit.

The tear glowed bright white, and I closed my eyes and waited.

...but nothing happened.

The tear remained, crackling and popping. I could feel the magical signatures of those on the other side in New Salem. It was open—Johanna's potion hadn't worked.

My jaw fell open and disappointment slammed into me like a ton of bricks. I'd been so sure it would work. In my gut, I'd known this was it. This was the thing that would work.

But it hadn't. And now...now I was back at square one.

"Oh shit," I mumbled to myself, rubbing my face. Mora was going to have a field day. *Irene* was going to have a field day.

But before I could dwell on that too much, a loud booming drew my attention. For a split second, I thought it was from the tear, but dismissed that as the sound had come from this side. I turned, spying a bright light in the distance. It looked like something had caught on fire...

My heart sank. It couldn't be my house.

And yet...

# Nineteen

I ran as fast as my legs could carry me, telling myself that it wasn't my house, but knowing—just knowing—that it was. I turned onto my street to see it filled with firetrucks and people. The sight was so jarring I couldn't process it—I was just mesmerized by the dancing orange flames.

Then, slowly, my brain kicked into gear. And I couldn't breathe.

I scrambled toward the house, calling out my wife's name, scanning the wreckage for their magical signatures. When nothing came back, I closed my eyes and scanned the surrounding area for my girls' signatures. No matter how far, if they were… No, they were alive. They couldn't be…

Marie's magic blinked at me in the distance, and I sagged. Nicole's was fainter but nearby. Mora's was…

I couldn't find her.

I transported myself as close as I could get to them—in a closet in a hospital. I rushed out, ignoring the looks of surprise from the nurses as I leaned onto the counter.

"My wife, where is my wife?" I rasped.

"Calm down, sir," the woman said. "Who is your wife?"

"Mora McKinnon," I said. "Please...please help me find her."

The woman checked her computer then her face fell. "Follow… Follow me."

Numbly, I followed her to a closed door with the blinds drawn. She opened the door. My wife was on the bed, bathed in darkness as if she were sleeping. But I didn't need light to know.

There was no magic—no life.

Mora, the love of my life, the mother of my children, the most beautiful, vibrant woman I'd ever met, was gone.

I sank into a chair, the breath gone from my body. Guilt threatened to drown me—the last words we'd said were in anger. Had she known she was my everything? Had she understood the depths of my love for her? How I'd do anything for my girls?

"Oh, I didn't realize anyone was in here."

The woman in the doorway wore scrubs. A nurse, I supposed. Nonmagical. I didn't want her around to see the depths of my despair.

"Are you...her husband?" she asked quietly.

I nodded. "Go away."

She wrung her hands then disappeared through the door, leaving me alone with my thoughts. My wife was gone, my...

Oh my God, my child.

I buried my head in my hands, grief anew. The child couldn't have survived. I'd lost them both.

A soft knock on the door.

"Damn it, woman, I said..." The words died in my throat. There was a small bundle in the plastic crib the woman had wheeled into the room. "Is that..."

"Your daughter," she said softly. "She's healthy—perfect, in fact. Your wife held on until she was born."

Carefully, I gathered the baby in my arms. She was so tiny—so delicate. But a Warrior as powerful as the one born in New Salem. Brown hair, my nose, my chin. Skin still pink from the birth. She opened her big eyes in my direction.

"Hi there," I said, tears leaking down my face. "I'm your dad."

She gurgled and squirmed, staring around and looking at nothing.

I sank back into the chair, her tiny body cradled in my arms, as more tears fell. "Look, Mora. She's...she's perfect. We did perfectly."

There was no response. There wouldn't ever be a response. I would never wake up to her beautiful blue eyes, or hear her laugh. I would never see her roll her eyes at me or taste her lips. She would remain like this—still, cold. Dead.

It was all my fault.

"You!"

Jeanie stood in the doorway, with tearstained cheeks and fury in her eyes.

"You got a lot of nerve showing up here," she snarled, walking into the room. "After what you did to my sister?"

"What I..." I swallowed, knowing even if I hadn't killed her, I might as well have.

"Well, you got what you wanted, I guess. Take your Warrior and get the hell out of here."

"Tell me what happened," I whispered. "Please."

Jeanie worked her jaw then softened. "You don't know?"

I shook my head. "I was… I wasn't home. How the hell did this happen?"

"A Warrior showed up," she said. "Mora drew him away from the clan while Mom beefed up our protections. We found her on the beach…" Jeanie swallowed. "She was barely hanging on. I think she… she stayed alive for the baby."

It was worse than I could've possibly imagined. "A Warrior…"

"Yeah, from *your* guild."

"Cyrus." I rose with the baby in my arms, the fury and guilt mingling into a massive storm. I hated myself more than I'd ever hated anyone else. I'd given Cyrus a chance—shown him mercy. And he'd repaid me this way. By killing my wife.

She must've been scared to death. She must've wondered if I'd abandoned her, or if I'd sent Cyrus. I wished I could wake her up and tell her everything. Tell her that when I looked into her eyes, I could find the whole universe. That when I came home and saw her on the couch with my girls, it was the closest to perfection a man could get. That I would regret my actions for the rest of my life—give anything just to have her wake up and forgive me for my idiocy. I had put the Guild above my family. I would never, *ever* make that mistake again.

Cyrus knew where the tear was. And I, like an *idiot*, had been so sure in my own brilliance that I had no way to close it. Back to square one, I thought angrily to myself. Cyrus wouldn't

rest until he'd destroyed everything I held dear, and there was…
there was only one way for me to stop it. Only one way to
contain him until I could permanently do so. But to do it…to
do it, I'd have to give up the only thing I had left.

"Jeanie," I began softly. "I have something very important to
ask you."

"W-what?"

"You and I have never been particularly close," I said, gently
brushing my little girl's soft cheek. "But what I'm asking you to
do… I would only trust you to complete it. Because I know,
deep down, you and Mora loved each other. And you love my
girls, even if you don't care for me."

She was silent, so I took it as an invitation to continue.

"I've made a horrible…" I shook my head. "Horrible doesn't
even begin to describe it. I should've closed the tear years ago. I
should have been more vigilant. I should've…" I closed my eyes.
"But in order to fix my mistake, I have to return to New Salem.
And I have to remain there."

"What are you saying?" Jeanie asked.

"I need you to take my girls," I said, surprised I could still
feel the sharp jab of pain in my chest. "Take care of them. Raise
them."

"I don't understand. Why can't you take them?"

"Because in order for the Guild to do what I ask, I have to
pretend like every horrible thing your mother ever said about me
is true. To protect my girls, I need…" I closed my eyes. "I need
to give you sole guardianship over them. I'll give you money to
disappear—move somewhere else. You don't even have to tell
me where you go." I hoped she wouldn't, so I wouldn't have to

see my daughters growing up without me.

Jeanie looked at the baby and shook her head. "I don't think I'm strong enough to handle them."

"Guardianship bestows upon it the weight of your clan," I said. "You'll be able to…contain them, if you need to."

"I meant…" Jeanie began softly. "I don't think I'm strong enough to handle three kids. I'm…Gavon, I'm just twenty. You can't ask me to do this."

"If there were anyone else, if there were any other way, I would do it. But if my kids grow up with your mother…" I closed my eyes. "I don't want to know what she'd do to them."

"Why can't you take them with you?" Jeanie asked.

"Because if they believe I know where the girls are, or have access to them, they'll come for them and kill them," I said. "Cyrus would take the baby and raise her into a cold-blooded killing machine like he is. He would use her as a vehicle to take over this world. There's much I can do as Guildmaster, but I can't…I wouldn't be able to stop him." I closed my eyes, praying Jeanie would understand, that she'd know I would never give up my girls unless there was no other option. "If your mother cared at all about Mora, she'll allow the girls to stay in Clan Carrigan. That will afford them some protection, even if you don't physically live here."

"Gavon, I can't do this…" Jeanie's voice was thick, and I was reminded of how many lives I'd ruined with just one stupid mistake.

"I'm begging you," I whispered. "Please take my girls. I don't trust them to anyone else."

She heaved a loud, wet breath, wiping her cheeks. "A-all

right. I'll take them."

I opened my wet eyes into hers and could've kissed her. "I'll give you whatever you need. Just please…don't bind their magic. At least not forever."

Jeanie nodded. "You make it sound like you'll never see them again…"

I couldn't tell her the truth, so I rose and placed the baby in her arms. "Have your mother cast a containment spell on her. Use the power of your clan to seal her up tight. And…" I closed my eyes. "And for good measure, just don't tell her about magic. I have a feeling she'll be as powerful as her sisters, and if she knows her magic is reachable, she could break the containment spell."

"Do you think…she could?"

"I think given the right incentive, sure. Better to wait until she's mature enough to understand what she is." I ran my hand across her soft skin, imprinting the memory of her in my brain.

"Did you guys ever decide on a name?" Jeanie asked, looking so young with a baby.

"Alexis," I whispered softly. If I'd another chance, I would let Mora name her whatever she wanted. But Alexis would do. "Alexis Renee McKinn…" I swallowed. "Carrigan."

Jeanie nodded.

I wished I had something to say. Wished I could tell my girls I loved them, or perhaps even give them a kiss. But if I didn't leave right then, I would change my mind. So I left Jeanie and my newborn daughter in that hospital room with my dead wife.

# Twenty

I arrived in New Salem ready to murder. Cyrus was in the Council room, along with the rest of them, and I didn't care who saw me punch him in the face. I stormed into the room, ripping him out of his seat and slamming him against the wall.

"Something the matter, old friend?" Cyrus taunted. His face was bloody—good. My wife had left some bruises on him.

"I'm going to kill you," I snarled. "Why? Why did you do that?"

"You should've killed me, Gav," he said in a sing-song voice. "Now your wife is dead, and there's no one to blame but yourself."

I released him and stepped back.

"And now, I have the joy of raising that daughter of yours. After all, what are you going to tell the Guild?" He laughed. "I'm going to make her *hate* you and then, when the time is right, I'll have her challenge you and kill you."

"G-Guildmaster?" Rogers whispered. "Guildmaster, what is

the meaning of this?"

"It appears our Guildmaster has been keeping more secrets than we thought," Cyrus said. "He's borne a Potion-maker and a Healer in that world, alongside the infant Warrior. And he thought he would raise that Warrior over there, outside the norms of this Guild."

"Of course," I said, too angry to show emotion. "That was my plan. Until you screwed it up."

Cyrus started. "What?"

"I'd infiltrated Clan Carrigan," I said, evenly. "Used the woman to have some children until she bore me a Warrior. I planned to train the girl and educate her in that world then use her to help lead us to victory. The only way I could do that was to pretend I came in peace, that the child's existence was a quirk of genetics."

Silence reigned—especially from Cyrus. It gave me a sick sense of victory. I hadn't been able to prevent the death of my wife, the sundering of my family, or the abandonment of my children, but I could finally shut him up.

"Unfortunately, thanks to Cyrus's idiocy, my plans have to change," I said, throwing him a glare. "The girl is now under a containment spell until she's fifteen. The clan's magic has overruled mine, and I'm unable to break it. Therefore, she's useless to us until she returns to her magic."

"What will you do then?" Rogers asked.

"Introduce her to the Guild," I said. "Perhaps. If she hasn't been completely swayed otherwise. She will be, in essence, a nonmagical until then, and I doubt they'll even tell her magic exists to keep the containment spell strong. She may be useless to us. Only time will tell." I rose. "Until then, I want the Council to enact a ban on entry to the world."

"Why?" Rogers said, as Cyrus choked in surprised. "We need to learn—"

"Clan Carrigan may kill the child if we take action," I said, knowing full well they wouldn't. But the Council understood ruthlessness. "It's better that we bide our time in this world. I will continue my research into the nonmagical weaponry and bring food to the village. We will grow strong. Train. And when our Warrior returns to us, we will make our move."

I arrived at the house that would become my home and collapsed in the library. In the privacy of my new home, the one I was yet again trapped in, I could let the rush of grief finally wash over me. In less than twenty-four hours, I'd lost the love of my life, my two precious girls, and a baby I'd held for nothing but a heartbeat. And now they would grow up believing I'd abandoned them.

My wife, my Mora, my partner…was gone. My girls, the light of my life, would be raised by a veritable stranger. Would Jeanie give them enough love? Teach Nicole the difference between lavender and thistle? Would she continue her potions tutelage?

And Marie, my brilliant, blue-eyed girl who'd just started talking and understanding the world. Would she even remember my face?

Alexis, my precious baby. All the plans I'd had, teaching her how to spar, watching her learn how to use that beautiful purple magic, were now gone. A little brunette who darted about the ring with the brilliance and quickness of the magical she was named after. Perhaps I'd never see her again.

Was it worth it to continue at all? I could find a way to close the tear then kill myself. It would be the same to my girls either way. Irene would fill their heads with lies about me, and they would hate me. They had every right to. I'd failed them in every sense of the word. I didn't have the right to be their father anymore.

There was a soft rap on the door and I readied myself to rage at whomever had disturbed me. I flung open the door to reveal Agatha, who carried her infernal child in her arms.

"M-Master Gavon," she whispered with a nod.

"Agatha," I said. "What do you want?"

"I thought…you would be taking the boy now."

Time for her to receive payment, I assumed. The boy was barely six months. "He's not old enough yet."

"Forgive me. He's begun to wield the Warrior magic, and I can't… I'm not…" She straightened. "I wish to live here and raise him under your roof."

I stared at her. That she could speak to me at all in the face of my horrific guilt was at once amusing and sickening. "Give me the boy, and get the hell out of my sight."

She handed me the child, and I magically slammed the door behind me.

The baby boy in my arms fidgeted and squirmed then opened his mouth to start wailing. I cooed at him, summoning a bottle and a can of formula from a grocery store. As the mixture warmed and blended, I rocked him gently, much the same way I'd done with Nicole when she was fussy. The bottle was exactly what he wanted, and he settled and ate.

"That's right, isn't it, James?" I said. "These idiots here don't know the first thing about babies, do they?"

The boy looked up at me with round eyes, reminding me painfully of my newest daughter. But I buried that guilt and that pain. If I sat in New Salem and thought about my children, I wouldn't be doing what I needed to protect them. I would continue to drown in my misery until I took my own life.

And if I killed myself, James would go to Cyrus—who'd fathered many children but had never been a father himself. He certainly didn't know anything about formula or changing diapers or soothing a colicky baby. Worse, in his care, James would grow up cruel and hateful. Even if I was successful in closing the tear, Cyrus would still wreak havoc on the people here. I couldn't be that selfish.

The baby opened his eyes and gurgled, giggling at me. I found a smile forming on my face as I tickled his stomach, eliciting more giggles.

I could never, *ever* replace my children. I would never heal from the pain of losing Mora. But perhaps, in this boy, I could find something to live for. I would raise him to be a good Guildmaster, to know and love his people as I did. Then, perhaps, when the time came to close the tear, I would let him have it.

# Twenty-One

That squalling baby had grown into a young man, the very man who sat before me on a chair, his head lolling as he recovered from the last interrogation. A young man I was profoundly angry with—who'd betrayed me and my daughters, who'd nearly gotten Alexis killed by tricking her into an induction match with Cyrus.

He'd always been a narcissistic child, but I'd hoped I had stomped the cruelty out of him. It appeared I hadn't known him as well as I'd thought—and Cyrus had been more influential. But for him to betray us like this? It made no sense. It wasn't the boy I'd raised.

When I'd finally been able to get him alone without anyone looking, I'd let him have it. But after a few moments of his painful stuttering, I'd realized he was under a curse. More prodding indicated he'd signed some kind of pact, which prevented him from divulging the details of it and also, it seemed, why it was signed in the first place.

I could piece together some aspects of it—he'd obviously discovered some devious plot of Cyrus's and, instead of coming to me, he'd seen fit to approach the man directly. Where had I gone wrong that both my apprentice and my daughter had become so cocksure in their powers?

He was certainly contrite now, fighting tooth and nail against a secrecy pact that would kill him if he continued.

"I want to try again," he ground out.

"Inadvisable," I said. "You were out for five minutes this time."

"Give me a healing potion, then. I want to beat this."

I sighed. "You may not be able to."

"But you have to know, Gavon," he said, his voice taking on the pleading note that told me more than his words could. "Please. Once more."

I handed him a vial of potion and he downed it in one gulp. Some of his color returned, and he wiped the blood from his nose.

"I'm ready."

"Name," I asked.

"James Malcolm Riley."

"Age?"

"Eighteen." He glanced at me and nodded, signaling he was ready for the harder questions.

Due to the pact, I had to be cautious of what I asked him. Without knowing what the agreement entailed, there was no way to know how to phrase questions to get around it. But in some cases, his inability to answer questions was a clue in and of itself.

"Did you approach Cyrus on your own?" I asked.

He nodded.

"Did you seek him out about Alexis?"

He shook his head.

"About something else?"

Again, he nodded. "M-m-" He released a sigh of frustration.

"It's all right," I said. "Let me guide the questions here." But an 'm' word. Magic, marriage, mule, military—none of those words were making sense to me so I set it aside. "Did you find him or did he find you?"

"S-second," James spat out with some difficulty.

"Did you find Cyrus doing something I don't know about? On the other side of the tear?"

He nodded, but it was clearly painful to do so. "Mmm—"

"Magic?" I offered, and James stared at me straight on, fighting the pact. "You saw him doing magic—"

A shake of the head. A trickle of blood dripped from his nose. "M-m-meeting."

I was almost sure I'd misheard, but the one word had been clear. "Meeting?"

James released a loud sigh and wiped his sweaty face.

"He was meeting with people? Who was he meeting with? For what purpose?" James gave me a tired look, and I held up my hands. "Withdrawn."

I turned away from him, mulling over this new scrap of information I'd gleaned, and how I could ask James more without killing the boy. Cyrus had only had access to the world for less than three years, but in that time, I'd kept a close watch on his movements. Had he still given me the slip? And if so, what could he be planning?

"All right," I said, after a moment. "I'm going to ask you a series of question that should be a yes or no."

"Okay," he said with an exhalation.

"Was he meeting with people from the other side?"

James made a strangled noise. I took that as a yes.

"Were they magical?"

Another noise. Another yes. But James was beginning to fade, so I rose.

"Okay, we'll stop—"

"I don't want to stop! I want to be able to tell you everything." His outburst was short-lived, and he slumped back in his chair.

"I know, son," I said, patting him on the shoulder. "But you'll have to be patient and take this one step at a time."

He nodded. "I want to keep going."

"Fine." I changed directions. "Were you coerced into signing this silencing pact?"

"No."

I turned. His eyes were clear but his expression disgusted. "No? You signed it willingly?"

"Not…exactly."

"So if you weren't coerced, why did you sign it?"

He swallowed and closed his eyes. "L-l-l…"

"Alexis?" I said. "Did he threaten her?"

James sighed and slumped on the chair, which I took for confirmation.

"How? He can't touch her, per the agreements I made in the Guild."

"He…can't…"

"So why…" I rose, the word *meeting* coming back to my mind. "He was meeting with other magicals. Magicals not under the same agreements we are."

The loud breath of relief was the affirmation I needed—but raised other questions.

"But Lexie can handle a few magicals over there. They don't have specialties. They can't use attack magic or—"

"For…now…"

I turned. "The Danvers Accord is foolproof. Magicals have been trying to undo it for centuries and have been un—"

"You." James spat out.

"Me? What do…" I froze. "You mean my daughters."

Of course. The Danvers Accord had prevented anyone born on that side of the tear from specialties, including Warrior magic. And in New Salem, no matter how much Cyrus tried, he'd been unsuccessful in creating more Warriors. But if he'd been trying to do what I'd done with Mora—to create a set of new Warriors in the other world…

"Has he created any Warriors?"

James shook his head and sputtered more before giving up. "I hate this. I hate that I can't tell you what I want to tell you."

"So there's more?" I asked. "More than just trying to create magicals?"

He nodded. "So much more. I c… I c…."

"James, don't push yourself…"

But he'd overdone it once more, and fallen unconscious. I crossed the room and pressed my hand against his forehead, much as I had when he'd slept as a young boy. I'd tried my best to be the sort of parent I'd always wanted, but perhaps I'd been too indulgent. He was cocky, too sure of himself. Much too much like Cyrus.

I'd often wondered what truly lay beneath the exterior, if he was heartless, like Cyrus, or something a little more human. Alexis (*Lexie,* that infernal name) had certainly become close friends with him, and I knew her to be an apt judge of character. And James's struggle against the pact was only partially to clear his name—the information he'd given me was crucial. Cyrus presumably remained confident in his magical pact-making abilities, so now, at least, I had an idea.

James stirred and blinked at me groggily. "Sorry, I—"

"No need to apologize," I said, handing him a wet rag to wipe his face. "I think we've done enough."

He nodded, staring at the floor forlornly. "I'm sorry, Gavon. I wish I'd…"

"There's no use in dwelling on what's been done," I said softly. "What matters now is that we move forward productively. I want you to find out more about what Cyrus is doing. Whoever he's meeting with, I want you to try to disrupt it."

"How will I report back?" James asked.

"Can you report back?"

James shook his head.

"Well, Cyrus can write a pact, I'll give him that," I said with a shake of my head. "I suppose we'll have to figure out a system."

"Can you tell her?" he asked, showing a pair of sad, puppy dog eyes I hadn't seen since he was a small boy.

"Tell Alexis?"

"She thinks I'm a monster. Please tell her I didn't mean any of it."

I didn't respond right away. Alexis—*Lexie*—was crushed, and despite all her assurances to the contrary. I'd had a little hope that she and James would become friends, if only so she'd have a fellow magical to talk with and he'd have someone on his level intellectually. But even I'd been surprised at how quickly they'd become inseparable.

As much as I wanted to return to Lexie, explain everything and wipe away the hurt, it wasn't the right thing to do. If I told her why James had seemingly betrayed her, she would go stirring up trouble with Cyrus. She had a big year ahead of her, with her freshman year at Georgetown a scant four months away, and I didn't want any New Salem hijinks to ruin what should be a fresh start in a new city.

"We'll tell her eventually," I said, placing a comforting hand on his shoulder. "But for now, we'll keep this between us. You and I both have mistakes to make up for. And even if it kills us both, we'll make it right."

To be Continued...

Freshman year isn't all it's cracked up to be

# illusion&
# indemnity

Available now

# Acknowledgements

As always, thanks first go to you, the reader, for picking up my magical book and reading it to the end. If you've got a spare minute, I'd appreciate it if you'd leave a review on Amazon, Goodreads, or your favorite eBook store. Even a short review is incredibly helpful to an indie author like me!

Thanks go to Kristin for helping me get through the beta process.

Dani, as usual, you're the best. One of these days, I might write a manuscript with no typos. But until that day comes, I'm so grateful for your careful eye.

Thanks also go to my typo checkers, Lisa Henson, Leeve, and Elizabeth F.

# About the Author

S. Usher Evans was born and raised in Pensacola, Florida. After a decade of fighting bureaucratic battles as an IT consultant in Washington, DC, she suffered a massive quarter-life-crisis. She decided fighting dragons was more fun than writing policy, so she moved back to Pensacola to write books full-time. She currently resides with her two dogs, Zoe and Mr. Biscuit, and frequently can be found plotting on the beach.

Visit S. Usher Evans online at:
http://www.susherevans.com/

Twitter: www.twitter.com/susherevans
Facebook: www.facebook.com/susherevans
Instagram: www.instagram.com/susherevans

www.ingramcontent.com/pod-product-compliance
Lightning Source LLC
Chambersburg PA
CBHW070824190726
48292CB00006B/2104